COMING HOME

THE BAYTOWN BOYS SERIES

MARYANN JORDAN

Coming Home (Baytown Boys) Copyright 2016

Cover by: Graphics by Stacy

Cover photograph: Eric McKinney 612Covered Photography

ISBN ebook: 978-0-9975538-3-3

ISBN print: 978-0-9975538-4-0

ISBN special edition alternate cover paperback: 978-1-956588-15-6

ISBN special edition alternate cover hardback: 978-1-956588-92-7

AUTHOR INFORMATION

I am an avid reader of romance novels, often joking that I cut my teeth on the historical romances. I have been reading and reviewing for years. In 2013, I finally gave into the characters in my head, screaming for their story to be told. From these musings, my first novel, Emma's Home, The Fairfield Series was born.

I was a high school counselor having worked in education for thirty years. I live in Virginia, having also lived in four states and two foreign countries. I have been married to a wonderfully patient man for over forty years. When writing, my dog or one of my two cats can generally be found in the same room if not on my lap.

Please take the time to leave a review of this book. Feel free to contact me, especially if you enjoyed my book. I love to hear from readers!

Facebook

Email
Website

Author's Note

Please remember that this is a work of fiction. I have lived in numerous states as well as overseas, but for the last thirty years have called Virginia my home. I often choose to use fictional city names with some geographical accuracies.

These fictionally named cities allow me to use my creativity and not feel constricted by attempting to accurately portray the areas.

It is my hope that my readers will allow me this creative license and understand my fictional world.

I also do quite a bit of research on my books and try to write on subjects with accuracy. There will always be points where creative license will be used in order to create scenes or plots.

All books have errors, no matter how many author, editors, proofers, and readers have looked at the manuscript. If the errors are minor and do not affect the story, please forgive and ignore. But, if you find errors that you deem necessary to report, please send me an email with your notations and do not try to report to Amazon.

Be kind to authors... we are human!

authormaryannjordan@gmail.com

DEDICATION

Years ago my husband and I discovered the Eastern Shore of Virginia and fell in love. The mostly rural strip of land forming the peninsula originating from Maryland has managed to stay non-commercialized. The quiet, private area full of quaint towns captured our hearts, and we rushed to buy a little place there.

It has become our retreat when we need to leave the hustle and bustle of our lives. I gather ideas, create characters, and spend time writing when not walking on the beach collecting sea glass.

My mother became ill and passed away during the writing of this book. She was my best friend, supporter of my writing, spent endless hours helping the homeless and refugees in our area, and was a selfless, devoted wife, mother, and nana.

This book is devoted to the woman who gave me life, taught me to dream, and gave me the courage to follow those dreams. I am so pleased that she was able to visit the Eastern Shore

*before she became unable to travel. She loved our little place
and knew it would spark my creative juices.*

1

It never gets old. I could stand here for a thousand years, watching it over and over...and it would never become less spectacular.

Mitch Evans sipped his beer as he stood on the weatherworn wooden back porch of his small cottage, his eyes never leaving the sun setting over the Chesapeake Bay. One hand wrapped around the warped board railing and the other curled around the sweat-beaded beer, he viewed the sun dipping lower and lower until the round, orange ball was no longer seen as the sky painted every shade of pink, red, and blue.

He walked a few steps to one of the Adirondack chairs, settling his tall body in, leaning back, continuing to appreciate the sky's ever-changing panorama.

Did I appreciate this when I was a kid? Did I even notice this when I was a kid? I sure as hell didn't when I was a teenager, too busy, chomping at the bit to leave this place.

Shaking his head, he could not help but smile at the

brash young man he had been. *Desperate to leave this small town and see the world. Well, I saw some of it all right,* he thought, his mind drifting to the tours in Iraq and Afghanistan with the Army. *Front lines. The dust, the dirt. Little sleep. Making new friends only to lose some...permanently.* Shaking his head once more, he pushed those thoughts out of his mind, preferring to note the darker blues drifting across the sky as the night morphed into brilliance.

The ever-present breeze coming off the bay offered a respite from the evening heat that sizzled. His mind drifted over his day, busy with moving a few belongings into the house, having driven over three hours from Charlestown. The house was furnished, but he brought clothes, toiletries, books, and a few personal items to place around.

After a few more minutes, he hefted his body out of the chair, the still sweating but now empty beer bottle dangling in his fingers, and walked inside his house.

The small cottage had belonged to his grandparents, before they moved into town. His grandfather, wanting to keep a place to spend weekends fishing, never sold the property. "That house was built back when people knew how to build houses," his grandpa would brag. "It was built to withstand wind and weather." Years later he left it to his grandson. Mitch used to wonder if he would keep it or sell it, but as long as his parents were living, it gave him a place to stay when he came to visit.

Who would have thought I'd end up living here? Stepping into the kitchen, he tossed his bottle into the recycle bin by the door. The kitchen was U-shaped, with a new black stove and refrigerator. The sink had been upgraded as well and a dishwasher took the place of a few bottom cabinets.

The remaining cabinets and counter space were not abundant but served his needs. Opening the refrigerator, he chuckled at the amount of food his mother had stocked. Reaching in, he grabbed a plastic storage container labeled **Lasagna** and popped it into the microwave.

A knock on the front door sent him walking past the dining table and through the cozy living room with the overstuffed sofa and chair filling up much of the space. He had left the front door open when he finished moving the boxes in earlier in the afternoon, making it easy to see through the screen door at the visitor standing on his front porch.

The blue eyes of the beautiful blonde met his, a wide smile filling her face. "Well, hello, stranger!"

Throwing open the screen door, he braced as his cousin, Jillian, bolted through, hurling herself at him.

Hugging her closely he smiled, having wondered when she would make an appearance. "What took you so long?" he teased.

She stepped back, slapping his arm and said, "Hey, some of us have to work for a living!" Winking as she headed into the living room, she tossed her bag onto the floor before plopping down into the chair, draping her long legs dangling over one of the arms.

Following her lead, he settled on the sofa, placing his

feet onto the well-worn coffee table still sporting the dents from the many games they played as children.

Looking around, she smiled, "The old place still looks the same. You going to change it? Make it your own bachelor pad?"

Chortling at her goofiness, he said, "Think I'm a little too old to have a bachelor pad, cuz." His gaze drifted around the room, assaulted by the memories of many family gatherings in the cottage. "I've got some furniture I put in storage and figure I can use it at some time if I move to another house."

The quiet of the evening settled over the pair.

"So, what's new?" he asked, knowing if anyone had the gossip of what was going on in the small town, it would be her.

"New?" she scoffed. "Baytown has hardly changed!" She twisted a long lock of blonde hair between her fingers and added, "Honestly, Mitch? Since you Baytown boys all left after graduation and joined the military, it's been kinda boring."

"Graduation was thirteen years ago, cuz. I know things have changed," he protested. "I've been back for family visits enough to know that!"

"Well, I guess I just meant that not much has changed over the years. Have you seen anyone since you got in?"

"I saw Aiden and Brogan when I visited the town council a couple of weeks ago, but I just got moved in today." Aiden and Brogan MacFarlane owned Finn's pub, handed down to them by their grandfather, Finn

MacFarlane. Brogan graduated with him and Aiden one year behind; both joined the Marines as Mitch went into the Army.

"Did you hear Callan was back?"

"No shit?"

"He's still with the Coast Guard and stationed here."

"Anyone else?" Mitch inquired, wanting to find out more about his old friends who had left Baytown.

"Well, Zac is with the Fire Department, but I know you talked with him the last time you were here. He took over as chief about six months ago, so now he gets to be the boss of the volunteers." Her gaze dropped to her lap as she added, "And of course you and Grant will be working together on the force."

Mitch smiled, thinking of the gang he hung out with as a teenager. Baytown Boys. That was what they referred to themselves as, all itching to leave one of the poorest counties in Virginia. *All of us wanting something... to go somewhere. Anywhere but here,* he thought ruefully.

Jillian and Mitch smiled at each other for a long moment, the silence comfortable between them. Finally, Mitch asked, "You come all the way over here just to sit and stare at me?"

Throwing her head back in laughter, Jillian cried, "Jerk!" As she sobered, she wondered aloud, "You okay? About everything?"

"Wow...way to ask a million-dollar question," he joked. Noticing her eyes were not sparkling, he added, "Hey, I'm good."

Swinging her long, tanned legs back to the front of

the chair, she leaned forward resting her forearms on her knees. "Mitch, I know you. You couldn't wait to move out of this podunk town. Hell, you left for boot camp the day after your high school graduation. And these last several years? You've been a big-shot FBI agent."

"Hardly a big shot," he interjected.

"You know what I mean," she said.

The silence fell between them once more, this time less comfortable. Leaning back in the chair, she pinned him with her stare. "Got all night, Mitchy boy."

Laughing, he teased, "Jillian, you were a pain in my ass as a tomboy kid always trying to do what us boys were doing. Stayed a pain in my ass when you had those same boys chasing you in high school. And you're still a pain in my ass!"

Meeting his grin, she retorted, "That's what cousins are for!"

Nodding, he finally answered her concern. "I'm really good. Honestly." Seeing her raised eyebrow, he continued, "Yes, I wanted out of this town when I was a teen. Joining the military with the guys was the right thing to do. But it didn't take long to figure out that watching some of your friends die or get blown apart in battle wasn't what I wanted to keep doing."

Jillian's face immediately softened, her blue eyes warm with concern. "I'm sorry, Mitch. I shouldn't have been so cavalier with my words."

"It's okay," he said, his voice gentle. "Back stateside,

being in the military police seemed safer, but the Army wasn't ever going to be my career."

She leaned back in her chair, eager to listen to him. Tucking a few wayward strands of long hair behind her ear, she smiled her encouragement.

"Couldn't figure out anything other than police science as a major and then, hell, the FBI was exactly what I wanted to do."

"Grandpa and your dad were thrilled for you to become an agent," she reminded. "The town's past Police Chiefs loved the idea of their golden boy working for the FBI. You know they'd never want you to give up your dreams...not for them...not even for this town."

Pinning her with his intelligent blue-eyed gaze, he said, "Dreams change, Jillian. What was once important sometimes becomes less important."

"Did your dreams change or did you just adapt?" she prodded.

Chuckling, he said, "If this had all happened two years ago I woulda given you a different answer. But yeah, my dreams changed. The FBI bureaucracy became ponderous. I was no longer able to be as effective as I wanted to be. Honest to God, if it hadn't been for a private investigation firm I partnered with, I woulda lost my mind at times."

"I thought last Christmas, when you visited, you were thinking about joining them."

"Yeah, I was. But...well, the call came in about dad's

heart attack..." he said shrugging. "And then the call came in from the mayor. So, becoming the Police Chief of my hometown seemed like something I would like to do." Hesitating for a moment, he looked down at his hands, deep in thought, before speaking again. "I know I made a difference as an FBI agent, but the Bureau was so large that I rarely got to see the good I was doing. Sometimes, I didn't get a chance to really connect with the victims of the crimes I investigated . But here," he looked back up at her, "I can get to know the townspeople again. I can make a difference in their lives." Chuckling, he added, "Maybe I'm still a small-town boy at heart."

Sighing, she evaluated his words, finding only truth behind his explanations. "Well, gotta say, Baytown is lucky to have you, but I think you'll find being the Police Chief here a lot more boring than chasing down terrorists and major criminals with the FBI!"

"No problem with a slower, simpler life, cuz," he agreed. "That's all part of the dream that changes with age. I'm ready to get back to the life I was so ready to run away from when I got out of high school."

The silence once more settled comfortably between the two as each slipped into their own thoughts. After a moment, Jillian asked, "Remember the great tailgate parties we would have on old man Tollin's farm? Or the bonfires on the beaches?"

"Yeah," Mitch admitted. "Drinking way before we were supposed to. Me trying to keep some vacationing kid from getting too fresh with you. Hell, that alone, kept me busy!"

"Me? I seem to remember you trying to get it on with a few of the vacationing girls!"

The two cousins laughed at the long-ago memories before Jillian stood and walked to the door. Turning to hug Mitch, she clung tight to his shoulders and said, "I'm glad you're back, Mitch. I'm sorry for your dad...I know he hates convalescing after his heart attack. Being forced to retire wasn't what he wanted. But Baytown needs a good Police Chief and no one's better than you to follow in grandpa's and your dad's footsteps."

He returned her embrace, showing his gratitude for her visit. As she strolled back to her scooter, he watched as she drove down his pea-gravel driveway, her hand lifted up in a wave as she disappeared into the night.

Closing and locking the front door, Mitch walked back through the house to his bedroom, turning off the lights as he went. Years of having a security system out of necessity had him wanting to arm his residency, but then he laughed. *Don't reckon anyone would even know I was out here, much less try to break in.*

Stripping, he took a shower in the miniscule bathroom before walking back into the bedroom with just a towel hanging low on his lean hips. Stopping at his dresser, he looked at the three, small, framed pictures he had placed on top. The first picture was of his family taken last Christmas. Grandparents, parents, aunt and uncle, and Jillian. All smiling. *Who woulda ever guessed that one month later grandpa would be gone and six months later, dad would be laid up with a heart attack?*

The next picture was one taken a month ago. The

investigation firm he mentioned to his cousin was the Saints Protection & Investigations, run by Jack Bryant, a former Army Special Forces sergeant. The ten men... and their women, had become not only co-investigators with him but good friends. He had planned on resigning from the FBI and working for Jack until the phone call from his mom came in.

The last picture...the Baytown boys. Taken at a tailgate party right before graduation, he peered at the fresh, young faces. All eager. All ready to take on the world. Most returned from the military like him. Hardened. Seasoned. A few returned in worse shape, both physically and mentally. And two did not return at all.

Turning sharply away from the dresser and the memories the pictures held, he jerked the towel off and tossed it into the bathroom before sliding under the covers. Lying on his back, his muscular arm tucked underneath his head, he wondered if sleep would come. Getting up to open the window in his bedroom, he slid back into bed, listening to the sound of the gentle surf, and fell into a deep sleep, dreams full of young friends partying on the beach, beers in their hands, watching the girls walk by...and hoping one in particular would appear.

2

Early the next morning, Mitch wandered into the kitchen, popping a pod into the coffee maker and a slice of bread into the toaster. Opening the refrigerator door, he stared at the eggs and package of bacon, knowing it would only take a few minutes to fix breakfast, but thoughts of hitting the diner flitted through his mind. The last time he had been to Baytown, after his father's heart attack, he had run by the diner and been pleasantly surprised to see Katelyn working there. Aiden and Brogan's sister was just as adept at keeping up with the local gossip as Jillian.

He would be keeping up with old friends in any instance, but as the new Police Chief, it would be beneficial to make sure he stayed abreast of comings and goings. Thinking that a stop at the diner for breakfast might be the perfect chance to see and be seen, he finished his coffee quickly.

Walking back into the bedroom, he headed into the

bathroom for a shower. While inside the tiny stall, bumping his elbows on the walls several times, he wondered about the feasibility of adding on to the old structure as opposed to renting a new place. *Time to think about that later.*

He dressed in a royal blue shirt and dark slacks, then locked the front door behind him as he jogged down the front step. Climbing into his Jeep, he drove the few miles to Main Street.

The oldest part of Baytown was built on a square grid, with Main Street on one side, closer to the small harbor. Another side faced the Chesapeake Bay where the public beach enticed townspeople and visitors, and a park sat in the middle of town. About fifteen years prior, a developer built a golf course community on a large farm, and it was annexed into the city as well. On the other side, another developer built large vacation rental homes as well as a marina and a seafood restaurant.

Formerly plantations, the land was purchased in the late 1800s by a man intent on running the Pennsylvania Railroad down to the end of the Eastern Shore of Virginia where a harbor would allow goods and passengers to travel by water to Virginia Beach or Norfolk. By 1885, Baytown was already bustling with commercial and residential buildings.

As Mitch observed the view as he drove, he knew this epicenter of North Heron County took a nose dive during World War II, when trucks and highways took over much of the carrying of goods after the Bay Bridge and Tunnels were built. Now, Baytown resembled more of a sleepy village until the warm weather vacationers came through.

Parking outside of Stuart's Pharmacy and Diner, he strolled in, his gaze wandering around the familiar interior. The restaurant resembled an old-fashioned drugstore and soda shop. The tourist items were in the front, while the drugstore sundry items for sale were on the right with the pharmacy in the back. To the left was a long counter with rotating stools and a small seating area filled with plastic covered booths. The kitchen was behind the counter and the smells of a greasy breakfast called to him.

Katelyn MacFarlane, serving platters of eggs, bacon, and hashbrowns to a group of fishermen, looked up as he walked in. Her long black hair was pulled back into a sleek ponytail and the pink and white blouse she wore with her name embroidered across the chest pocket did nothing to hide her lush figure. Her face registered surprise for only a second before she stood, her hands on her hips, and grinned. As usual her smile filled the room, with her white teeth and adorable dimples.

He observed a couple of fishermen ogling her as she stood, but no one would mess with her, or they would face the wrath of her two brothers.

"Well, if it isn't the long-lost Baytown Boy, returning as the new Police Chief!" she exclaimed before rushing into his arms.

Once her arms were around him in a tight embrace,

she whispered, "So sorry about your dad, Mitch. But really glad you came home."

She pulled back before he could respond and he watched as she twisted around to the diner's patrons and shouted, "Boys, be on your best behavior now! The new Police Chief is in town!" Giggling as he shot her a pretend glare, she ushered him to the counter and slapped her hand on the smooth surface. "Anything he wants. On the house!" With that, she squeezed his shoulder and hustled back to finish pouring the coffee for the others.

The girl behind the counter looked at him in awe, her eyes large in her small face. The teenager stood rooted to the floor as an older woman came from the kitchen, wearing the same white and pink blouse as Katelyn and the teen. Her face, still smooth in her sixties, had a few more crinkles on the outsides of her eyes, a tribute to the many laughs she shared with her patrons over the years. Her hair, now more gray than blonde, was still teased out and piled on top of her head.

"Betty?" Mitch called out, recognizing the woman who had been with the diner for as long as he could remember. She used to serve him and the other guys when they came in after high school football practice.

"Lord, have mercy!" Betty called out, a smile on her face matching Katelyn's. "I knew you were going to be back here for us, but didn't expect to see you so soon."

"Thought nothing would be better than starting off my first day with your breakfast in me!"

Betty noticed the blank expression on the teen wait-ress and snapped her fingers in front of her face. "Juleen, get a move on. The new Police Chief needs his breakfast and he ain't gonna get it with you standing here gawking at him."

The teen blushed and grabbed her pad and pencil, ready to take his order. She scribbled as he ordered scrambled eggs, a stack of pancakes, sausage, and hash-browns along with coffee and a tall orange juice.

"Lordy, that's a lot," she said, her eyes wide once more.

"I like to eat," Mitch grinned, seeing Katelyn walking back in as Juleen hustled to the back.

Katelyn finished pouring the fishermen their coffee before settling on the stool next to him. "Jillian called me last night, so I was hoping to see you. Glad you came in."

"I figured I needed to reconnect with the town as soon as possible," he replied, his eyes lighting up as the food was placed in front of him. "And, figured between you and Jillian, I'll learn the latest town gossip."

Throwing her head back in laughter, she nodded her agreement. "Yep, I guess between her coffee shop, the diner here, and the bar, we keep up on everything."

They were quiet while he began to shovel in the food, knowing he would need to run a few extra miles to work off the calories. She moved to refill coffees and then took care of the fishermen who walked to the counter to pay.

Giving them a wave goodbye, she returned to the stool. Looking thoughtful for a second, she said, "I honestly don't know a ton of new gossip, Mitch. Baytown's got some new vacation houses that have gone up near the marina. That great new seafood restaurant built near the harbor pulls in a big crowd. Of course, the bar brings in mostly locals all year and vacationers during the tourist season, but even that's not too exciting."

"I saw some new businesses on Main Street," he commented.

"We've got some nice new shops that have come in and the shop owners seem to get along well with the established businesses. The nursing home on the outskirts of town has expanded, which has brought in some new employees. Still have the newer hotel and a couple of bed and breakfast places scattered around. The schools got a grant for more teachers since the state test scores sucked, so some new, young, fresh blood is in town."

Grinning at her description, he asked, "Anything you can think of that I'll need to know before I head over to the Department building?"

She scrunched her face into a frown as she thought. "Some bar fights. Some shoplifting during vacation season. Some vandalism, probably by teenagers." Giving a look of distaste, she said, "Some domestic violence." Holding his gaze, she admitted, "Mitch, I think you'll be bored!"

Pushing his empty plate back, he smiled at her. "Thanks for the breakfast and news. Tell your brothers I'll be over as soon as I can."

"I only work here for breakfast and then I work the bar in the afternoons, so I'll be with them in a couple of hours. Don't be a stranger!" She moved over to take the order from some other customers who came in as he sipped his coffee.

The bell over the door sounded and his gaze automatically slid to the left, watching to see who was coming in next. A young couple. Another trio of fishermen. And behind them, all he could see at first was a mass of red hair. Long, reddish-blonde hair hung in a thick sheet.

The woman was bending over from the waist, hopping on one foot as she struggled with a strap on her sandal. Slipping it into place she stood, blushing as she realized the fisherman in front of her had been holding the door open for her to enter.

"Oh, I'm sorry," she gushed, tripping as she hurried into the diner.

By now, Mitch was mesmerized. Not only by the striking hair color and long, tanned legs showcased in khaki cuffed shorts, but also her noticeable curves in a hunter green, ribbed tank top. Unfortunately, her face was turned so he was unable to discern her features.

Swiveling on his stool, his coffee forgotten, he tracked her as she wandered into the store. Once inside, she searched the area before moving toward the drug store items, disappearing between the shelves. As she popped out the other end with a bottle of Calamine Lotion held up in front of her face as she perused the bottle's label, she glanced his way.

As his gaze viewed part of her face, he began to smile, hoping for an introduction. He watched in surprise as she ducked back into the aisle. Dumbstruck, he wondered what sent her scurrying.

Something familiar about her hair niggled at the recesses of his memory; of a long-ago child playmate he used to spend his summers teasing and the beautiful teen she had become. *Tori Bradford.* She had crossed his mind many times over the years, but he had never tried to contact her after high school. *She's long gone by now.* An incoming alert from his phone had him checking the time. *Damn, I've got to go.* Downing the last of his coffee, he slid off the stool, waving at Katelyn just coming from the back with more food to serve, his eyes traveling once more over the aisles, wondering where the beauty slipped off to.

Even though she had told him breakfast was on the house, he tossed money on the counter—plenty to pay for the meal and a decent tip for the teen. Slipping on his sunglasses, he headed out into the sun. Time to get to work.

Mitch Evans! Dammit, I would have to run into him on his first day on the job. Not that I was paying any attention to when his first day was. Dropping her chin to her chest, her unruly hair offered a curtain to her red face. *Who am I kidding? Of course, I would be keeping up with the town's Golden Boy coming home to be the new Police Chief.*

Victoria Bradford, known as Tori to her friends, had only been in town a couple of months...*two months, one week, and three days to be exact.* She knew exactly how long considering she had moved in one week to the day before her beloved grandmother had died.

Standing slowly, barely peeking over the drugstore shelves, she watched as Mitch walked out of the diner and toward his jeep. *Whew...coast is clear.* Tucking a wayward strand of hair behind her ear, she turned and almost ran into Katelyn standing right behind her, a twinkle in her eyes.

"Uh...are you okay, Tori?"

Face blazing once again, Tori stammered, "Yes! Um...yes. I was just...um...getting lotion." She held up the Calamine lotion gripped tightly in her hand as though needing proof that she had not been hiding from someone. "I...um...found some poison ivy when I was clearing off the backyard."

"Mmmm," Katelyn murmured noncommittally, a wide smile spreading across her beautiful face as her gaze moved from Tori's to the door. "You know, I seem to remember way back in high school, you had a crush on—"

"Oh, water under the bridge," Tori gushed. "My goodness, Katelyn, we all hung out with each other."

"Yes, but when we went to games, it was always Mitch you cheered for the loudest."

"Well, who wouldn't? He was the Golden Boy, you know!" Glad she was not Pinocchio for fear her nose would elongate with more lies, she rushed to say, "Anyway, my summers here at Baytown were mostly enjoying you and Jillian and my grandmother."

Katelyn's expression quickly changed to one of sympathy as she reached her hand out and placed it on Tori's arm. "I'm so sorry about your grandmother, Tori. She was loved by the whole town."

Blinking back tears she thought had long since left, she smiled in return.

"How are you doing with everything? It seems like you've had a steady stream of guests this month."

"It's going fine. So far, I haven't changed anything, and grandma already had these reservations. I thought maybe in the off-season, I would upgrade the Inn a bit. No major changes," she added. "Just a few things that I think some of the younger guests would appreciate."

"Well, I...in fact, the whole town is pleased as punch that your grandmother left the Sea Glass Inn to you. I think she knew you would love it as much as she did and not just sell it to someone who wanted to tear it down and build a million-dollar condo!"

"Oh, I could never!" Tori exclaimed.

Betty called out an order and Katelyn belted, "Be right up!" Turning back, Katelyn patted Tori's arm again and said, "It's always good to see you. Make sure to come in often, and we'll get the girl gang together soon!"

As Tori made her way to the front to pay, Katelyn glanced to the door Mitch just left from and then stared at Tori's back, a slow smile creeping across her face. Katelyn knew Tori was lying...Mitch Evans had been her friend's obsession.

3

Walking into the Baytown Municipal building, Mitch headed to the mayor's office first. The Police Headquarters' entrance was on the side of the building with its own lobby, receptionist—who also served as the dispatcher—a larger room with desks, conference room, and what would be his office. But first, time to meet the mayor, so he entered on the other side.

He visited the building a month before when talking to the Mayor and Town Council and noticed the building had not changed much since the time his grandfather had worked there. The vinyl tile gleamed just as bright, if not a little yellowed on the edges. The painted cinderblock walls stood straight. The garish fluorescent light fixtures still made a slight buzzing sound. Strangely, Mitch found comfort in the old building that was so familiar.

Before he made it to the receptionist's desk, she was already on the phone announcing his arrival. As he stepped forward, she stood, her hand stretched out to take his in a firm handshake.

"Chief Evans, good to officially meet you! You probably don't remember me, but I've been here so long, I was just starting when your grandfather was Chief, and then your dad."

"Mrs. Marten, I remember you very well," he greeted, her handshake warm and welcoming.

Still smiling, she nodded her head down the hall that passed by her desk and said, "The Mayor will see you now. You can go on back." Then, lifting her eyebrow, she leaned forward whispering conspiratorially, "Watch out for his new secretary."

His brow furrowed in question, but it only took a few steps down the short hall to discover what her warning was about—a young woman, with more makeup than a theatrical actress, wearing what could only be described as one of the tightest, shortest dresses Mitch had ever seen, and that included clubbing in a big city.

The woman's head, full of sexed-out and cement-sprayed hair, turned his way and she eagle-eyed him as he made it to her desk. Her blood-red lips matched her long-painted fingernails, and she quickly stood, leaning over the desk.

"You must be the new Police Chief," she breathed, affecting what he assumed was her sexy voice but made her sound asthmatic.

"Yes, I'm here to see Mayor Banks," he replied, adopting a formal approach, afraid anything friendlier might cause her to jump over her desk toward him. He was not sure her miniature dress would withstand the leap.

Slowly smoothing her hands down her hips in an effort to draw his attention, she pouted when his eyes moved to the mayor's office, the door already open.

"Since he's expecting me, I'll go on in."

Teetering on her heels, she rushed around the desk, her long talons grasping his arm. "I'm supposed to announce you," she purred, giving his bicep a squeeze. "Ooh, you're big, aren't you?"

Her eyes dropped to his crotch, and Mitch, afraid she was going to grab him there, pulled away from her grip, slipping by her. "I figure the mayor and I'll need to see each other quite often. I won't expect you to announce me every time," he said, hurrying into the office and shutting the door behind him.

Elected as mayor almost fifteen years ago, Corwin Banks took his role very seriously. As small as Baytown was, he enjoyed a large office, very different from the stark utilitarianism of the rest of the building. Dark paneled wood covered three walls with floor to ceiling bookcases taking up the wall behind his large, ostentatious desk. Heavy chairs, the padding covered in navy leather, stood in front of his desk.

Mitch had first been in the office the month prior when he had been offered the job his father had to vacate. Recognizing the attempt to be a big fish in a very small pond, Mitch stifled a grin.

Corwin had at one time been a handsome man,

marrying the town fair's beauty queen, but the years had not been kind to him. Struggling to stand, he heaved his girth from his chair. "Mitch, good to see you. Can't tell you how happy the town is to snag you away from the FBI and have you come back home."

Before Mitch had a chance to speak, Corwin nodded for him to have a seat while he plopped heavily back in his chair. "Yes, yes, indeed. Me snagging you for our Police Chief might make the next election go very easily for me," he chuckled.

Itching to start work, Mitch said, "Yes, sir. I'd like to meet with my staff this morning but wanted to come by first to say hello."

The door opened and a slender man walked quickly in the room. Thrusting his hand out toward Mitch, he clipped, "Silas Mills. City Manager. Wasn't here when you came last time. Vacation. Just got back."

The man's short delivery of pertinent information seemed odd in a small town full of residents who loved to talk. Mitch shook his hand, not surprised to find the city manager's handshake was like his communication. Short and quick.

"Nice to meet you," Mitch replied.

"Only been here a few months. Didn't get to know your dad much. Hear we're lucky to have you. Make sure to work within your budget. We're not FBI here."

Jesus, this man is wrapped too tight! "I grew up in this town," Mitch said, holding Silas' gaze until the other man dropped his eyes. "Think I know how to take care of the residents."

"Yes, well, the residents are one thing, but we need to make sure to do whatever we can to keep the vacationers coming."

Cocking his head, he was about to speak when Corwin jumped in. "Silas is a wonder with ideas to keep the money rolling into our little town."

Mitch noted as a glance passed between the two men but, while naturally good at reading people, he had no idea what just occurred. "Then I'll leave the politics to you and make sure my department fulfills its responsibilities without compromising anyone's special interests."

The silence in the room was thunderous.

"Right-e-o," Corwin said and reached to the side of his desk. "Got some things just for you to look over. Police budget files mostly. City budget. City Council notes concerning the Police department."

Mitch's patience plummeted as a stack of files were placed in front of him. Standing, he picked them up and said, "I'll begin looking these over."

"My wife and I are planning a welcome party for you at the new restaurant in town. We'll have some of the businessmen and women, as well as a few high rollers from the golfing community, present. It'll be a chance for you to meet some of the important people you'll be protecting."

"I appreciate that, but I plan on getting out as soon as possible to start meeting as many people as I can on the streets. Residents as well as the business owners."

Bristling slightly, Corwin nodded, his jowls shaking

with the motion. "Yes, of course. Mitch, I let your father run the Police department the way he wanted, and he served us proud. I'm sure you'll do the same."

"I plan on it, but I'm not my father. Can't say I'll be making too many changes, but with the ones I do make, I'll expect your support."

A bit of blustering came from the older man as he ran his hand over his thinning hair. "I'm sure you'll have all the support you need. Just remember, people 'round here don't take to change too much."

Nodding, Mitch walked out, the stack of files in his arms. As soon as he stepped outside, he dodged the mayor's secretary and stalked down the hall to the back entrance of the police station.

Entering, he breathed a sigh of relief. *This is more like it.* Moving down the short hall, he passed two interview rooms on the right, a hall leading to the small holding cell area, and on the left, his office. Stepping inside to drop off the files, he halted. It suddenly hit him. This very room had been his grandfather's office. *I remember thinking it was the greatest thing on earth to be able to come visit grandpa here when I was a kid.* Enthralled by the uniform, the respect others gave, and especially the gun his grandfather strapped to his side, made it a dream job to a little boy.

Setting the files on the desk, he heaved a heavy sigh. The last time he had been here was when he visited his dad while home for the holidays. Closing his eyes, he could clearly envision his father sitting behind the desk —one of his rare times chained to the desk since his dad preferred to be out and about the town. *If only I'd known then how close my dad would come to dying...I'd have stayed longer.* His father was straining at the restraints of the convalescence, but Mitch's mom was running a tight ship. A smile slipped out as he thought about his parents. A noise behind him startled him out of his musings.

"Oh, sorry sir. I didn't realize you were here yet."

Mitch turned around and viewed the man in the crisp uniform. He appeared to be in his early thirties, blond hair, and physically fit. Intelligent green eyes peered back at him, seeming to be sizing him up as well.

"You must be Burt Tobber," Mitch said, shaking the officer's hand.

"Yes, sir. I'm sorry I wasn't here to meet you last month when you came by. Good to see you now. We're sorry to lose your dad but real glad to have you here with us."

Mitch measured the officer, finding his words sincere. Smiling back, he said, "I was just getting ready to head out front and see when we could schedule our first staff meeting."

"I think Mildred was already expecting that this morning, so she's got the officers all coming in at eight for you to meet with us."

Grinning, he said, "Efficient as ever."

Burt laughed as he nodded. "We won't be as fancy as the FBI, sir, but I can't imagine even they could compare to Mildred."

"I thought my ears were burning," the spry woman

declared as she popped around the corner into his office. Her smile greeted the two men as she stepped up to Mitch.

"Good to see you again, Chief Evans. Lord have mercy," she exclaimed. "You now make the third man I've served under and called Chief Evans!"

"I'm glad to be here, Mrs. Score," Mitch replied. "My dad and grandfather always spoke of you with the highest praise." He watched her blush with pride and added, "I also remember your husband and all the extra runs me and my friends would have to do if we were late to practice."

Throwing her head back, her blue-gray curls shaking, she laughed. "Oh my, yes. Chester may have driven you hard, but he loved you boys like his own." Her gray eyes twinkled as she looked him up and down speculatively. "You've grown up, like all the ones he coached. And look how well you've turned out. An FBI agent. My goodness. Well, Baytown is certainly pleased as punch to have you back with us."

Before Mitch had a chance to respond, she clapped her hands together and said, "Well, enough chit-chat. You've got things to get to, and my job is to do what I can to make that easier. I've called a staff meeting to convene in fifteen minutes. There's a Keurig in the staff room, but for your first day, I've had coffee and goodies delivered from your cousin's coffee shop." She stopped her dissertation and turned to leave, stopping at the door. Looking back, she grinned, "Welcome back home, Chief Evans."

As her sensible shoes squeaked down the hall, Mitch turned to Burt. "You're right...she's way more efficient than anything I had at the FBI."

Laughing, the two men headed to the staff room.

Sitting at the round table, Mitch viewed his staff, still munching on his cousin's pastries. Ginny Spencer was his first officer. Smart, driven, efficient...but with a shadow in her eyes. She had been with the Army Military Police and served in Afghanistan. She was pretty, but Mitch could not help but think that she held men at an arm's length to maintain professionalism. Her expression was eager and more than willing to make any changes he proposed, wanting to move the BPD forward.

Sam Stubbis was the oldest officer. He had been hired almost twenty years prior by Mitch's grandfather and was a native to the area. Well liked, Mitch appreciated the history and knowledge he could gain from Sam. Although...*he seems to be a little willing to turn a blind eye to some things. Might be a little harder to get him to go along with any changes.*

Grant Wilder had been one of the Baytown Boys with Mitch. He was a year behind in high school, but they played ball together. He joined the Army after graduation. Mitch was pleased to find out that he had been with the Virginia Beach PD for several years before coming back home. *Grant still has a flirtatious, eye-for-the-ladies manner about him...I may have to rein him in to maintain the professionalism of the force, but we're damn lucky to have an officer like him here.*

Burt Tobber was not a native of Baytown, having only moved to the Eastern Shore about three years ago. Mid-thirties, he was a family man and involved in the community. He and his wife volunteered with the school, boy scouts, church activities, and the Baytown recreation center. Not able to discern any problems, Mitch was thrilled to have him on board as well.

"First things, first," Mitch declared, gaining the attention of the group. Seeing Mildred start to leave the room, he called out, "Mrs. Score, I'd like you to stay. While you might not be needed for all staff meetings, I feel that your presence is necessary today, since you are an integral part of the staff."

Accepting her appreciative smile as she took her seat, he continued. "I come to this job, having to fill very large shoes. My grandfather, and then recently, my father, were examples of exactly what a Chief should be...accessible to staff and public, civic minded, non-biased, and driven by a love of this town. I have no desire to walk in and completely change things, but I will want to upgrade the department where we can and work with the town council on our budget."

That gained him emphatic nods from the others gathered around the table, so he continued, "And, to begin with, I would like to be called Mitch by my staff. In the community, you can address me as Chief or Chief Evans. But in here...I'm Mitch."

The others smiled and quickly agreed to first names amongst themselves. And so, the first staff meeting began.

Two hours later, as the meeting came to a close, Mitch looked around the table at his staff, pleased with how the meeting had progressed.

He had quickly reviewed the budget items he wanted to address with the town, discussed the schedule and ways to make it more efficient. Flow charts of duty divisions were plotted and equipment needs were itemized.

Not wanting to make grand changes, he wanted to institute certain new policies, which had been met with agreement from all.

One of them dealt with uniforms. The officers wore the traditional police black pants and shirts, but with budget cuts, they were a line item that Mitch felt could be looked at. Putting it to the group, he asked for input.

Grant asked, "What changes are you thinking about, Mitch? Gotta say, I'm not wedded to the black police uniform."

"I like uniforms, sir...uh...Mitch," Ginny said. "I suppose I was used to the Army uniform and so having a uniform in civilian life was easy for me. It also makes us stand out in a crowd."

"Ever since the town said that we may have to start paying for our own uniforms, which have to be ordered from a catalog, it's an expense I could do without," Burt added. "With two little kids, every dime counts for me, so I'd be interested in what alternative you're talking about."

Mitch nodded and said, "Many small communities are going with a more casual uniform. Easier to maintain, easier to pay for since you're responsible for your own uniforms. Examples would be khaki pants and polos or shirts with the BPD logo clearly embroidered on them. You would still be responsible for the clothes, but you can buy your khakis anywhere as long as they meet certain requirements."

He observed them carefully as he added, "With the money saved to the town, I will go to them to add more equipment to our budget."

The immediate response was exactly what he had hoped he would garner. All four officers immediately began talking about the old equipment and what they would want to have.

"Make a prioritized wish list of what you think this department needs to have, and I'll go through it before taking it to the Council," Mitch said. "Next, I need you to bring me up to date on any on-going cases. I plan on spending as much time as I can out in the community. Communication is key in this job. Each of us need to know what all is going on."

It did not take long for the others to fill Mitch in on the cases that were still being investigated— graffiti on the golf course, a theft of women's underwear on clotheslines throughout the town, and they had all been keeping their eye on the group of teens hanging around the basketball court after dark.

"They're not bad kids," Sam began, but was interrupted by Grant.

"Not yet, but I'm seeing drugs among the young, and we'd be stupid to turn a blind eye to what could be right in our backyard."

Sam pursed his lips and Mitch wondered if the older officer was ignoring or not aware of what the youth might be doing.

Just then, Mildred moved to answer the phone and then popped her head back in. "Got a call from Rupert Cramer. Seems some teens are using his back field as a drag race strip."

Ginny and Burt hopped up from the table, looking to Mitch to see if he had any other instructions.

Smiling, he nodded and watched as they hustled out of the room. And the new job began.

4

That afternoon, after work, Mitch stopped by Finn's Pub, tired and hungry from a day of organization and not investigation. Desperate for one of their pub burgers topped with crabmeat, he stepped into the old establishment. Never changing, the entrance held a dartboard to the right and an old fireplace and sofa on the left. The original building had been one of the early brick structures in the town. While renovated, it retained much of the original brickwork walls and floor from years gone by. The bar ran the length of the right side with tall, mismatched, padded bar chairs up against the counter. The left contained tables already full of patrons and the kitchens were in the back.

"Hell boys, look who just showed up! If it ain't the long arm of the law, straight from the fuckin' F.B.I.!"

Hauling himself up into an empty chair, nodding at the smiling faces of the others already there, Mitch looked over at Aiden MacFarlane, one of his oldest friends. Long, dark hair pulled back in a ponytail was the look Aiden now sported, along with the tats on his arms. Before he could greet him, another man walked behind the bar, cuffing Aiden on the shoulder.

"Shut the hell up, asshole. You ain't gotta be yelling across the place. We got some kids here eatin' dinner."

Actually blushing, Aiden looked over at the tables and yelled, "Sorry folks. Just got excited!"

Brogan, almost identical to his brother, rolled his eyes, looking over at Mitch. "Good to have you back, bro. What can we get you?"

Giving his order, Mitch enjoyed watching the two brothers bicker amongst themselves as they expertly handled the bar and grill. Their sister, Katelyn, came from the back a few minutes later bringing his food.

"Well, this must be my lucky day," she exclaimed jovially. "I get to serve you breakfast and dinner on the same day."

Laughing, Mitch dug into his burger. "Can't do this everyday or I'd spend my whole paycheck on food...and not be able to fit inside my jeep."

It took a while for him to finish his food as numerous town patrons stopped by to say how glad they were he took over for his father. Taking the time to shake their hands and listen for a minute if they had a concern to share, he finally took the last bite of his fries.

"So, how'd your first day go?" Aiden asked.

Mitch pushed his plate back and settled in with his beer. "Not bad. Met with the staff. Reviewed some policies, brought some new ones up, and went over budget concerns."

"God, that sounds boring!" Aiden blurted.

"Well, not every minute of every day is for fun and games," Brogan said, walking over, throwing a dish-towel over his shoulder, his typical glower in place.

Aiden, as usual not paying any attention to his brother's mood, kept his gaze on Mitch. "I reckon Baytown is a step down from the FBI, but I sure as fuck hope you have better days than this one or you just might not want to stay."

At that statement, Mitch realized the three MacFar-lane's gazes were pinned on him. "Guys, I'm not looking for exciting days to keep me here. I'm here...I'm stay-ing." Inwardly pleased to see them visibly relax, he wondered how many other townspeople had the same thought.

Before he had a chance to ponder that further, Aiden leaned forward, resting his tatted arm on the polished, worn bar, his eyes twinkling with mischief and said, "So, did you meet *Celia*?"

A confused expression crossed Mitch's face as he noticed Katelyn roll her eyes and the normally taciturn Brogan fight a smile. "Celia?"

Aiden crowed, "The mayor's new *secretary*? Hell, if that woman can type, I'll eat that bar stool you're sittin' on!"

Laughing, Mitch nodded. "Uh, yeah. I had the *plea-sure* of untangling myself from her claws this morning."

As their laughter ended, he asked, "What's the deal with her anyway?"

"Rumor has it that Corwin's wife is pissed about her husband's new secretary but, since she holds the purse strings in the family, he'll probably keep it in his pants," Katelyn said. "I think he's going through a mid-life crisis, 'cause the next thing we know, he's hired a secretary just for himself and in waltzes Celia Ring. And," she leaned forward, "gossip has it that the new town manager and her might be having a fling."

"As long as she stays on her side of the building, we'll be fine," Mitch pronounced, remembering how he feared for his manhood.

As they laughed, a couple of older men approached Mitch, wanting to congratulate him on taking the police chief job.

"Knew your grandpa and your dad," one of them said. "Sure, was glad to hear you were coming home."

"Thank you, sir," Mitch replied sincerely.

"Heard you was in the Army," another one said. The man looked at the brothers behind the bar and added, "And you?"

The MacFarlane's answered in unison, "Marines, sir," as Mitch nodded.

"Well, this might not be up the Police Chief's alley, but this town's got a need, and it ain't gonna happen with old fogies like us here."

"Sir?" Mitch asked, glancing first to his friends, but seeing their questioning gazes, focused his attention fully on the older men.

"If we want to be part of a veteran's organization, then we gotta go north and the American Legion's building is gettin' ready to be sold, so we need to find another one. Ain't no reason why we can't have a chapter here. We now got a bunch of you Baytown Boys back from serving in the military and we ought to have one too."

Mitch nodded slowly and confessed, "Well, sir, I haven't given it any thought, but I certainly will. And that's not the Chief saying that…that comes from me, the former soldier."

The three older men puffed with pride and smiled, shaking his hand once more, pumping it up and down. As they filed out of the pub, Mitch turned back around and startled as the three MacFarlane's stared at him.

"What?" he demanded.

"You haven't been back in town a full day, and you're already getting all civic-minded!" Aiden accused. "Those old dudes have asked us several times about trying to get new blood into the American Legion, but…well, I guess we just blew them off."

"Mitch," Katelyn said, squeezing his arm before walking away, "good to have you home!"

Mitch gazed back at his two oldest friends and shrugged, "There's a lot of us who came back, and I don't think it's such a bad idea to have a meeting place. Granted, I don't have a lot of information about the American Legion, but I've got no reason not to check into them."

Brogan, wiping the bar with his dishrag, nodded,

"Let me know what you find out. I'd be interested in discovering what a former Marine like me could do with an American Legion. I'm in." Walking to the back kitchen, he left Mitch and Aiden staring at his back.

"Well, fuck me," Aiden said. "That's more than he's talked about the service since he came back." Meeting Mitch's gaze, he added, "and since that was only a sentence, you can imagine what a big deal that just was."

Mitch knew Aiden had his issues from the war, hidden behind bravado and jokes. But Brogan came back quieter than ever and never spoke of his service time. Nodding, he met his friend's eyes, saying, "I'll check. Maybe we can resurrect the Baytown Boys...as men now."

"Hell, yeah!"

Sliding off the stool, Mitch tossed down his money and waved as he walked out into the evening breeze coming off the bay. Sucking in a deep breath of the warm, salty air, he decided to walk toward the town's public beach.

As he got to the end of the sidewalk, he sat down on one of the concrete benches and pulled off his shoes and socks. Rolling up his pants legs, he stuffed his socks into his shoes and headed out onto the sand.

A few families were still wandering on the beach having celebrated the sunset. It always amused him that the beach and town pier would be filled with sunset watchers. And as the sun finally dropped behind the bay's horizon, people would clap. Most were now packing up their towels and chairs and herding tired children back to their cars.

It did not take long for him to be one of the few left on the beach, and he walked along, the soft, white sand under his bare feet. As he stood with his toes in the water facing the bay, he was struck as always by the way the ever-undulating surf calmed his soul.

When he returned from his tour in Iraq, he threw himself into studying police science and becoming an FBI agent, burying memories of his time overseas. Occasionally, they came back, but for the most part he battled them down into the recesses. *But a lot of my buddies didn't do that...or can't.* Turning to face the town with his back to the water, he thought, *and some of the Baytown Boys could use an American Legion.* Hanging his head for a moment, he wondered how he would find the time to learn everything he needed to learn about being a police chief and deal with some of the veteran needs in the community.

Glancing down at the white sand, a flash of green caught his eye. Bending, he picked up the piece of sea glass. Smiling, he remembered that Baytown was one of the best places for collecting the surf-polished shards and his mind rolled back.

"Whatcha got in your hand?" I asked the pretty little girl, whose red hair, escaping the two braids, was whipping about her shoulders.

Katelyn and Jillian ran from behind me and hugged the little girl.

"She's our new friend," my six-year-old cousin, Jillian claimed. "Her grandmother owns the Sea Glass Inn."

As the new girl turned, I was captured by her large, sky-blue eyes peering back at me. Little freckles ran across her nose, and she smiled at me.

Just then, some of my friends came running over, chasing Katelyn and Jillian. Screams of "Tag, you're it!" rang out on the beach as they all ran off, leaving the new girl still standing and staring at me.

"I'm Tori," she said, her smile illuminating her face as the sunset colored the sky behind her head. Lifting her hand, she exposed a tiny piece of sea glass resting on her palm.

"That's sea glass," I said. Seeing her confused expression, I stepped closer. At eight, I already towered over her. "Do you know what sea glass is?"

Shaking her pigtails, she raised her blue eyes to mine.

"It's bits of glass that come from ships. They toss out their glass bottles and, once in the ocean, the glass gets broken and then tossed with the waves and sand. It polishes them so that the pieces are smooth."

Eyes wide, she breathed, "Ooh, how pretty." Fingering it in her hand, she asked, "Should I put it back on the sand?"

"No. You can keep it," I told her, loving the smile that greeted my words. She looked up at me as though I had given her permission to hold a priceless gem. "I'm Mitch, by the way."

Just then the gang ran back, still chasing each other and squealing in the evening sunset. "You wanna play?" I asked.

Grinning again, Tori tucked the piece of sea glass into the pocket of her shorts and nodded.

Reaching down, I grabbed her hand as we ran across the beach toward our friends.

His memories were interrupted by a light in the distance. An upstairs light shone from the third-story attic room of the Sea Glass Inn. French doors led to a balcony that had been built from that room, and the light poured forth. The building was an old, stately home facing the bay and he remembered the older woman who used to own it. *Mrs. Bradford. Tori's grandmother.* Her husband died in the Vietnam War and his widow ran the Inn ever since. *I wonder if she's still around? Or still alive?* Tori would cross his mind occasionally over the years, memories of her always bringing a smile. He chalked it up to nostalgia, much like the Baytown Boys. His feelings for the little, red-haired pigtail girl grew until, as an adolescent, he discovered his body responding just at the sight of her. *I thought at one time...well, I was just a kid then. Life intervened. War intervened.*

Before his memories were able to go down that road, his attention was diverted when a woman stepped through the glass door of the attic room onto the balcony. The evening was too dark to tell her features, but he discerned her long hair blowing in the breeze. She stood with her hands on the railing, facing the water for several minutes, before dropping her head as though looking at the beach below.

The distance kept him from seeing where she was looking, but as she halted her perusal, he could swear it was as though she pinned him with her gaze. His pulse jumped and, before he could stop himself, he raised his hand to wave.

The woman suddenly whirled around, her hair flying about her shoulders with the motion. She hustled back through the doors, pulling the curtains over them.

Stunned—and rooted to the spot—Mitch realized his hand was still in mid-wave. *Wow...never had that effect on a woman before.* Shaking his head as he made his way back to his car, he thought, *hell, from that far she probably didn't even see me. And certainly didn't know who I was.*

That night, as he lay in bed, his mind filled with the events of the day, he thought back to the Inn and the mysterious woman on the balcony. As he drifted off to sleep, he dreamed of the blue-eyed, red-haired little girl he used to play with when she would visit her grandmother and, when they were older, how his adolescent blood ran hot at the sight of the pretty teenager she had become that last summer.

Tori sat on the end of her bed, her head hanging down with her red hair falling all about. *I am such a dork! There's no way Mitch could have seen me up here in the shadows of the building, but now he'll think whoever is here is a complete nincompoop!*

Flopping back on the bed, her legs still hanging off the side, she stared at the ceiling fan in her room. Mesmerized by the motion, her mind wandered down memory lane.

Summers in Baytown were my favorite part of the year. Time with grandma. Time away from arguing parents who failed miserably at hiding from their two daughters how much they wanted different things. Dad wanted to move back to tiny Baytown, and mom wanted him to stay in Virginia Beach, move up the corporate ladder at the bank, and finally be able to give her the country club living she desired.

I never met friends back home like the ones I had here. A fun group of girls and boys always swarmed over to the Sea Glass Inn during the summers and included me in their games. My sister, Vanessa, rarely there, tried to hog attention like she did at home, but the kids in Baytown never liked her more than me. Maybe that's why Vanessa used to be so mean to me and refused to spend summers here.

I loved my friends. I loved the acceptance. I loved spending time with my grandmother. A smile crept across her face as she admitted to herself...*I loved Mitch Evans.*

Sitting up, Tori looked around her beloved room. By the time she was a teenager, Vanessa did not want to stay in Baytown for the whole summer, but Tori begged to stay. When she was fourteen, her grandmother said,

"I'm going to turn the attic into a nice room and you can stay there when you come, if you'd like."

She had been thrilled, and even more excited when her grandmother let her help decorate. The walls were painted a soft blue with white wood trim. The lace curtains were white as was the comforter on the queen bed. The antique dresser and chest of drawers were painted distressed white as well. A small window over-looked the back of the property and underneath sat a desk, perfect for writing—something Tori loved to do. But her favorite change was the balcony and glass doors her grandmother had added.

It was Tori's, and she didn't have to share it with her sister. *Vanessa was never enthralled with the charm of the Sea Glass Inn.*

The thought of her grandmother brought a familiar pang to her heart. Moving to the dresser, she brushed her hair; the memory of her grandmother doing the same act had her soon laying the brush down. Looking at her reflection, she said, "You're trying not to think about Mitch Evans, aren't you?"

Refusing to answer herself aloud, she nonetheless knew what the answer was. *Of all the friends I had here, Mitch Evans was the one who I wanted to give my heart to.* By the time the kids had become teens, Tori had fallen for Mitch. Afraid to tell him of the depths of her feel-ings, she tried to pretend she did not care for him more than the others. *He must have liked me too...at one time.* She remembered how he would always manage to sit next to her at ball games or picnics in the park. She even caught Aiden making kissy faces at them once behind Mitch's back.

She never liked to think about the girls he may have dated during the school year when she was back at home, but he was always single during the summers, and she would pretend that was because of her.

Wrapping her arms around her waist, she remembered the last spring break before his high school graduation when, visiting her grandmother again, Mitch had asked her to the town picnic. Vanessa and mom left the day of the picnic but as soon as her sister found out her plans, she had to ruin everything.

"Why, Tori, I had no idea you liked Mitch. He's a great kisser," Vanessa crooned.

My heart jolted at her words. How would she know?

Continuing to stab at my heart, Vanessa leaned in so that mom couldn't hear her words and said, "Little sis, you should know he's been after me for over a year. Begged me to give up my virginity to him." Smiling as though in the throes of a sweet memory, she continued, "I finally gave in and had sex with him last summer when you were laid up with a cold. Of course, after I found out he slept with lots of girls, I broke it off."

My face, unable to hide my hurt, seemed to give Vanessa pleasure.

"Oh, honey, it's so much better for you to know that he's a player." The corners of her lips turned up, as she drove the knife in a little further. "But I gotta say that sex with Mitch

Evans may have ruined me for any other man." Patting my shoulder she added, "But if you don't mind your sister's castoffs, go for it."

Mom called, and Vanessa turned to climb back in the car. Mom yelled that she would be back to pick me up in a couple of days. I don't remember waving. All I remember doing was going up to my room and crying.

When Mitch showed up to take me to the picnic, I had grandma tell him I was sick. And I stayed sick for the next two days. My adolescent heart broken, I left Baytown and did not go back that summer. First college, then a job. I knew Mitch had joined the Army and then the FBI. Grandma would always fill me in on the comings and goings of Baytown and especially the Baytown Boys, as they were known.

But I never saw Mitch Evans again. Until today.

5

"So, Chief Evans, do you play golf?"

Mitch gazed out of the clubhouse over the emerald-green expanse of grass, bordered with flowers and pines. He had to admit, the golf course was beautiful and the surrounding houses and condos in the gated community gave a boost to the economy of Baytown. Looking back at the three men he dined with, he wondered how many more meetings like this he would need to endure before he settled into the routine of his job.

Having been the Police Chief since Monday, it was now Friday and he had met with the Rotary Club, Town Council, PTSO, Clergy of Baytown, Lions Club, Business Men & Women of Baytown, Board of the Boys and Girls Club, Eastern Shore National Wildlife, Commercial Fishermen's Organization, and now the board members of The Dunes Golf Club.

He was about at the end of his patience, considering

every organization had their own agenda concerning what they wanted and expected from the Police Chief, not to mention that in such a small community, many of the same people populated the different groups.

Plastering on a smile, he nodded politely and said, "Yes, I do occasionally. I'm afraid I haven't had time recently and won't in the near future, but I certainly appreciate what has been built here."

His answer appeared to placate the members of the board, and he was grateful to take his leave, nodding at the waitress and bartender as he walked out into the bright sunshine. He drove through the gates, then meandered through the harbor, making a circle in front of the new seafood restaurant, The Seafood Shack. A popular eatery, he had not dined there yet and put it on his list as next to visit. Leaving the harbor, he waved as some of the fishermen were coming in from their day on the bay.

Taking the bridge that spanned the train tracks, he drove by the beach and then turned by the town park, noting families out and about. On his way through town, he waved to residents out on their porches or walking in the evening sun as he drove to the other side where large, bayside vacation rental homes stood next to the yacht marina and an upscale restaurant. At only five square miles, it did not take long to cover the town. He had been wined and dined at Sunset View restaurant a few times during the week. Instead of stopping, he glanced at his watch as he turned the jeep around and decided it was time for a detour.

Ten minutes later, he pulled into his parents' driveway. Alighting from his vehicle, he barely rounded the front when the door opened, and his mom came out onto the porch. At five feet five inches, she was towered over by her husband and son, but what she lacked in height she made up for in what Grandpa Tolsen used to call gumption. Fair to the bone, tenacious, and the most giving woman Mitch had ever met. Her brown hair, streaked with a little gray, was bobbed to her shoulders. Her smooth complexion had her appearing ten years younger and, except for a few pounds that his father lovingly patted every chance he got, she was the same wonderful woman Mitch remembered from his childhood.

"I thought you'd never have a chance to come over," she joked. "I remember a lot of nights when your dad would come home late from everybody in town wanting a piece of him." Drawing him into a hug, she opened the door and ushered him in. "I know you've had dinner but how about some dessert?"

"Oh, God, mom, do you have pie?"

"Do I have pie? What kind of a question is that? Have you ever come home for a visit, and I didn't have pie?" she asked, pretend scolding.

"No, but this isn't a visit anymore. I live here."

She stopped in the entry foyer and turned, piercing her son with her warm gaze. Placing her hand on his cheek, she said, "I'm glad you have come home, Mitch, but I know what a big life change this has been for you. So, as long as you're here, I'll always have something special just for you." Leaning forward to whisper, she said, "But I have to keep your father on a strict diet, so he can only have a little piece. If you'll have a little piece too, I'll send the rest home with you."

Smiling, he peered down at the indomitable Nancy Evans. "No problem, mom. Now let me go talk to the former Chief."

Walking into the comfortable den, Mitch found Ed Evans sitting in his recliner, a baseball game on. His father was an older version of himself. His light brown hair was speckled with gray. The only difference from when Mitch visited at Christmas would be his slightly gaunt appearance from several hospital stays. It was hard to imagine his dad anything but in the most robust health.

Seeing his father about to rise, Mitch rushed over to take his hand. Shaking it, he quickly said, "Dad, don't get up. I'm just here to visit for a bit."

Thirty minutes later, after the pieces of pie were consumed, Nancy stood and said, "I'm going to let you two men talk shop for awhile. I'll be back after I clean up the kitchen." Winking at her son, she bent to kiss her husband before leaving the room.

Mitch watched as his father's eyes never left his mother until she was completely out of sight. *Funny, he's always done that, but it never used to mean anything to me... until recently.* Heaving a sigh, he realized he wanted that kind of relationship. At thirty-one, he was ready to find someone. *God, but I sure as hell don't have time now to even think about it!*

Bringing his attention back to his dad, he noticed his father's gaze now on him. "Son, tell me all about it. I just might be the one person in this town that can understand what you're going through."

Laughing, Mitch agreed. Leaning back on the comfortable sofa, he shook his head. "Dad, I had no idea how much of your time was spent glad-handing everyone in town."

"I promise it'll get better," his dad assured. His eyes stared down at his hands for a few minutes, lost in thought. "You know, when my dad became the Police Chief, it was 1960. I was six years old and thought he was a god."

"You became the Chief right before I was born so I grew up always thinking you were a god as well," Mitch confessed.

The two laughed, sharing the experience of growing up as the son of the police chief.

"But I had no idea that my dad had to spend time working on things as boring as budget meetings and all the other things you had to do. I guess I just thought you chased bad guys."

Mitch nodded, having felt the same thing about his dad.

"I became an officer in 1974 and finally figured out that dad had a job that was way more than what I ever imagined."

"Did you ever fear taking over as Chief?"

Ed grew thoughtful before he answered. "I grew up here in Baytown. Well, we lived out in the county, but this was home. When I was a teenager in the late 1960's, I couldn't wait to leave this little place and see the world. Of course, the only place I saw was Vietnam."

Mitch held his breath, realizing his father almost never talked about his two years in the Army.

"By the time I got back, I was ready to come back to this little town and wanted to put down roots here. I'd met Nancy Tolsen in high school and had no idea if she'd still be available, but after I saw my parents, she was the first person I looked up. Couldn't believe my luck, but I wasn't about to let anyone else have a shot at that wonderful woman. Put a ring on her finger and joined the police force. I didn't have to be educated in police science beforehand...not at that time, but I studied at night to get my degree. I think my dad would have kept working but, when mom got cancer, he wanted to spend every minute with her. The mayor and town council asked...and well, I said yes and never regretted it. Dad had big shoes to fill, but I was determined to put my own mark on the job."

At that, Mitch's gaze jumped up to his father's smiling face. "That's right, son. You took the job and it's time for you to make changes to put your own mark on it. And I promise that once you get this initial round of meet-n-greets over with, the job will settle down to more of what you'd like it to be."

The two were silent for a moment and then Ed, watching his son carefully, said, "It'll never be as exciting as your FBI job, but it'll have its own rewards."

"Dad, you have no idea how maddening my job was

at times. Had some good cases and met some great people, but I never thought of coming back to Baytown as a step down."

With his father's smile, Mitch felt a weight lift off him. He looked up as his mom walked back into the room, wiping her hands on a dishrag. "You men through with your pow-wow?"

Patting his lap, Ed grinned, saying, "Come on over, darling. Have a seat."

Laughing, she sat down on her husband, her legs dangling over the side of the recliner, her arms around his neck. The three of them sat for a while, reminiscing about Baytown and especially the Baytown Boys. Mitch mentioned the idea of an American Legion and Ed's eyes lit up.

"You need help with that, I'll be more than happy to help you."

"And I know that the American Legion has an Auxiliary for family members," Nancy added. "I'd love to help start that up as well."

As Mitch walked out of the house, his mom walked him to the front porch. As she hugged him goodbye, she said, "I haven't seen your dad that excited about anything in a long time."

"I'm a long way away from setting up anything about an American Legion now, but I promise to involve him when I do."

As he jogged off the porch, a sudden thought of the woman he saw at the Inn came into his mind. "Does Mrs. Bradford still run the Sea Glass Inn?"

Nancy shook her head sadly. "No, she passed away a few months ago. Such a sweet lady. I remember how you kids used to always head over to her house for treats, especially when her granddaughter was there. I was real pleased when Tori came back to run the Inn now."

At the name of Tori, Mitch startled. The image of red hair and sky-blue eyes slammed into him. *Tori Bradford. The woman at the diner. The one who almost tripped over herself to hide from me.* Before he had a chance to process that piece of information, his mom waved goodbye, and he climbed into his jeep.

As he drove home, his mind slipped back to memories of Tori Bradford. The red-haired, pigtail girl with the cute freckles that always came to stay with her grandmother every summer. She was funny, goofy, and never minded climbing trees or playing soccer.

By the time he was in his house and locked in for the night, he remembered the adorable teenager she had become. Thick hair, a sweet body, and a shy smile that shot to his teenage heart.

Lying in bed, he remembered asking her to the spring break picnic when she visited before his graduation. He remembered her smile when she agreed. If he were honest, in his memories, he was going to ask her to wait for him until he got back from the Army— *adolescent and stupid, but hell, I was eighteen and thought she might be the one.* Aiden and Brogan teased him, but he knew they were secretly envious.

Walking up to the Inn that day, he was surprised

when her grandmother met him at the door and said Tori was not feeling well. He tried to see her the next two days of spring break, but she never came out of the Inn before she went back home. And three months later, he left Baytown.

6

Waking early as the dawn pierced the sky, Tori dressed quickly, pulling her long hair back with a headband and slipping into a green sundress with little flat sandals on her feet.

Making coffee, she filled several carafes, placing them on the sideboard of the dining room. The large brick house, originally built in the late 1800's, had been painstakingly restored and maintained by several owners, ending with Tori's grandparents.

The beveled glass around the front door sent light shining down on the polished wooden floors of the entry foyer. Oriental rugs led the way into the formal living room, complete with comfortable furniture mixed with antique pieces. A wide staircase split the house with a hall beside it leading to the back rooms and kitchen. It boasted a formal dining room, but the guests had their breakfasts in the glassed-in sunroom at the side of the house, through double doors leading from the dining room.

Each morning, one of Jillian's coffee house workers would deliver pastries to the Inn while Tori whipped up scrambled eggs, bacon, sausage, and English muffins that she kept on the dining room table with warmers. Apple, orange, and cranberry juice pitchers were set on the table as well. Her grandmother's china sat, ready for guests to fill their plates, along with the antique collection of mismatched floral coffee cups.

Breakfast was available for guests from eight to nine in the morning. Just as she placed fresh flowers from her garden into a vase, the first couple came in. Greeting them, she showed them where to serve themselves and motioned to the beautifully decorated sunroom where small tables and chairs were placed.

The doorbell sounded just as the next couple came down to eat. Excusing herself, she walked to the door, not looking out before throwing it open. It took a few seconds for her mind to catch up to the sight that filled her eyes. Mitch Evans stood on the stoop. All six feet, four inches of him. Khaki pants, a navy polo stretched tightly over his muscles, with the letters BPD embroidered over his chest. As her gaze traveled upward, his face filled her view. Chiseled jaw, much squarer than when he was a teenager, now covered with a deliciously trimmed beard. His hair, slightly more brown than blond, was now cut shorter and no longer hung down in his face. His lips, once an object of her dreams, now formed a smile around perfect teeth. And lastly, his eyes. Blue. Intelligent. Piercing. And staring right at her.

Gulping as her mind finally caught up to her gaze, she felt her face flame as she stuttered, "M...Mitch? Um...I mean, Chief Evans?"

His eyes sparkled as he watched her stammering her response. Chuckling, he said, "Mitch is fine. Tori, it's good to see you again. I think I saw you the other day in the diner but didn't put two and two together until mom told me you were back."

"Oh," she said, blushing more. "I must have been distracted. I didn't see you," she lied. *God, what's wrong with me? I'm acting like I have no sense!* Plastering a smile on her face that she hoped covered her fumbling and pounding heart, she asked, "Can I help you? Is there something you need?"

"I just wanted to come by and see you. It seems as though we've both come home." Seeing her eyes flash with grief, he fought the urge to pull her into his arms. When she had first opened the door, he was struck once again by her quiet, understated beauty. Long red hair, held away from her face with a wide green headband matching the sexy-as-hell green sundress that show-cased her figure to perfection. The lips that once enticed the adolescent boy nearly sent the blood rushing south in the adult man.

"Tori, I'm sorry about your grandmother. She was a wonderful woman and a great loss to our community," he said, his voice sincere as he stepped forward into her space, sending her backward so he could enter and close the front door.

Sucking in a cleansing breath through her nose, she blinked rapidly for a few seconds, barely noticing how he maneuvered her back inside her entry foyer. Now the sunlight coming through the beveled glass panels cast a glow behind his head, making his features stand out more.

"Thank you," she whispered. "It's still hard to believe she's gone." Cocking her head to the side, she cleared her throat and corrected, "But you're the one who came home. This was only my vacation home."

"I always got the feeling that this was more home to you than Virginia Beach was."

She wanted to deny his words, but if he had any memory of her the way she did of him, he would know it was a lie. Nodding slowly, she agreed, "You're right. This always did seem more like home. I was always happy here."

Just then, another guest came down the stairs for breakfast, and she quickly glanced at them and then back at Mitch. "Um...I...have to...do breakfast."

Mitch observed as the man at the bottom of the stairs eyed Tori's ass with a smirk and he bristled. "Go ahead and do what you've got to do. I'll wait."

"Wait? Um...did you need something?"

His wide smile met her uncertain expression, and he replied, "Just you."

What on earth does that mean, she wondered, then hoped she did not say the words aloud.

"Miss, Miss?" came a call from the dining room. Before Tori could process what Mitch meant with his words, she turned and hustled to make sure her guests had everything they needed.

After thirty minutes of moving amongst the small tables of breakfast guests and sending them on their way, she began to clear the dishes, assuming Mitch had left. Carefully lifting the large tray containing precisely stacked antique china, she turned, only to find a large body right behind her.

Yelping, she stumbled, the tray teetering precariously. Strong hands whipped out to steady the tray as she watched, horrified, as one of her favorite teacups toppled to the edge. Before she could blink, the tray was held in one strong hand while the other grabbed the delicate cup placing it back securely on the tray.

Jerking her stunned gaze from the perfectly balanced tray to the man standing in the sunroom, her mouth dropped open. *Mitch? He stayed?*

"Let me carry this for you," his deep voice rumbled, awakening a long dormant need inside.

"I've got it now," she replied, but found that his hands did not leave the tray.

Nodding toward the dining room, he said, "I'm sure you've got plenty to take care of. I'll just set these on the kitchen counter."

Smiling her appreciation, she tried to ignore the ping-pong balls bouncing in her stomach. If she thought the teenage Mitch had been a dream come true, the adult version was a female wet dream. *God, how long has it been since I've had sex?* Too long was the only reason she could come up with for her response to having him in close proximity again.

As he headed into the kitchen, she gathered what was left of the bacon, noticing the sausage and egg casserole was empty. Walking into the huge, upgraded kitchen with its mixture of old décor and new appliances, she held her breath as he placed the heavy tray expertly on the counter. *Mitch Evans in my kitchen.* As much as she hated to admit it, her adolescent crush came rushing back, but she battled to push it to the corners of her mind. *That was years ago...lots of water under the bridge.*

Mitch turned, leaning his hips against the counter, one muscular leg crossed in front of the other. Folding his muscular arms across his chest, he peered at the woman in front of him—the same one that filled his teenage dreams.

"You look good, Tori," he smiled. "How have you been?"

"Fine." She hesitated for a moment before a chuckle slipped out. Catching his questioning gaze, she explained, "Isn't the word *fine* such a ridiculous way to answer a question? I haven't seen you in thirteen years, so I suppose a lot has happened, and yet I answer with *fine.*"

Throwing his head back in laughter, he said, "I forgot how funny you can be...or how totally honest. Gotta say, I missed that."

Licking her lips nervously, she said, "Uh...you never said why you came over today."

Shrugging, he replied, "You're right...it's been a long time. But, honestly, Tori? I remember you fondly and we were good friends a long time ago. We're both in the same town now, and I wanted to see if we could get to know each other again."

Gifting him with a shy smile, she could not think of a reason not to. "I suppose that makes sense." She wished the pain of her sister's revelation thirteen years ago did not still sting, but her sister had proven that betrayals by those close to us cause heartaches that hurt the most. *Geez, get ahold of yourself—it's not like he's here because he's carried a torch for you for years. More like the new Police Chief needs to check on the community.*

Fiddling with the platter in her hands, she said, "Have you had breakfast? It would only take a moment to heat the bacon and scramble a couple of fresh eggs. I still have a few of Jillian's pastries as well."

"Sounds like a plan," he grinned, reaching for the carafe of coffee and pouring it into a mug. Popping it into the microwave, he heated it up while Tori went to the stove. Five minutes later they sat at the informal kitchen table eating as the sun streamed through the back sliding glass door onto the deck.

After silently filling their bellies, Mitch pushed the plate back and said, "So tell me, what's gone on in your life?"

Almost choking on a sip of hot coffee, Tori sputtered

and coughed for a moment. As he slapped her back, she finally caught her breath, tears streaming. Wiping her face with a napkin, she laughed, "Sorry. I guess I was not prepared to give a thirteen-year dissertation on my life."

"Yeah, I guess that was a little odd," he admitted, his eyes never leaving her face. "Well, how about you give me the abbreviated version?"

Before she had a chance to answer, his phone rang. Answering it, an expression of irritation crossed his face. "Right. Be there in five minutes."

Standing, he said, "I'm so sorry to have to rush out. Seems there's a bit of a problem with a couple of teenage shoplifters from one of the shops on Main Street."

Hiding the disappointment of losing his company, she smiled as she walked to the front door. "You're the Police Chief now, so of course I understand."

Mitch followed her, noting the slight sway of her hips, and barely jerked his gaze back up before she turned around and caught him ogling. At the door, he reached out and squeezed her hand. "I'd like to continue…my schedule's kind of crazy right now."

Holding his gaze with her blue eyes, she replied, "It's a small town, and you know where to find me."

Fighting the urge to capture her plump lips with his, he simply nodded and jogged down her front steps toward his jeep.

The sun was setting over the bay, painting the evening sky between fluffy clouds. Walking down toward the beach, Tori slipped off her flip-flops when she reached the sand. Families were packing up the children and couples were lounging on blankets, ready to snuggle as the night sky encroached.

Realizing she forgot a towel, she found an isolated patch of sand and sat down, stretching her legs out in front of her as she leaned back, resting her hands on the sand behind her. Lifting her face, she closed her eyes as the light breeze tossed her hair.

"Hello," a deep voice sounded.

Twisting her head, she saw the man standing right next to her, but she had already recognized his voice. Unable to keep the smile from her face, she acknowledged. "Hello to you too."

Mitch plopped down on the sand next to her, managing to align his body so his hips were touching hers.

Part of her wanted to push him away, thinking that a friendship with Mitch Evans would never work. Not when his very presence made her girly parts tingle and the knowledge that he could never be what her heart had desired him to be to her made the idea of friendship a disaster. *If I thought I was hurt as a teenager, what would the adult Mitch do to my already damaged heart?* But she peered into his deep blue eyes and knew that if friendship was the only thing he offered, she wanted to at least be able to say hello to him in town without having to duck behind every aisle.

Mitch noted the doubt cross her face and held his breath, waiting for her to speak. Having only been in her presence for a little while, he decided that this time she would not run away. *This time...I'm no longer a teen with a crush.*

He cleared his throat, causing her to jump. "Sorry," she mumbled, gathering her thoughts. *How much do I tell him? Oh, hell, if we're living in the same town, I doubt there will be many secrets.*

Holding his gaze, she sat up straighter and said, "Well, the Reader's Digest version of the last thirteen years, is that while you left for the Army, I went to college at Old Dominion. I majored in Hotel Management." Hesitating for a moment, she added, "I'm not sure why, but helping grandma with the Sea Glass Inn was my favorite thing to do. I never imagined I would be doing it here, but I liked the idea of working with people on trips or vacations. I ended up at a couple of hotels in the Richmond area and, by then, I was married, so I settled for jobs I wasn't really happy with."

Mitch was visibly startled. *Married? She's married?* He looked down at her hand and observed no wedding ring. His eyes jumped back to hers and found her gaze directly on him.

Lifting her hand, wiggling her fingers, she grimaced. "As you can see, I'm no longer married."

Unable to think of what to say, he stared numbly at her.

"I landed a job at the historic Virginia Beach Hotel." Giving a little shrug, she admitted, "By then I was newly divorced, moved to Virginia Beach and had a really nice job in a prestigious hotel. I had only worked there for a year when grandma became ill."

"So, you came here to work?"

"Not at first...she was able to keep working for a long time with the help of some friends who provided the breakfasts for guests and did the cleaning. But when her health went down, it went down fast. I was here at Christmas and knew she didn't have long."

Her eyes dropped to where her fingers played in the sand. Sighing, she said, "Grandma told me that her Will had been written a long time ago and that she was leaving the Sea Glass Inn to me entirely. She had some money set aside for my sister, but considering Vanessa never visited after graduating from high school...and well, some other things, um...grandma left it to me."

Clearing her voice as the emotion of the moment threatened to take over, she smiled tremulously, declaring, "And that sums up the last thirteen years of Tori Bradford." Hoping Mitch would reciprocate, taking the spotlight off her, she turned her expectant face to him.

Instead, he just sat. "Wow, that's quite a tale."

"I hardly think it compares to your story," she prompted. "Won't you tell me more about you?"

Making a decision, he shook his head, standing. "Nope, not now." Before she could protest, he added, "I'll take you to dinner tomorrow...then I'll share." He held his hand out to her, waiting for her to place her smaller hand into his. She did not disappoint.

Standing, leaning her head back to keep her eyes on

his, she placed her free hand on her hips. "That's kind of like coercion."

Laughing, he agreed. "Yep. I'll pick you up at six o'clock. I'll take you to the Sunset View Restaurant for dinner." Leaning over, he placed a kiss on the top of her head, saying, "Glad we've got a chance to re-connect, Tori." With that, he walked back toward his jeep parked on the street, leaving Tori to stare at his delectable backside.

Oh, lordy...what have I agreed to, she wondered.

7

Mitch headed into the office to try to get some work accomplished, even though he was not on duty. With four officers underneath him, they worked a rotating shift of four ten-hour days on and two days off, always having two to three officers on each day. Mitch worked Monday through Friday but knew that he would spend most of his weekends checking in with his staff. Mildred also worked the weekdays, and the town paid for a weekend receptionist to handle the non-emergency police, fire, and rescue calls.

The office was quiet as he moved past the staff room, seeing Ginny eating lunch. Stepping back, he greeted her.

Smiling, she said, "Sam's down at the beach and Grant's patrolling through town, so I thought I'd grab a bite."

"No problem," he replied easily, deciding to sit with

her for a few minutes. "So, can I ask, informally, how you think things are going with me in charge?"

Chuckling, she said, "Well, for starters you've gotta know the townspeople are thrilled to have their golden boy back."

"Jesus, I hate that label," he growled.

"Hey, don't knock it." Seeing his incredulous expression, she continued, "Look, Mitch. The Evans have filled police and Chief roles here for fifty-five years and have done so without a bunch of drama or problems. That's given the town stability. From what I hear, you were a good kid, a good athlete, weren't a troublemaker, and then you went off to join the Army."

Her eyes flashed dark, before shuttering, and she continued. "So, you come back, giving up a job with the FBI and, face it…the town sees you as a returning hero." Kicking his leg under the table, while grinning, she said, "Don't fight it…just live up to it."

"Damn, you lay it out, don't you?"

"Life's too short not to be real all the time," she explained, the specter of darkness flashing once more.

"Anything else?" he queried.

"The town seems to love the new uniforms and well, we officers are thrilled with the choice. It's more laid back, while still being professional. I thought the older townspeople might not like it, but they seem to." Standing, she tossed her sandwich wrapper in the trashcan but turned at the door and chuckled. "Of course, rumor has it that the mayor thinks we look too casual."

Grinning at the idea of the pompous mayor hating

the casual uniforms, he realized that maybe the title golden boy would keep the mayor off his back. Making his way to his office, he spent a couple of hours reviewing cases, signing off on reports, and working on statements due to the state. Finally looking at the clock when his stomach growled, he decided to see what was at Finn's.

He walked the four blocks to the bar, greeting people as he went. Several townspeople who had not had a chance to meet him stopped him to chat. He appreciated the goodwill, but with his stomach continuing to growl, he was glad to step inside the cool interior.

Right away, he saw Aiden and Brogan behind the bar, as well as Zac and Callan, two more of the original Baytown Boys, eating lunch.

"Damn, man," Zac called out. "You've been back a week and I've hardly seen you!" The two man-hugged before Mitch grabbed Callan in a hug as well.

"Good to see you all. It's been way too long." Looking up at Katelyn walking over, he said, "Can I get a burger and fries?"

"Coming right up," she grinned.

"So, how's the new job going?" Callan asked, cutting to the chase.

Nodding, Mitch replied, "My dad left some big shoes to fill, but I'm finding my way." Eyeing Callan's uniform, he added, "I see you're still with the Coast Guard."

Callan opened his mouth to answer when his radio

alarmed. Hopping off the stool, he said, "Fuck, I gotta run." His eyes viewed his half-eaten burger longingly.

"You free tomorrow?" Mitch asked. "If so, be at my place at about two. Beer and steaks."

"Hell, yeah, I'll be there!"

Katelyn ran over with a box and scooped up his leftovers, including fries, and put them in a bag for him. "I threw in a couple of cookies as well," she added.

He grabbed her arm and pulled her forward over the bar, kissing the top of her head. "You're the best, babe," he called out as he ran out the door.

As Mitch dug into his meal, he said to the others, "You all too. Beer and grilling at my place."

"You thinking about trying to start an American Legion?" Brogan asked, cutting straight to the chase.

"Figured it was time for the Baytown Boys, all grown up, to do something worthwhile together. What better than something that'll benefit us and other Veterans in the community?"

Nodding, Brogan offered a slow smile. "You got it."

Jillian and Katelyn arrived at the Inn at almost the exact same time. Looking at each other, Katelyn asked, "Do you know why Tori needs us?"

"No idea," Jillian admitted, "but I'm curious."

Before they could surmise any more, the front door opened, and Tori welcomed her friends inside. "Come on back, girls," she invited, leading them to the covered private deck behind the kitchen. This was one of her places that guests did not wander to. The deck overlooked the backyard, full of landscaped flowerbeds while broad trees provided the shade. Tall, sweating glasses of sweet, iced tea and a platter of small, sugar cookies sat on the small table in the middle of the chairs.

After sitting and serving the tea and cookies, she took a huge breath and said, "I have something to share with you two…something no one else knows."

Jillian and Katelyn, eyes wide, leaned forward hanging on her every word.

"I…I have a date this evening with Mitch."

Silence. Except for the distant sound of children playing on the beach and the birds in the trees. Utter silence.

"Um…didn't you hear me?" Tori asked, her eyes darting between the two.

"Oh, my God!" Jillian exclaimed. "I thought you were sick or something!"

"I thought you were going to say you were selling the Inn and moving away!" Katelyn accused.

Blinking, Tori said, "Why would I sell the Inn?"

"That's not the point," Jillian huffed. "Anyway, a date with Mitch? Jesus, it's about time!"

"Definitely!" Katelyn added. "I'm surprised it took almost a week of him being back in town to find you and ask!"

Leaning heavily back in her chair, Tori appeared stunned. Before she could speak, Jillian spoke up.

"Tori, Mitch has been sweet on you since you were six years old! He'd never let the other boys tease you about having red hair or freckles. He'd always be the one to find you when we played hide and seek. And, as we got older, you were the first to get boobs and believe me, he noticed!"

"I...I...just thought...well," Tori stammered.

"I'm surprised he didn't ask you to wait for him when he left to join the Army!" Jillian said. "He was completely over the moon for you, even back then."

"No, no, you've got it wrong. It was my sister Vanessa he liked." She hesitated before adding, "I...we were childhood friends, and I was really into him, but um...well, I guess Vanessa won out."

Snorting, Jillian rolled her eyes. "What gave you that idea? I mean, hate to be rude, but Vanessa? She was the biggest bitch to all of us, and honestly? The boys hated her!"

Katelyn observed Tori closely before leaning over to place her hand on Tori's arm. "Did Mitch tell you that or did Vanessa?"

Her gaze bouncing between the two women, she said, "Vanessa told me they slept together."

Breaking out in a hoot, Jillian snorted again. "Now I know she was a bitch! Believe me, the boys may have had their hound dog ways back then, but I can promise you, Mitch never slept with Vanessa."

Sighing, Tori shook her head slowly, a new reality crashing into what her old reality had always been. "I should have known. Vanessa never could be satisfied with having the attention taken away. Some things never change."

Now, it was Katelyn and Jillian peering at her in curiosity. "Why do I get the feeling there is more to this than just a teenage Mitch?" Katelyn asked, her comforting hand still on Tori's arm.

Her face twisted in a grimace, and she sat silent for a moment. Finally, she admitted, "I knew something was wrong in my own marriage. I got with Thomas when I was working in Richmond, and we married after only dating six months. I thought we were in love, but he was always after the next big deal, sure that his happiness rested on making more money."

"So, what happened?" Jillian asked, her voice now soft with empathy.

"I caught him cheating. He tried to hide it, but I found the hotel receipt that he left in his suit pocket." Blushing, she said, "Actually, I didn't find it. The dry cleaner did and when I went to pick the suit up, they had the receipt taped to the plastic bag. God, how embarrassing!"

"Oh, my God," Katelyn breathed. "What did you do?"

"I hired a PI who had no problem giving me proof. I then surprised him with the proof, moved out, and filed for divorce that week."

"Tori," Jillian said gently, now leaning forward like Katelyn, her attention completely on her friend. "You said 'some things never change'. What did you mean?"

Licking her lips nervously she pierced them with her

gaze and answered, "The other woman was my sister, Vanessa."

Tori stood nervously in the entryway of the Inn, checking her appearance in the mirror time and time again so that when the knock on the door occurred, she jumped, almost in relief. Opening the door, she was once again stunned into silence at the tall, muscular frame filling her doorway. His beard, closely trimmed, made her fingers itch to reach out to touch him. Instead, she stood rooted to the spot as though her feet had grown into the old wooden floor.

Mitch grinned, noting her obvious appreciation as much as he viewed the vision in front of him. The green sundress of the morning gave way to a flirty black dress, with her reddish hair piled on her head with sexy tendrils framing her face. *Stunning...just stunning.*

Cocking his elbow out, he said, "May I escort you, Ms. Tori?"

Laughing, she took his arm and, making sure the door locked behind her, she allowed him to walk her to his jeep. He assisted her inside, making sure she was buckled safely.

Raising an eyebrow, she said, "I could have buckled myself, you know?"

"And take away my chance to be even closer to you?" he smiled. Adopting a joking seriousness, he added,

"And how would it look for the date of the Police Chief not to be buckled in properly?"

"Oh, my, they'd run you out of town in disgrace!"

The two laughed together as they drove the few miles to the upscale restaurant and, upon entering, were escorted to a corner table overlooking the bay with a perfect view of the sunset.

He kept his hand lightly on her back as they walked to their seats, but she felt each fingertip as it burned against her dress. Assisting her into her chair, she could not take her eyes off him as he sat across from her, his long legs touching her knees.

After their drinks were placed on the table in front of them and the waitress took their order, they talked, finding the years falling away.

"Do you remember climbing the apple trees over on Milligan's orchard and how he'd come out and yell at us to get away?" Mitch began.

"Yes, and how you'd dare me to climb higher each year," Tori accused. "And then the one year I went too high and got scared and started crying." Chuckling, he nodded, but she kept going. "What I remember most was how you came up to calm me before helping me down."

"I would have always helped you," he said. "Even when I was a goofy kid."

He held her gaze until they were interrupted by the waitress bringing their food. Moaning orgasmically, she dove into the delicious seafood. "I haven't been here yet, so this is a real treat."

"Me either," he commented, then, catching her eyes again, he added, "And I'm glad it's with you."

"You still haven't given me the Reader's Digest version of your last thirteen years," she accused with a smile.

"God, I feel as though everyone in town knows what's gone on. Since being considered for Chief, I feel like I'm an open book."

"Maybe I've heard the newspaper version, but I want the real Mitch."

"The real Mitch," he repeated, touched by her interest. "Okay, well, I did join the Army after high school. And no, I wasn't anything special. Just regular Army. Did a tour in Iraq and one in Afghanistan and then called it quits."

"You say it wasn't special...just regular Army...I don't know what that means."

"I was with the Military Police. I'm not downplaying what we did...our asses were on the line every day, but Hollywood loves the tales of Special Forces, snipers, Navy SEALs...so a lot of people start thinking that's what we all did."

Nodding slowly, she tried to imagine what his Army life had been, but before she could ask more, he continued.

"Most of the time, we were hot, tired, dirty, moving around. And I longed for the peace of home. When I got out, I went to a community college to earn a degree in Police Science, then got on with the FBI. I did the training at Quantico and became an agent. I was based out of Charlestown where I spent the last six years."

"And now? Was your job hard to give up?" she queried softly, reaching out to touch his hand.

He turned his hand up and she linked fingers with his, unable to tear her gaze away from his.

"Nah. Granddad died last summer and when I came home, it was...nice. It no longer seemed like the small town I escaped from." Laughing he said, "Don't get me wrong. Baytown is still tiny, but it held familiarity and comfort that my life in Charlestown didn't have. Plus... well, I needed a change."

"What kind of change?"

"The FBI is such a large agency, change comes slowly. And I got so angry when the left hand didn't know what the right hand was doing. Anyway, I was already thinking about quitting and joining a private investigation company that I worked with. Good men, everyone, and I was looking forward to joining them."

Understanding dawned on Tori and she squeezed his fingers. "And then your dad's heart attack."

"Yeah, but don't think that coming back to Baytown was a bad thing. The timing was perfect. I have a chance to give back to the town that gave me so much. A chance to make a difference. A chance to reconnect with old friends and help mom and dad. So, it's all good."

Tucking a wayward strand of hair, she asked, "Old friends?"

Giving her hand a little pull, he leaned his face

closer, holding her gaze. "Yeah, Tori. I came back having no idea you were here. You're like icing on the cake."

Leaning the rest of the way in, he placed a whisper-soft kiss on her lips. Desperately wanting more than just a taste, he forced his body back, willing to wait for a more private place to delve into her warmth.

Opening her eyes slowly, her lips curved in a smile as she leaned back in her seat. Just then the waitress came by.

"Dessert, anyone?" the young woman asked sweetly.

Glancing over at Tori and noting the slight shake of her head, he looked up and smiled, "We'll pass on dessert." As the waitress walked away, his heart pounded as he brought his gaze back to hers and added, "At least not a dessert here."

8

Reaching her front door, Tori leaned her head back, unable to keep her eyes off Mitch's face. *I thought he was cute at ten. I thought he was handsome at eighteen. But nothing...nothing is like Mitch, the man.*

"I hate for the evening to end," Mitch admitted.

"You can come out to the back deck for some wine, if you'd like," she offered. "It's my private retreat...the guests don't go out there."

"I'd like to." Following her through the wide hall by the stairs, he nodded to an older couple sitting in the living room. He whispered, "How does this work, Tori? I never considered it when we were kids, but now that I'm really thinking about this setup, you've got strangers living in your house!" Suddenly protective, he was unhappy about the living arrangements of a bed and breakfast Inn.

As they made their way into the kitchen, she said, "It really isn't bad. The guests use the front door that has a card reader lock—I'm the only one with an actual key. The front room, including the living room, dining room, and the sunroom are all pretty much for the guests. They are not allowed in the kitchen, but they have a mini fridge in their room. When they check in, they have to sign that they understand the kitchen, the deck off the kitchen, the back study, and of course, my attic rooms are off limits. I show them the snack pantry in the dining room. I keep it stocked with snacks they may partake of, but everything else is mine."

"But what if you get rowdy guests and they—"

"Mitch," she said with exasperation. "Rowdy people don't fork over the money it takes to stay here. I'm more expensive than a hotel so that helps." Grinning, she teased, "Plus, I happen to know the Police Chief."

"How can you keep them away from your private rooms?" he pushed, not giving in to her joking attitude.

She pointed to a closed door near the back of the kitchen. "There are two sets of stairs. When the house was built, there was a separate servant's entrance. Of course, my room is two levels up, so I have lots of stairs, but my bedroom suite is in the attic. It can also be reached from the second floor where the guest rooms are, but again, I keep the door locked as well. I also have an intercom into my bedroom for emergencies."

So, it was you I saw the other night from the beach. Not wanting to embarrass her, he did not mention it but instead followed her out onto the deck. He breathed in the sweet floral scent of the summer flowers mixed with her honeysuckle shampoo. They sat together on the glider, and he wasted no time putting his arm around her shoulders.

Sipping the wine, they relaxed, letting the years drift away, finding once more that time was easy between them.

"You never married?" she asked, curiosity overriding common sense.

"Nope. Never found the right woman to spend my life with. When I get married, it'll be for life...like my parents."

As soon as the words were out of his mouth and he saw the hurt flash across her face, he wanted to pull them back in while simultaneously kicking himself in the ass.

"Jesus, Tori. I'm sorry."

The silence was no longer easy but strained. Finally, he said, "Can you tell me about your marriage?" He paused, and then added, "Only if you want to."

She grimaced but forged ahead. "There's not much to tell. I married a man I met through work. I think we were actually more friends than a great love, and I was too naive to understand the difference."

"So, what happened? Did you just grow apart?"

Her gaze drifted over his shoulder, as she admitted, "No...like you, I planned on being married for life. But, well, he...um...well, he cheated, and I found out."

"No fuckin' way!" Mitch cursed, hating the insecurity he heard resounding in her voice.

Sitting up straighter, she met his angry stare. "Yep. I found out and hired someone to follow him to make sure. When I had all the evidence I needed, I confronted him. Told him I was leaving, and I wanted a divorce. He didn't want one. Swore it was all a mistake, and he'd never stray again."

She suddenly turned sideways, facing Mitch on the glider, bringing her face close to his. Taking a deep breath, she said, "As hurt as I was, I wasn't tempted one little bit to take him back. You want to know what I discovered? Grandma always said I deserved someone special and Mitch, right there, at that moment, I knew he wasn't special!"

Mesmerized by the strength in her words, he pulled her in for a kiss. Unlike the one at the restaurant, this kiss went from soft to a hard, wet kiss almost instantly. Delving his tongue inside her warm mouth, he tasted the wine and essence of her...drinking her in.

She relaxed into his embrace as he moved her closer. Reaching up, she cupped his face, finally allowing her fingertips to move over his close-shaven beard. His lips were strong and supple, moving over her mouth while his tongue tangled with hers.

Just when she slipped into a dreamlike state of kissing bliss, he moved away slightly. Her lips tried to maintain contact, but she opened her eyes to find him staring deeply into hers.

"You are special, Tori. I knew that the minute I saw you when I was eight and you were only six years old. And all these years later...I still know that. And your grandma was right."

Tucking her under his arm for a few minutes, they

once again fell into an easy silence as they rocked back and forth in the glider.

After staring at her profile in the moonlight, Mitch said, "I hated that you got sick the last time you came to visit during my senior year in high school. I knew I was heading to bootcamp two days after graduation and spring break was going to be the last time I was going to see you for a long time."

His FBI interviewing skills kicked in as he noticed her change in breathing. Lifting his hand to her soft cheek, he pulled her gently so she was facing him. "I was surprised you left without saying goodbye."

"I was...well...oh, hell, Mitch," she said with a sigh. "I can't lie...in fact I never could lie to you, that's why I had grandma talk to you."

"What happened, Tori? I really wanted to go to the picnic with you."

"Do you remember my sister Vanessa?" She felt his fingers on her jaw flinch as a scowl crossed his face.

"Uh, yeah. I have no idea what she's like now, but I always hated how she acted like she was so much better than us *hicks* as she used to call us. I hated how she was so mean to you. I even threatened her once to keep her mouth shut when she was calling you names."

Eyes wide, Tori said, "I had no idea! Well, to make matters worse, she discovered how much of a crush I had on you and told me that...uh...well...this is embarrassing now, but well, she told me that you slept with her."

Mitch reared back at her words. "Jesus, I'd rather have slept with a rattle snake!"

A slight grin curved her lips at the reptile comparison as Tori shook her head. "I had no idea. Back then, Vanessa with her perfect blonde hair and tall, tanned body...I always felt frumpy." Peering into his irritated face, she said, "I'm sorry for believing her." Thinking back, she continued, "Since we're being honest, I have to tell you the rest of my story." Seeing that she had his riveted attention, she said, "My ex-husband's affair was with my sister, Vanessa."

Whatever reaction she expected, his response was not in the realm of her thoughts. He immediately leaped from the glider, stalking to the edge of the porch before slamming his hand down on the railing, threatening the innocent piece of wood. Whirling around, his eyes were stormy, anger pouring off him.

"Are you telling me that piece of shit, low-life, son of a bitch man you married, slept with your over-inflated ego, lying, bitch of a sister?"

His voice growled so low, she would have been afraid if his words had not forced a gasp from her, at his vehement anger toward the two people that had one time gutted her. Inwardly pleased, Mitch hated the situation for her.

"Um...yeah, that's exactly what I'm saying. But it was a while back. Believe me, after the initial tears and tantrums...I realized I was better off. And that was when I realized I deserved better."

Stalking back over, he knelt on the deck, taking her

face in his hands. "Tori, I'm so sorry you had to go through that. And even more sorry that because of your sister, I wasn't able to talk to you that day. There was so much I wanted to say." Sighing heavily, he added, "But we were young then. And we have now."

Pulling him in for another kiss, she let her lips speak the words still embedded in her heart. *For me, that better man is you.*

As he walked back through the house toward the front door, with her tucked under his arm once more, he reveled in how right she felt there. By his side...just where he used to envision her.

At the door, she stopped and twisted her body around to face him. "I had a really good time tonight, Mitch. I'm glad we can be friends again."

Cupping her cheek, he gazed into her wide, blue eyes. "Is friendship all you want, because I've got to tell you, I want more."

"It's a start," she admitted hesitantly.

Nodding, he smiled. "Yeah, it's a start."

"Grandma used to say all things happen for a reason. I cared about you a lot when I was sixteen years old, but to be honest...I needed to grow up. Make mistakes, find out who I was and really like myself. So now...I think it's the perfect time to reconnect."

"How'd you get so wise?" he asked. Seeing her smile, he nodded, "I understand what you mean, though. I was hot-blooded at eighteen, and if I'd acted on what my desires were with you...well, at only sixteen, let's just say we both needed to grow up."

Holding her gaze as her body pressed up against his, he added, "But Tori, we may be friends now…but I'd like to see where this friendship can go."

"I'd like that," she replied rising on her toes to capture his lips once more. Ten minutes later, lips swollen from his kisses, she waved goodbye as he headed back to his jeep. Smiling, she locked up and moved to the back staircase, climbing to her room. Stepping out onto the balcony overlooking the beach across the street, she recognized his jeep still parked out front. Waving once more, she smiled as he flickered his headlights.

Laughing, she remembered he used to do that whenever he dropped her off at home all those many years ago. Finally, closing the lace-covered doors, she twirled a few times before getting ready for bed. Sliding under the covers, she fell asleep easily and for once, her dreams were not stuck in times gone by…but rather in things to come.

9

Tori carefully lifted the hot quiche into her food travel tote. She had cleaned up the breakfast dishes from her guests, tidied the kitchen, and was ready for some more girl time. The chicken salad she had made for herself had been shoved back into the refrigerator, knowing it could be tomorrow's lunch. Driving to Jillian's house for brunch, she was grinning with excitement. *Girl time!*

Arriving at the small house, a few blocks from the beach, Tori noticed a couple of cars parked out front. *Hmm, I wonder who else is here?*

Entering the refurbished house with the wide, Victorian front porch, she headed back to the kitchen after hearing Jillian's voice calling out, "Come on back!"

Jillian's kitchen was sunny and bright, decorated in yellow and green. She noticed the kitchen table was filled with fresh fruit, deli sliced meat, and a vegetable tray, as Jillian took the quiche from her hands.

Katelyn stood near the refrigerator, mimosas in her

hands as she looked over her shoulder. Smiling as she placed them on a tray, she made her way to the table as well.

Another woman stood by the table, her thick, black hair pulled back from her somewhat familiar face and Tori smiled, wondering where she had seen the woman. "Hi, I'm Tori," she greeted.

"I'm Belle. Isabelle Gunn. I remember you from the summers when you would come visit your grandmother, but I was a few years behind you in school."

Smiling widely, Tori replied, "That's right. I do remember you now. Do you live in Baytown?"

Belle, a shy smile on her face, explained. "I never left. I got my LPN at the community college and work in the new nursing home in town."

"Let's eat, girls. I'm starving," Jillian announced, placing the quiche wedges onto plates.

The women filled their plates, and each grabbed a mimosa before moving out onto the stone patio. The sprinkler shot water across the flowers near the back corner of her yard as butterflies flitted amongst the blooms. A few trees and a large yard umbrella provided shade for the gathering as they dug into their food.

The conversation was light while they ate, reminiscing about childhood in Baytown and how it had changed over the years. Finally pushing their plates back, refilled mimosas in hand, they leaned back enjoying the pleasant summer morning.

"So," Jillian began, piercing Tori with a grinning

stare, "are you going to tell us about your date last night with Mitch?"

"Um...I..." She gazed at the others, seeing interested and unwavering looks from them all. Laughing, she agreed, "I guess I am!"

Taking a sip of her champagne-heavy mimosa for fortification, she said, "We had a nice dinner. We went back to my place and talked for a while. And then he kissed me goodnight."

Silence greeted her and she widened her eyes in fake surprise. "What?"

Katelyn slapped her hand down on the table and, with exasperation, demanded, "Dirt, girl. We want the dirt!"

Laughing again, Tori replied, "Well, ask me questions. I don't know what to say on my own."

"Well, for starters, what did you talk about?"

"Our jobs, our families. I told him about my marriage and disastrous divorce."

"Did you tell him what Vanessa said?"

Belle seemed confused, then added, "Oh, I forgot about your sister. She was much older than me and, if I remember correctly, she wasn't very nice."

Katelyn snorted, "That's an understatement."

Nodding, Tori said, "Yep. I told him that she claimed to have slept with him in high school and then, many years later, actually had an affair with my husband."

Belle's eyes bulged out of her head at this proclamation, as Jillian and Katelyn shook their heads.

"Good!" Jillian proclaimed. "I'm glad you told him."

Then, leaning closer, she asked, "So tell us about the kiss."

Blushing, Tori smiled. "Ladies, let's just say that the years have not diminished his ability to take my breath away."

Settling back in her chair, Jillian nodded approvingly. "My cousin deserves you, Tori. He deserves the best and that's just what he's got."

"All the Baytown Boys deserve that," Katelyn added.

"Tell me about the Baytown Boys," Tori asked. "I remember that nickname when we were kids, but I guess I'm surprised it stuck."

Jillian and Katelyn were quiet for a moment as Tori and Belle waited patiently on them, both eager to learn.

"Part of it had to do with being raised in a small town. Our high school was the county high school of North Heron, so we had friends from all over the county. But when Mitch was in elementary school, there was a group of boys that were just...I don't know...they must have been different. They hung out, inseparable, together all the time. Whenever you saw one, you saw them all."

Katelyn laughed, "I was sometimes jealous, so Jillian and I would try to sneak off to find their secret clubhouse, but the boys would find out and chase us away."

"Yes, but they were never mean," Jillian added. "They weren't exclusive. They played with anyone, even us girls."

"That's what I remember so much about my

summers here growing up. There was always a fun group to play with."

"Everyone saw them together, running through town, playing with each other, down on the beach or at the fishing pier. It was Mitch, Aiden, Brogan, Zac, Callan, Grant, Phillip, and a few others as well. Somehow, they became known as the Baytown Boys."

Nodding, Jillian agreed. "Unlike many childhood friendships that dissolve with maturity, those guys stuck together. In fact, when they played baseball for the town's recreation club, the team was named Baytown Boys, and that's when the title really stuck."

Katelyn's eyes darkened as her memories came back. "Then, the whole group of them decided to join the service after high school. Aiden and Brogan went into the Marines. Callan with the Coast Guard where he still serves. Mitch and Grant enlisted in the Army, and Zac went into the Navy. I think a couple more guys that were a year or two younger than them were also Army and Air Force."

"The town was so proud of them," Jillian added.

"And now, most are back," Belle said, shooting a quick glance toward Katelyn.

Katelyn sighed heavily, "Yes, some in better shape than others. Brogan was never a very talkative guy, but he can be downright surly now. And Aiden...I sometimes wonder if he doesn't try to drown out memories with too loud laughter, too much talk, and too many women."

"Hell, Grant and Zac are worse than Aiden!" Jillian said, her eyes flashing with a disguised pain.

Katelyn hesitated before adding, "Phillip Bayles didn't make it back. At least not alive."

Tori's sudden intake of breath indicated the memory flooding back. "Oh, Katelyn, I remember he was the one who asked you to the prom that spring and you were so excited."

Nodding slowly, Katelyn's gaze drifted to the flowerbeds at the back of the yard, her expression far away as the other women sat quiet. After a moment, she spoke. "I'd been chasing after Phillip ever since we were kids...kind of like you and Mitch," she said, smiling at Tori. "I'd hoped that when he got back from the military, he'd come for me, and we'd leave Baytown. Go somewhere big. Have a fancy job and live in a city somewhere." Scoffing, she admitted, "That was so stupid. We were just silly kids."

"What happened?" Tori asked, her voice barely a whisper.

"He was killed in service. His body was brought home to be buried. He's at the town cemetery over near the resort."

Leaning forward, Tori grasped Katelyn's hand. "I'm so sorry. I had no idea."

Sighing again, Katelyn said, "Well, it's been a few years and doesn't sting as much as it used to." Slapping her hands on her knees, she shrugged saying, "But, thank God, most of our boys returned."

Jillian continued, "I overheard them talking about

starting an American Legion chapter here. I hope they do. I looked into it, and there are a lot of good things that they could do for their fellow servicemen. I think it would be good for them to have an outlet."

The women quieted for a few minutes, before Katelyn jumped up and said, "More mimosas?"

Soon, easier conversation and laughter filled the small gathering once more.

"Hell, the smell of steaks on the grill had me drooling about a mile away!" Zac called out, stepping onto Mitch's back deck.

Grabbing a beer from the cooler, he nodded to the others gathered there. Callan had arrived and was dragging the corn hole boards out into the yard. Brogan sat with his feet up on the rail, his eyes closed as the sun beamed down on him. Grant carried more beer out and reloaded the cooler.

Aiden stood, surveying the group. "It's been a helluva long time since we've all been together." Holding his beer high, he said, "Here's to the original Baytown Boys."

Here, here and *fuck yeahs* rang out amongst the gathering.

Turning back to Mitch, Aiden said, "So, I hear you finally got your chance to take the pretty Victoria out last night. It's about time. Hell, you chased her from the time you were eight years old! You are one seriously slow mover!"

Mitch had to laugh along with the others. "Yeah, well, like a fine wine, some things take time and only get better with age."

The men settled down with their steaks and the baked potatoes Mitch pulled out of the oven. Brogan set down a platter of corn on the cob and Callan pulled more beer from the ice in the cooler. The conversation and camaraderie flowed easily between the life-long friends and soon the discussion moved to the idea behind an American Legion.

"I've heard about them, but just thought that they were for old men," Grant admitted, pushing his plate back, patting his stomach. "Damn, that was good."

"Well, of course the American Legions had old men in them when we were younger…that's who had been in the service," Callan said. "Now it's us."

"Lot of my friends came back in not so good shape," Mitch noted. "Got a few that I try to keep up with, but we're lucky to have had most of us come back in one piece."

Brogan's eyes grew dark as he added, "Saw a lot of shit over there. Thought the stain of it would never wash off."

"And has it?" Zac asked.

"Working on it," Brogan replied.

"Hell…the heat…the sand…" Aiden said.

"I was in the goddamn mountains for a while," Mitch added, "training the Afghans on basic police skills."

The men sat for a moment, lost in their memories... and nightmares, before Aiden piped up. "So, what does the American Legion do exactly? I mean, if it's just a place for old war horses to get together, hell, we can do that at the bar!"

"I've been doing some research. They do more than swap old war stories. They set up programs that offer comfort to veterans, homeless veterans, give scholarships to teens, a lot of work with families, youth, and the community."

The men were quiet for a moment, allowing the gentle breeze to flow from the ocean, soothing their memories. Brogan was the first to speak, surprising Mitch.

"Mitch is right. We got back. We got a chance to help some of our other brothers and sisters who didn't come back so good. Ain't got a good reason not to do this."

The others looked over at Brogan, his face giving away nothing. Mitch smiled, knowing if Brogan were on board, the others would easily follow suit.

Propping his feet up on the railing, Grant added, "It's a good life out here."

"Remember when we couldn't wait to leave?" Zac grinned.

"Yeah...but we had something to come home to...a place to call home. I've got a couple of buddies that don't got that," Brogan added. "I was kind of thinking about asking one or two of them to consider moving here."

Mitch nodded as he added, "The American Legion

here might be a good enticement, if we're able to get it up and running and effective." Glancing over at Aiden, he smiled, "And not just a place for old war horses to share their stories."

The others laughed, then Callan said, "I've got buddies right now in the Coast Guard here in Baytown that served overseas, me included. I'm in and I can get them interested as well."

Mitch looked around, the afternoon sun moving lower in the sky, and knew he was part of something special. Old friends, most since early childhood, all wanting to escape their tiny town and now returned, they had a lot to give. "Okay, I'll contact the closest American Legion and find out what it would take to move the charter here."

"We need to include the old timers," Brogan said. "I'll pass the word around the bar."

With those plans in place, the group headed down to the sand to begin playing rounds of corn hole, betting quarters, drinking beer, and laughing over old times.

"Mr. Dumfries, there's water in the mini fridge in your room," Tori explained for the third time to one of her guests.

The large man grinned sheepishly and said, "Well, don't tell my wife, but I was hoping to raid your refrigerator."

Smiling while losing her patience, she replied, "Yes,

but the price of the room only includes breakfast. There is a snack pantry, as I pointed out, in the dining room, but the rest of the kitchen is off limits. This is still my home, and this is my food."

"Oh, now darling, you wouldn't begrudge an old man a sandwich, would you?"

Knowing Mr. Dumfries ran a large corporation, Tori bit her tongue from giving a retort about how he could buy twenty sandwich shops with his money. She firmly shut the refrigerator door and said, "I'm sorry, but those are my rules."

The grumpy guest left the kitchen and Tori walked into the laundry room to load another pile of sheets into the washing machine. The Dumfries were staying all week, but she had two weekend guests check out this morning. Thinking back to her hotel management days, she was glad for only four bedrooms in the Inn.

The front doorbell rang, and she headed through the entryway, seeing the shape of a man through the beveled glass. *I'm not expecting another guest today.* Hoping to see Mitch, she threw open the door, only to immediately scowl at the person standing on the porch.

"Thomas?"

"Hey, sweetheart," he said, a warm expression on his face.

Incredulous, she stood rooted to the floor, momentarily stunned into silence. Blinking twice, she asked, "What do you want? I thought I'd made it perfectly clear that once I let you off the hook about alimony last year, we weren't supposed to have any contact."

"Oh, come on, Tori, don't be like that." The congenial expression began to slide from his face as he continued to wait on the front porch. "Aren't you going to let me in?"

"Nope," she said. "We've got nothing to say to each other."

"That's where you're wrong. I really need to talk to you." Seeing her only lift her eyebrow in response, he continued. "I know we had our problems—"

"Our problems?" she barked. "Our main problem was that your dick found its way into my sister! I'd call that more than a rather serious concern."

Thomas blushed while grimacing, taking a deep breath. "I admitted I screwed up, Tori. I knew it at the time and was willing to fight for our marriage."

"But I wasn't," she replied, more softly this time.

"That's a rather harsh, unforgiving attitude," he accused. "Wasn't I worth your forgiveness?"

"Wasn't I worth your faithfulness?"

He pinched his lips together, looking down at his shoes.

"I have to add, Thomas, that while I would not still be with you no matter who it was, the fact that it was my sister totally sealed the deal. You knew how she was with me...always trying to make sure I knew I wasn't as good as her. Always trying to one-up me. Always trying to belittle me. I never understood why you were unfaithful to me...but especially with her."

Turning his gaze back to hers, he pleaded, "I swear, I never meant for it to happen. She just kept coming on to me every time we were together. And when you were back here visiting once, we were at—"

Throwing her hand up in his face, she said, "Please, spare me the details. This is old news. What you need to do is turn around and leave. Now."

Tucking his hands in his pockets, he started to speak when a deep voice from the side growled, "I'd advise you to do as the lady requested."

Mitch stepped onto the porch from the driveway and moved past Thomas and right up to Tori. With a gentle hand on her belly, he pushed her back a step, allowing himself to slip around beside her. Leaning over, he kissed her lips chastely, but possessively. He knew it was an alpha move but couldn't help himself.

Thomas glanced at the BPD logo on Mitch's shirt and sputtered, "Who is this? The police? You've got someone else—"

"We've been divorced for over a year, so I hardly think this is pertinent."

Before Thomas could speak again, Mitch observed Tori and, seeing the irritation on her face, turned back to her ex-husband and repeated, "You've been asked to leave. Now, you can leave of your own accord peacefully or I can escort you off the property. If the lady feels threatened, then I'll advise her to file for a restraining order."

Thomas stood, the warmth, gone from his expression, replaced with red-faced fury. Turning quickly, he moved down the steps but fired a parting shot over his shoulder as he hustled away, "We're not finished, Tori!"

Mitch started to follow him, but she grabbed his arm, pulling him back. "Leave him alone. I'm sure we've seen the last of him."

Whirling around, he retorted, "That could be considered a threat!"

"No, he's not the threatening type. He's just pissed and trying not to lose face."

Feeling impotent, and angry at that emotion, he stood rock steady, his hands on his hips, breathing hard. Finally, the small, warm hands on his chest penetrated and he looked back down at the woman he knew he was falling for. Her sky-blue eyes focused on him, concern in their depths.

Releasing a breath, he said, "You okay?"

"I should be asking you the same thing."

Leaning down a whisper away from her mouth, her scent filling his mind, he admitted, "I am now." Closing the miniscule distance, he captured her lips, this time in a soul-searing, claiming kiss.

His lips moved expertly over hers as his tongue slipped deep inside her warmth. She tasted of sweet syrup and strawberries, and he wondered if he found his nirvana just inside her mouth. Finally pulling back, he heard her mewl in discontent and grinned as he kissed her forehead. "Oh, Tori, I'd love to stay here, but I've got to get to work."

Giving his waist a squeeze, she said, "I'm glad you came by this morning."

His eyes darkened as he said, "Is that ass-hat going to be a problem?"

Shaking her head, "I actually have no idea why he's here. I haven't talked to him since the divorce over a year ago. Him showing up today was a totally unexpected surprise."

"People don't just do things for no reason, so he's got some motive for being here. I've got to go, but I'm going to have a friend do some checking into your ex. And if you have one tiny bit of a problem, you call me or the station – got that?"

"Got it, but I'll be fine," she assured. "In fact, I'll be cleaning most of today—that's my Monday routine."

Kissing her goodbye, Mitch headed back to his jeep, a plan already in action. *Her cheating ex doesn't just show up for no reason. I'm going to find out what it is!*

10

By the early afternoon, Mitch and the Baytown officers had arrested a teenage shoplifter, directed traffic around a fender bender, met with some school-age children for an anti-drug campaign in the library, and policed the public beach, filled with summer families. Most visitors obeyed the beach rules, but glass bottles and dogs not on leashes were always a concern, and usually those in the wrong liked to argue with the police. Throw in a meeting with the town council and mayor about the upcoming Fisherman's Fair in the harbor, and Mitch was ready to call it a day.

Sitting in his office, he finally had a chance to work with his computer. Doing a search of Thomas Porter, he began delving into Tori's ex. Scrolling through his basic information, he discovered he was a real estate broker, originally from the Williamsburg area. He had been named as one of the top realtors for several years but noticed that distinction had not been bestowed on him in the past two years. His address was a condo in an exclusive neighborhood in the outskirts of Williamsburg, and he had only lived there since the divorce. According to his social media, he was a very active man —golf tournaments, constant twitters and Facebook posts, social events, and a large number of realtor site pictures. But in searching his friend list, he noticed Thomas and Vanessa were friends. Her name was now Vanessa Hurkamp, but Mitch recognized her bleached blonde hair and heavily made-up face. The large diamond on her finger as she hung onto the arm of an older man was not hard to miss as well.

Leaning back, he twisted in his chair and glanced out the window. Recognizing Tori's hair, he watched as she walked down the street and considered jogging after her. Sighing, he knew he had work to finish and she seemed to be on a mission as she hustled along.

Twisting back around to view his computer monitor, he picked up his phone, calling Jack Bryant, of Saints Protection & Investigations.

"Hey, Jack," he greeted.

"How's life back home?" Jack asked.

"Busy," he replied. "My cases are a lot less stressful than with the FBI, but I gotta say the small-town life is still keeping me busy. I just found out that I have a private investigator in town but haven't met him yet. It sure won't be like working with you Saints."

"It goes without saying, but if you need us, give me a call. The Saints are still ready to help out, Mitch, whether you're FBI or the police chief."

"That's just what I needed to hear. Thanks, man. I might take you up on that occasionally, if needed. But I'm hoping the PI in town will be an ally. If not, I might have Luke do a little searching for me."

"Absolutely," Jack agreed. "You need my computer expert or any of us, just let me know."

Hanging up, Mitch breathed a sigh of relief, knowing he had the big guns at his disposal if needed to find out about Tori's ex and sister. Looking up, he saw Ginny and Burt at his door.

"Come on in," he called out.

The two sat down across from his desk and he leaned back, expectantly, watching the two of them eye each other nervously. "What's going on?"

"Sir," Ginny began, falling back to her military days, "we've noticed on beach patrol that Sam tends to let some things go and turn away, such as groups of men drinking alcohol on the beach, both in cans and in glass bottles."

"He's also harder on the kids that are playing basketball in the church parking lot than he is on the vacationer kids who are drag racing their golf carts on the streets and sidewalks."

Mitch stared at Burt for a long minute before sliding his gaze over to Ginny. "You think there's a problem?"

Ginny and Burt glanced at each other before she answered, "I think he takes his orders from the top."

Letting out a sigh, Mitch nodded. "Mayor Corwin Banks. Keep the vacationers happy while coming down on his own townspeople in the process." Leaning back, he scrubbed his face for a second. "Image. It's all about image to him."

Nodding, Burt joined Mitch with a sigh of his own. "I wouldn't discount Silas Mills either."

Wiping down the guest bathrooms, Tori walked by a bag of healthy snacks in the Dumfries' room and could not help but grin. *I guess that's why he's trying to sneak food from my refrigerator. His wife is trying to keep him on a diet.*

Walking out, she headed down the stairs, cleaning supplies in the bucket she carried. Her mind slipped back to the unexpected visit by Thomas and the subsequent arrival of Mitch. Her thoughts warred between irritation that her ex would just show up and pleasure at knowing Mitch was dropping by to see her before his day got started. Hoping she would not have to deal with Thomas anymore, she reached the bottom of the stairs just as her doorbell rang again.

Eyes jumping to the visible profile, she was pleased to see the image of a woman standing outside. *Good, no more ex!*

Throwing open the door, she stood stunned once more. If she thought Thomas standing on her stoop early that morning had been a shock, nothing could have prepared her for the sight of her sister. Only a year older than her, obvious, but unnecessary, plastic surgery had occurred since Tori had last seen her. A designer suit, designer heels, designer sunglasses, and a huge diamond wedding band on her left hand indicated Vanessa had hooked herself to someone with money. *Her lifelong goal,* Tori thought, irritation on her face. *Mom told me Vanessa had gotten married again...of course Vanessa told mom that since it was a whirlwind wedding in Aruba, they hadn't had time to involve family...as if I'd go anyway!*

"Tori!" Vanessa called out, a brilliant, dentist-whitened smile on her face.

Just like the morning with Thomas, she stood with one hand on the doorframe and the other still on the doorknob, blocking the path. "What do you want, Vanessa? Surely, you know you're not welcome here."

Immediately dropping her fake smile, Vanessa bit out, "Aren't you going to invite me in?"

"No."

"Tori, this was my grandmother's house also, you know."

"One you only visited when mom made you come here, and one you never visited after you left high school. Not even when grandma was sick."

Her botoxed lips twisted in an ugly grimace, Vanessa tapped her foot in irritation. "Look, I just wanted to come visit my sister. You know, let bygones be bygones. I don't understand why you're hanging on to the past."

"Maybe because when you slept with my husband, you stopped being my sister. So, you can turn right around and go back to your new husband and leave my property."

"This was our grandmother's property. She should have never left it just to you. I should be part owner."

Angry heat scorched Tori as she stared incredulously at Vanessa. "How dare you try to intimate you are owed something. Grandma left this place, in its entirety, to me. Only me. I'm so done with unwanted visitors today. Between you and Thomas showing up, I'm done. Get off my property, and don't come back!"

Ignoring the warning, Vanessa looked genuinely shocked. "Thomas was here? What did he want?"

"Don't know, don't care."

Tori watched as her sister's face grew thoughtful but interrupted her before she had a chance to speak. "Leave, Vanessa. You can't come in, and we have nothing to say to each other."

Closing the door in her face, she leaned against the polished, heavy wood, her heart pounding. *Thomas...and now Vanessa? What the hell is going on?* Peeking around the door, she observed her sister stomping down the front steps and moving toward her car. Breathing deeply, she glanced at her watch. *I wonder if Katelyn's at the bar? I need a friend...and a drink!*

Before she left the Inn, she placed a call to her grandmother's lawyer. "Mr. Benfield, it's Tori Bradford. I know it's getting late in the day, but my sister just showed up, and I'm pretty sure she's getting ready to contest the Will."

"I assure you, Miss Tori, your grandmother's Will is rock solid. She made the Will many years ago and it did not change. It always had you inheriting the Inn and the property. What she left for Vanessa was cash and some bonds. So, even if your sister has gone through that money, she cannot lay her hands on the Inn."

Breathing a sigh of relief, she apologized for bothering him, receiving his assurance that she was in no trouble at all. *Vanessa and Thomas...coming the same day. But Vanessa seemed truly surprised that Thomas had been here. So, what's going on?*

The Dumfries walked through the side door, greeting her as they made their way up the stairs, coming in from a day of sightseeing.

Calling out to them, she said, "I'm heading out to see some friends. I'll see you in the morning for breakfast. Oh, and by the way, I have a nice blueberry cobbler in the dining room if you would like some." Catching the gleam in Mr. Dumfries' eyes, she smiled.

Taking the stairs two at a time up to her room, she quickly changed and ran a brush through her hair before heading out.

"How dare that skank and your asshole ex show up! And on the same day!" Katelyn yelled, earning a glare from Brogan.

He walked over, looking at Tori, and said, "If you have any problem with them, let me know."

Before she could answer, Jillian came blowing into Finn's, yelling, "I can't believe this shit!"

Katelyn just shrugged when she caught Tori's raised eyebrows. "Hey, she needed to know, too."

Aiden, having finished serving some beers to a group in the back, sauntered up, throwing his arm around Tori. "Babe, if either of them tries to come in here, I'll kick both their asses."

Giggling, Tori smiled looking at the group. Before she could thank him, the door slammed open, and Mitch's large frame filled the doorway. As soon as her eyes landed on him, her heart began to pound. From his booted feet, up to his khaki pants covering his thick thighs, to his BPD black polo straining to contain his muscular arms as they crossed in front of him, ending at his strong jaw and glaring eyes...*glaring eyes?* Jolted out of her admiring perusal, she realized the man standing in front of her was pissed.

Opening her mouth to speak, Mitch crossed the floor reaching her side in a few steps. Before she could greet him, he said, "Your sister show up?"

"Uh...well—"

"Easy question, Tori. Yes or no."

Narrowing her eyes, she said, "Now just hold on a minu—"

"Did your sister show her face at your Inn today?"

"Yes, but—"

"You didn't call me," he stated. "Had my phone with me all day but got no call."

"Mitch, stop being so alpha," Tori groused. "Why on earth would I call you just because my sister came by? I didn't let her in. I didn't let her talk to me. What I did do was call my grandmother's lawyer to make sure Vanessa can't try to get her claws on the Sea Glass Inn. So, I handled it!" she huffed.

At that, the group grew silent, and she looked around at the stunned faces of her friends. "Wh...what?" she asked.

"Vanessa wants to get her hands on the Inn?" Jillian asked, wide eyed.

"No, no," Tori rushed. "Mr. Benfield assures me that the Inn is mine completely, and there's no way she can contest the Will."

"But she wants it?" Mitch growled beside her.

Glancing at the angry expression she nodded slowly. "Well, she said it wasn't fair, but she got money and bonds from grandma." Placing her hand on Mitch's arm, feeling the tense muscles underneath her fingertips, she said, "It's okay. Really."

"You shouldn't have to be in the presence of either of those snakes," he said, "much less in one day. And I expect to get a call the next time someone...anyone... shows up that you don't want to deal with."

"Mitch," she began softly, unwilling to let their friends hear her uncertainty, but before she could continue, he stepped in closer.

Placing his hands on either side of her face, he pulled her in and kissed her forehead. "I told you that we were friends but that I also wanted to take this as far as we can. I'm not willing to ignore what we have. My friends know how much you meant to me years ago and what we're starting now."

Nervously glancing to the side, she saw the grins from the group around. Sliding her gaze back to his, she smiled as he kissed her lips. Soft. And full of promises of more kisses to come.

Pulling back, he said, "You are a completely capable woman, running your own business, but babe, I do not want you dealing with either of those two. They're poisonous. So, you call me if they so much as wave in your direction. Got it?"

Nodding, she said, "Okay, but I have a feeling they both left town as soon as they didn't get from me whatever they wanted to get."

An hour later, after relaxing fun and drinks with friends, Mitch walked Tori back to the Inn. Accepting her invitation in, they made their way up the back stairs to her room. Slightly tipsy, she immediately moved into his body as soon as the door was closed. Pressing herself against his hard body, she threw her arms around his neck, pulling him down to continue the kiss he started in the bar.

He let her take the lead, not minding the feel of her hands in his hair, her lips moving over his, or her body pressed against his. Enveloping her in his embrace, he angled his head for better access to her warmth as her tongue flicked out and licked his lips.

Feeling the jolt, he fought the urge to grind against her soft curves. Taking over with one hand sliding up to cup the back of her head, the other hand slipped down to grip her hip.

It had been a while since he had been with a woman,

not wanting to start something in Charlestown when he knew he was moving, and random sex with a stranger had never held much appeal. *But this? Perfection.*

With their bodies clinging to each other's, pressed from knees to lips, he walked her backward until her legs hit the mattress.

The thought shot through Tori's mind that things seemed easier in her romance novels as they fell backward on the bed, their legs slipping on the floor, and his body landing with somewhat of a thump on top of hers. Her breath left her in a whoosh, and their lips separated as his head moved higher.

He rolled slightly to the side so she could catch her breath, and then they both scrambled to scoot farther up onto the bed. Finally, just as she was giggling nervously, their lips met again, and the kiss once more ratcheted to white-hot.

She felt the slight abrasion of his beard compared to the strong, silkiness of his lips. His tongue slipped into her warmth, and she groaned at the sensations tingling throughout her body. As her body began to spark, she realized this kiss was more than what she had ever felt. She had been kissed before...but this was a *KISS*.

Mitch, keeping his weight off her by lying partially to her side, allowed his hand to roam reverently from her jaw, over her shoulder, and downward.

The images filling his mind threatened to overtake all other thoughts, and he tamped them down, slowing the kiss. He glided his hand to her shoulder as he tapered the kiss.

Ending with a few nibbles on the corner of her mouth, he leaned back, gazing down into her lust-filled eyes. Seeing the question forming in her gaze, he said, "I want this. You were the first girl I ever wanted this with when I was younger. But I respected you then…and I'll respect you now."

"But—"

Kissing her objections away, he continued, "This is going to happen, babe. But at the right time. I want you, sure. I want you to be completely sure…because Tori, when I claim you, there's no going back. You'll be mine. So, it's gotta be right."

She lifted her hand to cup his face, rubbing her thumb over his stubbled jaw. Sucking in a deep breath, she let it out slowly before speaking. "I know what I want. What I've always wanted. But you making sure it's right means a lot to me. I've never had someone put me first. So, as hard as it is to resist you-"

His bark of laughter interrupted, and his smile remained as she finished, "We'll make sure it's perfect."

Kissing her one last time, he moved off the bed, pulling her with him. "Come lock up behind me so I'll be able to sleep knowing you're safe while having sweet dreams."

Tori was awoken at two a.m. by screaming in her intercom.

"My husband, my husband! He's not breathing!"

Stumbling out of bed, Tori grabbed her robe and ran down the connecting stairs to the second floor, racing into the hall. The call came from the Dumfries in the Blue Room, and the door was open as she careened around the corner, seeing Mrs. Dumfries being consoled by Mrs. Tolliver from the Green Room. Racing into the Blue Room, she recognized Mr. Dumfries prone on the bed, not moving. Not breathing. And what appeared to be blue vomit around his mouth.

Grabbing her phone, she dialed 911.

"Emergency at the Sea Glass Inn," she cried, trying to still her erratically beating heart. "Yes, yes. One of the guests. He's not breathing."

Handing the phone to Mr. Tolliver standing in the hall, she said, "They say to stay on the line. I'll go let them in." Racing downstairs, she glanced into the dining room on her way to the front door. Half of the blueberry cobbler was gone.

11

The ambulance and fire truck pulled into the drive of the Inn and Zac alighted first. Grateful it was someone she knew, she began babbling immediately.

"I don't know what happened. His wife found him and called me, and I went running in, and then I—"

"Slow down, slow down," Zac said. "Just show me where to go, then I want you to call Mitch."

"Mitch? But I—"

"Honey, call Mitch now."

Leading Zac and his partner up the stairs, she hustled the other guests back to their rooms. "I know you all are concerned, but please give the rescue workers some space." Turning, she was halfway down the stairs with her phone in her hand, dialing Mitch, when he came through the front door, a female police officer by his side.

"Oh, Mitch—umph,"

Her words were cut off as he slammed into her body,

wrapping his arms around her. He felt her quivering and held her for a few seconds before pulling back to peer down into her face. Her wide, blue eyes registered shock as they searched his.

"Mitch," came the soft voice of the police officer next to him, and as much as he hated it, he knew he needed to let her go. Pulling back, he glanced down, seeing her long legs barely covered by her sleep shorts, her breasts outlined perfectly in a pink camisole, and her silk robe hanging open. Grabbing the edges of the robe, he pulled them together and tied the belt again.

"Tori, stay down here. Fix a cup of tea for yourself, and I'll be back as soon as I can."

With those simple instructions, she watched as he and the other police officer jogged up the stairs. Staring numbly after them for several minutes, she jolted when another person showed up at the door. Opening it, she was surprised to see Dr. Warren, one of the two medical doctors in the town.

"Doctor?" she asked hopefully, thinking that his presence must surely mean that Mr. Dumfries had revived.

"Miss Bradford," he replied congenially, stepping into the house. "Can you show me the body?"

"B...body?" she stammered. "Uh..."

His kind face relaxed slightly as he said, "Is he upstairs?"

"Who?"

Just then the female police officer appeared at the top of the stairs and called out, "Up here, Doc."

He patted Tori's arm as he passed her by and jogged up the stairs. Ignoring Mitch's instructions, she followed the doctor.

Standing outside the doorway, she listened to him ask, "What have we got?"

"Male, sixty-two years old. Wife noticed husband was not breathing when she got up to go to the bathroom. She takes sleeping pills and had not heard anything even though it appears he had thrown up. His skin is pink, and the wife claims they had not been in the sun much today. Also, the odor..."

Tori leaned closer to the door to try to hear what was being said, but several voices chimed in making it impossible to discern clearly.

Inside the room, Mitch observed as Dr. Warren proceeded with his initial examination. "I'd say he's been dead less than an hour. Can't tell much from his skin color, since there is the possibility that he had been in the sun. But the smell," he stood and looked over at Mitch. "Could definitely be poison. I'd say you need to treat this place as a possible crime scene until I can do an autopsy." Looking over at Ginny, he said, "And you'd better bag up the food."

Mitch rubbed his hand over his face in frustration even as he nodded to Ginny. "Call in Grant and Sam to assist. We'll have to talk to all the guests and get food samples of what he ate. I'll talk to Tori first and then join you in interviews."

"Mitch," Ginny said, gaining his attention. "Should you be the one to interview Ms. Bradford?"

Irritation shot over Mitch, but he knew she was right. "I just want to tell her what's happening, and then I'll have you interview her."

Stepping out of the room, he turned quickly and slammed into Tori. "What the hell are you doing up here?" Seeing the shock on her face, he softened his voice. "We need to go back downstairs." Looking at the other guests standing in their doorways, he announced, "Mr. Dumfries has died, and we'll need to interview all of you, so that we have our facts straight."

"I thought I heard you say something about poison," one of the guests said. "We've all been eating food here, so I want to know what happened."

"Poison!" shrieked another guest.

Tori's heart pounded as she watched the other guests begin clamoring for explanations.

"I'm getting out of here."

"Get dressed honey, we'll go check into a hotel."

"How do we know what he ate?"

"Quiet," Mitch shouted, hushing the others. "Calm down. At this time, we have yet to determine the cause of death. You will remain here until we can interview everyone." Turning, he grabbed Tori's arm and escorted her down the stairs with him.

At the bottom, she looked up at him reproachfully. "You're hurting me," she accused.

He immediately dropped her arm. "Shit, I'm sorry, babe. Okay, listen, I need you to get dressed. I've got more officers coming over. We've got to interview the occupants of the Inn, and we've got to bag up any possible food that he may have eaten."

Sucking in her breath quickly, she cried, "Oh, my God. He was poisoned?"

"Babe, we don't know that, but the medical examiner has suspicions, and until they can be proved or disproved by the autopsy, we have to assume the worst and be prepared."

They were interrupted by a flurry of more activity as Grant and Sam arrived while Zac and his partner were bringing Mr. Dumfries' body down the stairs on a stretcher. Mitch squeezed her hand and regretfully walked away. He had work to do, and the sooner he got the scene processed, the sooner he could get back to Tori.

The sun had risen in the Eastern sky by the time the police left the Inn. Tori had slipped back to her room a few hours earlier to dress in capris and a T-shirt, running a brush through her hair and pulling it back into a ponytail. As she stared at her reflection, she was stunned at the events of the previous day. First, Thomas appearing out of nowhere wanting to talk...then Vanessa coming by to imply that she wanted a stake in the Inn...then one of her guests was possibly poisoned and had died. *If there were ever a contest for the suckiest day of the year, this would win.*

As soon as that thought hit her mind, she was immediately contrite, hanging her head. *Poor Mr. Dumfries... and oh, Jesus...his wife!*

Straightening up, taking a fortifying breath, she went back downstairs to her kitchen, now being dissected by Sam. He looked at her sympathetically as he bagged up the food she had served from breakfast and anything from the snack drawer available to guests. Ginny walked in with the remains of the cobbler in her hands and set it on the counter.

"We haven't been introduced yet. I'm Officer Ginny Spencer."

Tori accepted her hand and returned the pretty officer's greeting. "Is there anything you need from me?"

"Sam, bag this please," Ginny directed, before turning back to Tori. "Can you tell me about the cobbler here?"

"Um..." Tori's eyes sought Ginny's, uncertain what she was supposed to say.

"Tell you what," Ginny elaborated, "why don't you simply explain the food service here and that will help us out."

"Okay," Tori agreed, looking around the kitchen as though seeing it for the first time. "The kitchen is for me, and the guest rooms have a mini fridge in each one. I do keep a snack pantry in the dining room, for when guests get the munchies. And will sometimes leave goodies on the dining room table for them. Like that cobbler," she nodded her head toward the half-empty baking dish.

"So, they aren't supposed to eat the food in here?" Ginny clarified.

Shaking her head, Tori said, "No, but sometimes they do. In fact, I had to chase Mr. Dumfries out yesterday."

"Do you prepare food in here for them at any time?"

"The guests are provided breakfast...that's part of their payment."

"What time is that served?"

"Between eight and nine in the morning. I place it in my grandmother's silver warming trays and put it on the dining room table. The guests serve themselves... um, I have coffee and juice there also."

"The guests aren't served individual plates of food to their tables?" Ginny queried.

"No."

"So, she couldn't have poisoned his food directly," Sam said.

Tori whipped her head around so fast her ponytail smacked her cheek. "What? Me? Poison—"

"Sam!" Ginny growled, shooting him a death glare.

Sam shot Tori an apologetic gaze and muttered, "Sorry, Ms. Bradford. I wasn't implying it was you. Could have been the wife...or one of the other guests."

The room began to darken as Tori's knees buckled, and she crumpled to the floor.

"Come on, Tori, baby, wake up."

The words came from far off, but slowly crept into her consciousness as her eyes fluttered open. Mitch's face was directly in her line of vision, worry lines emanating from the sides of his eyes. Her hand involuntarily reached up to smooth away the chiseled creases.

"Babe? You with me?" His voice caressed her as she blinked a few more times, awareness crashing back.

Bolting upright, she was trapped by him as she reclined on the living room sofa, curled on her side as his hip sat in the crook of her body. His hand jumped to her shoulders quickly, stilling her movement.

"Whoa, slow down, babe. You hit your head pretty hard when you passed out. I want the doc to check you out."

Her eyes cut over to a young man standing in her living room, watching her from over Mitch's shoulder. His dark hair, slightly long and curled on the ends, stood up at odd angles as though he had just gotten out of bed. *He probably did.*

The new man in the room gave Mitch a shove on the shoulder, saying, "Let me in, man. Let me check her out."

Mitch reluctantly stood and stepped back, but just enough to allow the doctor to slide in closely.

"We haven't met yet. I'm Dr. Turner. William Turner. I'm fairly new in town and work with Dr. Warren at the Baytown clinic. I hear you've had quite an exciting night."

His voice was warm and soothing, opposed to the vibe coming off Mitch. Before she could speak, the doctor reached behind her, his hand gently probing the side of her head.

Wincing, she jerked, and he apologized. "Do you faint often?"

"Only at the sight of blood...or needles," she replied. "I...I remember being in the kitchen and the room began to sway."

Nodding, he checked her eyes, pulse, and blood pressure. "You seem to be in good health. I have a feeling that anxiety, and probably dehydration, caused you to faint. If this is the first time, then I'm not as worried about the fainting as I am about the bump on your head from when you hit the floor. I'm leaving you with a list of things to watch out for. I want you to rest and make sure to—"

"Miss! Miss!" One of the couples was dressed and standing at the front counter in the entryway. "We're checking out now and want to make sure we get a refund for the rest of the week that we won't be here."

Pushing past the doctor and Mitch, Tori rushed over. "I understand this was upsetting, but please don't leave. I assure you—"

"We are leaving! A man was poisoned right across the hall from us! We've been up all night, being interviewed by the police!"

Shoulders slumping, she nodded as she took the keycard from them and watched them as they walked to the front door, luggage rolling along behind them.

Mitch stepped up to the couple and said, "Until we

have completed our investigation, you will need to remain in the area."

The man rose to his full height but still had to look up into Mitch's unhappy face. "Fine. We will be at the Baytown Hotel for the rest of the week." With a parting glare at Tori, he and his wife walked out.

Mitch turned around to move toward Tori, but two more couples were coming down the stairs, wanting to check out as well. He watched, helpless and hating the emotion, as Tori went through the obligatory motions.

Ginny, Grant, and Sam walked into the front foyer as well, watching the last of the guests leave. As Tori stared dumbly at the crowd, she recognized their sympathetic expressions, which only made her tears fall more.

Mitch stalked over, pulling her into his embrace. Tucking her tightly against his body, he looked over her head to give instructions. "Sam, make sure to bag the food in the Dumfries' room as well and get the samples to the coroner's office until we know more as to what needs to be sent to the lab. Ginny and Grant, I'll meet you in the office in a few minutes." The three officers left the Inn, and Dr. Warren walked over to Mitch.

"I'll check on her again this afternoon," he said softly, patting Tori's back.

Mitch nodded and, after he left, he walked her back over to the sofa. Settling her down, he crouched in front of her, his hands at her jaw. "Tori," he called softly, drawing her anguished eyes back to him. "I hate like hell to leave, but I have to. I'm calling Katelyn and Jillian to come stay with you until I can come back here."

"I...how...?"

"I don't know. But we'll find out what happened and then you can get your life back."

Her gaze shot up to his and she said, "I didn't poison him—"

"I know that, babe, but I have to find out if he was poisoned and, if so, how. And I need to find out who did it. Let me do my job and then you can get your Inn back."

Her gaze left his as it wandered over the room. "I...I have no guests."

She turned her tearful eyes back to him, and he swore he felt the punch right in his heart. "I know, and I promise to find out what happened. Then we'll work on damage control for the Inn."

Kissing the top of her head, he walked out, hating himself for leaving her arms. Standing at his jeep, looking back to the peaceful Inn, thinking of all the wonderful times he had had here as a child and the beautiful woman hurting inside, his jaw tightened in anger. *No one gets away with murder in my town. And, especially, no one messes with my girl!*

12

Stopping by Baytown's Medical Clinic later in the day, Mitch walked straight back to Dr. Turner's office. The older man appeared fresh even after the long night and morning he had.

"Whatcha got for me, Doc?"

"I had his body taken to the morgue at the North Heron Hospital. My initial evaluation is the strong possibility of poison in gestation, so the medical examiner there worked on the autopsy today. I went up late this morning to work with her and I've got the initial report right here."

He handed a file to Mitch but, before Mitch could open it, Dr. Turner began to summarize. "Internal examination agrees with the possibility of cyanide poisoning, and she agreed that the time of death corresponds with the wife's account."

Mitch said, "The wife claims that she had her husband on a strict diet and he never strayed from it."

Catching the doctor's raised eyebrow, he smirked. "Yeah, I know. I also know that Tori said she had to remind him several times that the kitchen was her domain and he wasn't supposed to forage."

"According to his stomach contents, he had eaten some of the blueberry cobbler late at night, so we can assume his wife must have been asleep then."

Nodding, Mitch agreed. "She said she takes sleeping pills, so I'm guessing either last night the call of the dessert was too much of a temptation or her husband made a habit of sneaking food at night."

"Had others eaten any cobbler?" Dr. Turner asked. "Because the poison acts fairly fast, if it was indeed cyanide."

"According to the other guests, a few of them had some early in the evening, but it was left on the table, open, so anyone could have gotten to it."

"Any idea who?"

Mitch rubbed his beard. "The most obvious would be his wife. She appears to be the only one there who knew him and therefore the only one with motive."

"How's Tori?"

Sighing heavily, he replied, "With her guests checking out, she's reeling from it all."

"Damn."

"Yeah." Nodding, Mitch headed back to his jeep. Glancing at his watch, he saw that it was almost three o'clock. He'd called a meeting for the officers to work the intel they had and was going to have just enough time to get there. Driving, he called Jillian.

"Hey cuz," she answered softly.

He knew Katelyn had spent the morning with Tori before Jillian took over when the bakery rush slowed down. "How's it going?"

"Physically? She's doing okay. Doesn't seem to have any side effects from a concussion. Emotionally? She's a mess."

"Damn."

"I've kept her busy, though. We can't clean the rooms until Grant gives us the go-ahead. I think he's finishing now, 'cause he said he needed to get to a meeting at the station."

"I have no idea how long we'll be meeting, but can you—"

"Of course. You don't even have to ask."

"Thanks, Jillian," Mitch offered sincerely.

"Hey…" she replied, gently, "I really like her. I always have. And the two of you together…well, I just wanted to say, it's perfect."

Hanging up, he slammed his hand down on the steering wheel, shouting, "Fuck!" All he wanted to do was be with Tori…*but until she's cleared from the investigation, I've got to keep my distance.*

Mitch walked into the staff room, immediately getting down to business. "Here's the initial autopsy report. Dr. Turner said that his initial suspicions seem to be correct, but we'll know more when the results come back from toxicology. Tissue and blood have been sent to the Virginia Department of Forensic Science. They've put a rush on it, but it could still take a week to obtain the results. In the meantime, if we go on the medical examiner's assumption that it was cyanide poisoning, what else have we got?"

Ginny said, "Mrs. Dumfries was hard to get much out of. Sobbed all the way through the interview, which is understandable. But she was completely unwilling to concede that he might have eaten some of the cobbler, even when the evidence in the vomit was right in front of her."

"Does she have an explanation?" Grant asked.

Rolling her eyes, Ginny said, "She claims the sausage casserole was undercooked yesterday morning and that everyone knows that undercooked meat can contain bacteria that can kill a person."

Leaning back in his chair, Mitch shook his head. "That's what everyone was hearing and why all the guests checked out."

"Partially. Also, because I think they were all just upset and scared," Sam added. "And before you ask, I went through the garbage and retrieved samples from the leftover sausage casserole."

"But it was sitting out on the table for everyone. If there was a problem, it wouldn't only hit one person," Burt argued. "And certainly not eighteen hours later!"

"Gotta be the wife," Grant said. "She had opportunity, she's the only one who might have had motive."

"What'd you get on their finances?" Mitch asked Burt.

"Retired store manager. She had been a housewife, and they retired with a decent nest egg. Not extravagant, but reasonably well off. He did have a nice insurance policy to the tune of one million dollars, and she's listed as his only beneficiary."

"Any children? Relatives?"

Shaking his head, Burt said, "No kids. They have a nephew that's had to declare bankruptcy, but he lives in Texas and, according to the wife, they haven't heard from him in a couple of years."

"Keep looking into the wife," Mitch said to Burt. "See what more we can dig up." Turning to Grant, he asked, "What about the Inn? What did you find?"

"Nothing, Chief. Absolutely nothing you wouldn't expect to find. The place is clean, neat, and orderly. The cleaning supplies are locked in the pantry in the laundry room. There were no hidden bottles of anything unexpected in the Inn proper or in the individual guest rooms."

"Sam, what about the kitchen?"

"I bagged up samples of just about everything poison could be in. It looks like Tori eats light, because the refrigerator did not hold a lot. There were things that she would use to fix the guests breakfast, but other than that, some lunch meat, cheese, some leftover lasagna, and some chicken salad she must have had for lunch. I sent samples to the lab as well."

"Okay, obviously this is our first priority. We'll pull

back on the beach shifts and make those only two-hour patrols with one officer, once in the morning and once in the afternoon. Town patrols can stay as usual and the rest of the time we work this case."

Mildred stuck her head in the doorway, an irritated expression on her face. "Celia rang from next door. The mayor wants to see you and says it needs to be now. He has a dinner at the clubhouse and doesn't want to be late."

Mitch caught the sympathetic expressions fired his way from his staff as he stood up. Stopping at the door, he turned back and said, "You all did good today. Keep it up."

Walking through the back hallway connecting the station with the mayor's office in the Municipal Building, Mitch hesitated for a second before pushing the door open. He hoped that the mayor's clawing secretary had left for the evening, but it appeared she kept her boss' hours. *Great...just fuckin' great.*

Celia's eyes lit as soon as he approached. His attempt to sidestep her desk and proceed directly to the mayor's office was hindered as she hustled on her stilettoes and managed to plaster herself against his side, her long fingernails digging into his arm.

"Mitch," she purred. "I haven't seen you in so long."

"Ms. Ring, I've been doing my job. Now if you'll excuse me, the mayor is expecting me."

Digging her fingernails in a little deeper, she pouted, "But I thought surely you would make time for me."

Seriously? Take a hint, lady. Tired, irritated, and

wanting to get to Tori, he carefully grabbed her arm and firmly moved it off his. Glaring down at her surprised expression, he said, "Ms. Ring, you're the mayor's assistant, and that is all you'll ever be to me. Now stop the pretense of something happening and let go of my arm."

Walking past her as brusquely as his words, he stepped into the office, firmly closing the door behind him.

Corwin looked up, a scowl on his face. Silas was also in the room, his expression mirroring the mayor's. Before Mitch had a chance to speak, Corwin jumped in.

"A murder? A murder of a vacationer in Baytown? What the hell are you going to do about this?"

Sighing at the mayor's histrionics, Mitch cocked an eyebrow. "I'm going to do my job. We've already had an initial autopsy performed and the results, as well as some of the food, have been sent to the lab. We've interviewed the wife, the other guests, and Ms. Bradford."

"Speaking of Ms. Bradford, my wife tells me that the two of you have been seen together in town. You need to watch your step! I can't have the Chief of Police cavorting with a possible murder suspect!"

"We don't want property values going down because one of our Inns can't be run properly," Silas added.

Stalking from the door to Corwin's desk, Mitch placed his fists on the desk and leaned in. "You let me do the job you hired me to do and keep your mouth shut about suspects and members of this town. The last thing we need is for rumors to run amuck hurting innocent people." Mitch swung his head around toward Silas, pinning the man with his glare.

Corwin swallowing deeply, unused to the full anger of a furious man aimed directly at him, backpedaled. "Well," he blustered, "I didn't mean to imply that she was guilty. I just meant we have to think about our image. We need to uphold the town's confidence."

"Don't worry about me," Mitch said, straightening to his full height before heading toward the door. "But, um...you might want to think about your image and the new secretary out there." Smirking, he took pleasure in seeing Corwin swallow deeply several times more but noted Silas' appraising glance. Throwing open the door, he ignored Celia's stare and headed back to the station, each step bringing rising fury.

Arriving at the Inn, Mitch hustled to the front door, hesitating just enough for Jillian to open it before he knocked. Giving her a quick hug, he glanced around, noting Tori was not in sight. "How is she?" he asked, worry lacing his voice.

Jillian tossed her blonde ponytail over her shoulder as she sighed. "She's trying to be positive, but as the day wore on, she had three cancellations."

"What the hell?"

"It seems one of the guests that left this morning works for a radio station in Virginia Beach, and they ran a news piece about the *suspicious death at the Sea Glass Inn*," she groused, using her fingers as quotation marks as she recited the title. "Plus, Sam told her that as long as the Inn was a crime scene she shouldn't have guests anyway."

His hands on his hips, Mitch gazed at his boots for a moment. Looking back up when his cousin placed her hand on his arm, he offered a tight smile. "Where is she?"

"She's resting in her room right now. I'll leave and let you take care of her." Receiving his nod, she grabbed her purse off the table by the front door before smiling up at Mitch. "Tori and you have been destined to be together since she was six years old. Don't let this screw things up, Mitch. Just ride it out and sweet things'll come."

Locking the front door behind her, he walked up the main stairs and through the door leading to her room. Ascending to the third floor, he entered her suite, seeing her lying on her bed, eyes closed.

As he approached, she opened them and turned toward him. The fading sunlight from the lace-curtained French doors cast a glow on her pale face. Moving quickly, he sat on the bed, gathering her into his arms.

Adrift in a sea of swirling emotions, Tori wrapped her arms around his neck tightly as she held on to her lifesaver. Neither spoke for several minutes, just pressing their bodies as close together as possible. He stroked her long hair, slightly rocking her body.

Finally, she leaned back and gazed into his eyes. "How are you?" she asked.

"I should be asking you that," he admonished.

"You're the one who's been up all night and working all day. I've just been lying around in my big Inn, unable to do anything. I can't even clean the rooms."

"Babe, the processing should be done. I'll confirm with Grant tomorrow. Then you can get back to what you need to do. And don't worry about me. This is nothing compared to my former jobs, so I'm good."

Snorting, she said, "Why clean the rooms when there's no one coming to the Inn. I've had three cancellations already."

Placing his hands on either side of her face, he brought her gaze directly to his. "Listen to me and listen well. We will get through this. I promise."

Feeling his assurance seep into her very core, she nodded slowly. "Okay. You're right. It'll be fine." Taking a deep, cleansing breath, she said, "Are you hungry? I know there's not a lot probably left, but I could fix you a sandwich. Um...well, I don't know if there was any food left after it was all taken actually. I made some chicken salad yesterday and didn't even get to eat any before your office had to take it for sampling. I could fix—"

"Nah," he said, "I grabbed a sandwich at the diner earlier." Looking around, he said, "I probably should go and let you get some rest since you were up all night as well."

Tori hesitated, hating to feel clingy, but still shook

up over the events. "Mitch," she began, sucking in her lips, her sky-blue eyes turned up to his.

"Yeah?" he said, holding her gaze.

"Would you consider staying with me…just to sleep, but I…I really want you near me."

Fuck keeping a professional distance! "Babe, I can't think of any place I'd rather be." Seeing her shy smile, he added, "Why don't you go on and get ready. I'll check to make sure the Inn is secure."

Moving with a purpose for the first time all day, Tori grabbed her sleep shorts and camisole to take into the bathroom. Hurrying through her nighttime routine, she washed her face, moisturized, and brushed her teeth. Exiting, she saw Mitch was just walking back into the room.

The expression on his face as he perused her from the top of her head to her pink-painted toenails warmed her to the core. Sucking in her lips, she wanted to jump up and down, wave her arms, and scream, *'Mitch Evans likes me!,'* but managed to smile instead. Unsure what to do, she stood in the middle of the room, fingering the bottom of her shorts.

Noting her uncertainty, he walked over, wrapping her in his strong embrace. Kissing the top of her head, he said, "I want you to be comfortable, Tori. Nothing is going to happen tonight. We're both exhausted and, when we finally get together, I want no shadows between us."

She grinned into his chest before leaning her head back and gifting him with her smile.

"You with me, sweetheart?"

Still beaming, she simply nodded.

Bending, he touched his lips to hers and gave her a little squeeze. "Go on and get in bed. I'll be there soon."

A few minutes later, after finishing in the bathroom, he walked out having shucked off his shirt and jeans. Turning off the light, he moved toward the bed.

Tori wasn't sure if she would ever get the image of Mitch stalking toward her in only boxers out of her mind. *And I hope I don't!* The view of his bare chest with a smattering of hair, leading down to ripped abs and into his narrow waist made her mouth water. His muscular arms encircled her, pulling her tightly into his hard body. *I will never be able to fall asleep with him holding me this close. This is my teenage dream come true.*

Mitch slid one arm under her head while the other circled around her waist.

The exhaustion overtook them and without another thought, they both fell asleep.

13

The sun cast patterns across the bed as it beamed through the lace curtains. Tori, always an early riser, opened her eyes to a sight she never thought she would see—Mitch Evans asleep in her bed. He was lying on his back, one arm thrown behind his head and the other curled around her neck. As her gaze drifted downward, she admired the muscular chest and defined abs rising and falling with each breath. She yearned to reach out and trace her fingertips along each ridge, but did not want to wake him.

Trying to even her breathing, she still let out a deep sigh at the sight of him relaxed in slumber. For a moment, she cast her mind back to the summer when she was fifteen and he was seventeen, ready to start his senior year.

. . .

Calling out to grandma that I'd see her for supper, I ran two blocks over to Jillian's house. Katelyn was already there and the three of us hopped in Katelyn's dad's golf cart. I loved being able to travel about Baytown in a golf cart, but grandma had never gotten used to driving anything except her old Chevrolet.

We laughed and giggled as we headed to the ball field on the other side of the train track bridge. Jillian was sweet on Grant and Katelyn always had her eye on Phillip, but for me there would never be anyone like Mitch Evans, the town's golden boy. His blond hair had darkened with maturity...and that wasn't the only change I noticed.

Parking, we ran to the bleachers and watched as the Baytown Boys easily defeated the North Heron team. And then my favorite part of the whole game...Mitch and the others would pull off their shirts and splash water over their tanned skin to cool off. They were all teenage gods, but Mitch...I noticed how much more defined and ripped he was this year than last.

A group of girls to the side of us began to giggle and preen...I hated them all, but didn't need to worry. Phillip's eyes were on Katelyn, but the big flirt hopped the fence and gabbed with some of the other girls. Grant, flexing his muscles, did the same. I could never understand why they didn't go straight to Jillian and Katelyn without having to flirt right in front of them. By the time they made it over to my friends, Jillian and Katelyn pretended not to notice them. And so, the flirting game continued.

But for me...Mitch simply came straight over. He would

lean his body on his forearms, propped on the short fence and stared right at me. Throwing his legs over the fence, he'd then take the bleachers two at a time until he was towering over me. I know he preened also, but the view was great. I looked up expectantly...hoping against hope he would lean down and kiss me. But he would just smile and—

"Good morning."

The words startled Tori out of her walk down memory lane. Jerking, she focused on the blue eyes staring back at her.

A grin played around his mouth as he pulled his arm from the pillow behind him and tucked a strand of hair behind her ear. "What were you thinking about?" he asked. "You were staring at me, but your expression was far away."

Blushing ten shades of red, she admitted, "I was thinking about the summers when we were teenagers and the girls and I would watch you play ball."

"Anything in particular you remembered?" he asked with a grin.

Hesitating for only a second, she replied, "I liked how you would come straight to me and bypass the other girls. I always thought Phillip and Grant were mean for flirting in front of Katelyn and Jillian, even though I knew they liked them."

"Why would I want anyone else when I had the prettiest girl coming into town each holiday and summer?

The one who had eyes for me?" He cupped her face in his large hand, the feel of her soft skin against his palm.

Leaning into his warmth, she closed her eyes and asked the question she had always wanted to ask but was too afraid of the answer. "I always wanted you to kiss me, Mitch. Why didn't you?"

"Look at me, Tori," his gentle voice ordered.

Obeying, she opened her eyes and saw his staring back into hers, a touch of regret filling them.

Rubbing his thumb over her cheek, he said, "I always wanted to. I wanted so much to kiss you every time I saw you sitting in the stands, cheering me on. I wanted to hop the fence, race up the bleachers, and claim you for myself."

She cocked her head to the side, waiting for him to continue.

"We'd been friends since you were six years old, and I found you one day playing on the beach with my cousin. Your visits with your grandmother were what I looked forward to most each summer." Sighing, he rolled over so that his body was aligned with hers, now closer than ever. "By the time I was fifteen and you were a teen, I used to get a hard-on every time you were near."

Eyes wide, a small laugh erupted from Tori's lips. "Seriously?"

"Hell, yeah."

"So, why didn't you kiss me?"

"At first, I thought you were too young. I also wasn't sure I would be able to stop at just a simple kiss."

"And here I thought Mitch Evans had such control," she teased.

"By the time you were sixteen, I was eighteen and my dad had the big talk about how I had to be careful. I was an adult, and he warned me about not taking advantage of a younger girl."

"All I wanted was a kiss, Mitch," she pouted.

Chuckling, he said, "I know, but you were special, Tori. I dated some girls in high school here, but that's all they were...just dates. I think you had hold of me with your red hair and little freckles."

"Ugh, I hated them! Even though I didn't have many, I thought they were ugly."

He leaned forward and kissed the tip of her nose. "I loved everyone. And you were...and are, the prettiest girl around.

"The next spring, I planned on making my move, but that spring break when you visited changed everything." His face took on a serious expression as he admitted, "I wish I'd known what Vanessa said to you. I hate that you thought I was that kind of guy."

"I'm sorry, Mitch. I was young and insecure, I guess."

"I left right after graduation and life took me a lot of places. I never forgot the little red-headed girl from long ago though. And I'm so glad we're both back to stay."

With that, he kissed her lips, soft and slow. Pulling her body into his, he felt every curve against his.

She answered back with her body as well, moving

her hips against his, sliding one leg over his so that her warm core was settled on his thigh.

A vibrating sound from the nightstand caused them to jerk apart. Blushing, she tried to move back, but he kept her in place with one arm while the other snagged the phone off the table.

"Evans," he answered, his voice still rough with a mixture of sleep and desire. A pause. "Got it. I'll be in. Give me twenty."

Disconnecting, his lust-filled eyes were now filled with regret.

"You have to go," she whispered, hating to lose the moment but accepting it was already lost.

"Yeah."

"You can take a shower in there. There's no food in the kitchen right now, but I can make some coffee for you to take with you," she offered, moving to slide out of bed. His arms stilled her, and she looked toward him again.

"Tori, I told you why I waited when we were teenagers. When I left home, I never thought I'd see you again and convinced myself you were just a childhood crush. But now that we're together here in Baytown...I plan on you and me becoming an *us*. If you'll have me," he added.

Smiling, she leaned over, touching her lips to his. "I think you've held my heart for twenty-three years, so I'll definitely have you." Sobering, she said, "But I know the investigation takes precedence right now...so go do your cop thing, and hopefully I can get my business back on track and weather this storm."

Another quick kiss and she was out of bed on one side, moving toward the stairs as he headed toward the shower, her kiss still warm on his lips.

———

That afternoon Mitch walked into Finn's, hauling himself up onto a bar stool, shooting a nod toward Brogan. A minute later, he was joined by Aiden, Zac, Callan, and Grant as Brogan set a beer on the bar.

"How's it going?" Callan asked.

"Waiting on lab evidence to come back is always a pain in the ass," Mitch replied, "but this time it's pure torture. Tori has had almost no guests this week and she's terrified of what'll happen with the Inn."

"Got any leads?" Aiden inquired.

Brogan cuffed his brother on the back of the head. "He can't talk about an open case."

Mitch and Grant nodded, but neither could hold back a grin at the antics of the two MacFarlane brothers.

Zac, usually jovial, had a serious expression on his face as he rubbed his hands over the water droplets on his beer.

Mitch, observing his friend, asked, "You got something on your mind?"

"I've been thinking about the American Legion and

had an idea, but it's just dawned on me that it might help Tori out for a bit, too."

Mitch's attention was snagged, as were the others.'

Zac explained, "I've got a couple of buddies that had been in the Navy with me but had no family to return to and no hometown to welcome them. I've already been in contact with one and told him about Baytown. I think I've got him interested in moving here, and maybe he could stay at the Inn for a couple of weeks until he gets a place." He looked at Mitch and said, "She'd have to be willing to give him a special rate, but it'd be some income."

Mitch nodded, appreciating the thought. "I'll talk to her and see what she says. I know she's had some cancellations, so she'd probably be glad for the guest."

"Where are we with the American Legion?" Aiden asked.

"I've started the process and have put an ad in the Baytown News, as well as the North Heron newspaper, about a meeting."

"Next Thursday night?" Grant confirmed, pulling out his phone.

"Yep," Mitch answered.

"What does your friend do?" Brogan asked Zac.

Chuckling, Zac admitted, "Well, he's kind of a Jack-of-all-trades, but he's a tattoo artist." Observing Mitch raise his eyebrow, he hurried to say, "He's a good guy."

"Hey, no problem here," Mitch said, "but I was wondering if he'd have enough business to make a living."

"He's also an ace mechanic," Zac said, capturing everyone's attention.

"Thank God! Ever since old man Zucker died and the auto shop along with him, Baytown's been desperate for a mechanic."

"He's interested in the property and says he'd like to have a tattoo shop as well."

Callan added, "I've got someone who worked on engines in the Coast Guard, and they also work on cars. Sounds like a similar situation...got out, no family...no real home."

Brogan eyed Mitch, watching the wheels turning in his friend's head. "You thinking this is a good thing?"

Nodding, Mitch replied, "We get an active American Legion that offers programs, not only for Vets, but for Vets to participate in to help others, we could bring some new blood into Baytown."

***

The next week crawled as Tori tried to go about her normal routine. She was pleased to be given the go-ahead to clean the Inn, so she spent two days doing all the laundry, scrubbing the guest bathrooms, vacuuming, dusting, and cleaning out her refrigerator. There was little food left that hadn't been sent to the lab, even though she told Sam that this was her private stock, and the guests did not eat from it. On the third day, grocery shopping and visiting Katelyn and Jillian helped pass the time. Finally, on the fourth day, two couples checked in and she breathed a sigh of relief. And, more importantly, there had been no sign of Thomas or Vanessa. *Maybe, just maybe, things will get back to normal.*

In opposition to her hope that life was getting better, Mitch grew increasingly irritated waiting on the toxicology reports to come in. Sitting in his office he picked up the phone once more to call the forensic lab when Mildred came running in.

"Got the initial results," she said. "They came through the fax, and the report said if you'd verify your email and secure login with them, they'd send the rest directly to you."

Mitch reached out, almost grabbing the papers from her hand. Flipping through them quickly, he scanned to see what they reported. Cyanide was found in Dumfries' body. Glancing through the blood and tissue testing, the report confirmed death by poisoning. Flipping some more, he looked through the initial food testing. Comparing the numbered and tagged bags of food to the report, he read that there were no traces of cyanide in the leftover breakfast food Sam had taken from the garbage, the food in Mr. Dumfries' room, nor the cobbler. Nor was it in the water bottles in his room. Nor was it in the food that Tori would have used to make breakfast for the guests. *So, where the hell did it come from?*

"Chief, we heard the report came in," Burt said, standing in his doorway. "The others are in the staffroom. Can we hear what it says?"

"Sure," Mitch confirmed, standing with the report in

his hands, still trying to flip through the papers. Moving down the hall, he saw Grant coming in wearing civilian clothes.

"Mildred called and said the report was in, so I hurried over," Grant explained, sliding into the seat next to Sam. Burt and Mitch sat down, Ginny in between, and Mitch began telling them what he had learned so far.

"So, how did Mr. Dumfries ingest the poison?"

Continuing to go through the report, he read which sample the poison was discovered in and then quickly checked the tag numbers. *The chicken salad in the refrigerator.* Looking up at Sam, he asked, "The chicken salad in the refrigerator? What was it in?"

"Um," the flustered officer stuttered, "It was um…a plastic container. It was homemade and in a plastic container in her refrigerator. Ms. Bradford told me that it was her personal food and not for the guests."

"Was the container disturbed? Did it look like anyone had eaten any?"

Sam thought for a moment, rubbing his chin. "Yeah, someone had been in it. It looked like a large amount from the side had been scooped out of the container. I assumed she fixed it for herself and then ate some."

"The cyanide was in the chicken salad," Mitch said, his voice as cold as his blood. "She told me she had not had any because she decided to have lunch with some friends instead."

"So, how did someone try to poison Mr. Dumfries —" Sam began.

"He wasn't the intended victim," Ginny stated, as the others caught up to Mitch's thoughts.

"Oh, fuck, Mitch," Grant bit out, seeing the Chief already pushing himself from the table, a hard expression on his face.

"Right," Mitch growled. "Someone was trying to kill Tori!"

14

One of the advantages of living in a small town was that it only took Mitch five minutes to pull up in front of the Sea Glass Inn. Jogging up the steps, he barely noticed Ginny and Burt were right behind him. Banging on the door, he glanced over his shoulder, saying, "Is this necessary?"

"Chief, you're too good an investigator to fuck up a case because you're involved. We're here to talk to Tori."

Just then, the woman in question opened the door, a look of pleasure followed quickly by surprise, crossing her face.

"Uh...hi...everyone. Is there something—"

Mitch moved into her space, forcing her to take a step backwards, allowing Ginny and Burt to follow him in. Once the door was closed, he held on to her shoulders and said, "We've gotta talk."

Her gaze darted among the three and, swallowing deeply, she nodded, turned, and led the way silently to the living room. She sat on the sofa, hands clasped in her lap, noting Mitch sitting next to her with Burt and Ginny taking wing back chairs facing them.

"Guys, you're scaring me. What is it? Was there something in the cobbler? I swear I had nothing to do with Mr. Dumfries' dea—"

Mitch's arm was around her shoulder, and he gently turned her so she was angled toward him. "Tori, there was nothing in the cobbler. There was nothing in any of the guest rooms either."

"But—"

"You need to listen carefully, babe." When he had her attention, he asked, "Tell me about the kitchen and the food in the refrigerator." Seeing her about to speak, he said, "I know you've told me, but Officers Spencer and Tobber need to hear and will ask more questions."

Sucking in her lips for a moment, she tried to steady her quivering. Taking a deep breath, she said, "Many years ago, when my grandparents ran the Sea Glass Inn, they allowed guests to roam a bit more freely. It was a different age and time…and well, quite frankly, people had a few more social skills." Licking her lips, she continued, "But about ten years ago, grandma had to make the kitchen off limits. She would shop for herself or us when we were here or for the next day's breakfast, only to find guests had raided the kitchen as their own three-meal-a-day place. And sometimes they would eat out of a container and that's not sanitary. So, she created the off-limits area, and it made for a better use of our space."

Shaking her head, she said, "Everyone should know bed and breakfast means just that—breakfast is served, but no other meals. She'd find families would use her food to make lunch to take to the beach or come back from a day at the beach and again, raid the kitchen. So, as much as she hated to add rules, she made it part of the contract. Guests are advised the kitchen is off limits. So is the back patio."

Looking at Ginny and Burt, she explained, "The guests have the lovely front porch to sit on and another patio off the breakfast sunroom. The patio off the kitchen was for our family only."

"And you said, this is in a contract?" Ginny queried, taking notes.

"Yes, and I have every guest sign the contract as they check in that says they understand the rules. Plus, there is a sign outside the kitchen. We provide mini refrigerators in each of the four rooms, so they can keep their own snacks. And we provide a snack pantry in the dining room."

Mitch observed Tori twisting her fingers together and placed his hand over hers.

She whirled around, eyes wide, and said, "Am I in trouble? Is there something I did wrong?"

"No, babe. But let's keep going over everything first." He hated the expression of fear in her eyes but wanted to make sure they covered all the bases in the investigation. Nodding jerkily, she looked back to the others.

Burt asked, "Do any of the guests ignore the rules?"

Grimacing, she nodded. "Not too much, because I

offer the snack pantry and mini fridges, but yes, I have to shoo out some guests." Her eyes bugged wide as she remembered, "In fact, Mr. Dumfries was one of the ones!"

The officers' eyes jumped to hers. "Tell us," Ginny demanded gently.

"He was in the kitchen twice, and both times I shooed him out. He was nice about it, but I was very irritated when I caught him the second time." She thought for a moment and said, "It's probably due to his wife's restrictions."

"What do you mean?"

"He told me he'd been to the doctor and well, as you could see, he was overweight. So, she had him on a low-salt, low-carb diet, and he was most grumpy."

Ginny said, "Can you tell me about anything you noticed him getting into?"

Cocking her head to the side, Tori tried to remember specifics. "It's hard to recall what exactly he got into. I've been so busy lately I hardly remember what was there."

"Just tell us what you can. The food that you've had recently, for example. When was it made? Who made it? Who was it for? That kind of thing," Ginny clarified.

"Oh, well, um...I made chicken salad two days ago; it was supposed to be for my lunch, but I went out and met some friends instead."

Mitch, wanting her to be exact, prompted, "So, who exactly was the chicken salad for? Did you make a large amount to serve the guests, saving some for yourself for later?"

Twisting around to face him, her face scrunched in confusion. "No. I made it. It was for me. Just me. I only prepare breakfast for the guests...and certainly not chicken salad. I can tell you exactly what I made for the guests for breakfast and what was left for snacks, but that's all I'm sure of. I'm sorry, but I honestly don't remember all the contents of my fridge, only what I made myself."

"Hang with us, please," Ginny said, her voice softening.

Dropping her chin to her chest, Tori willed her breathing to steady. She felt Mitch's strong hand on her shoulders, rubbing some of the tension out.

Finally, raising her head back up, she said, "Everything in the refrigerator was for me. The eggs, bacon, sausage, cheese...all of these things were used for the breakfasts, but then I ate them also. I keep those things on hand all the time. I made the chicken salad and that was two days ago but had not had a chance to eat a bite."

"Do you know if anyone else ate it?"

"I...well, I...uh, I don't know. I didn't look at it before Officer Stubbs took the plastic container away," she admitted. "I can tell you that I didn't eat any and none of the guests were supposed to. So, if someone did, then—" Gasping, she jerked out of Mitch's hand and jumped from the sofa. "Oh, my God. You're trying to tell me Mr. Dumfries ate some of my food and the poison was in it! And the only thing I made was chicken salad so . . ." Whirling back around to Mitch, she said, "You think I poisoned him with my food! But I swear I had no idea—"

Mitch stalked over, placing his hands on her shoulders again, and said, "No, Tori. If you fixed the chicken salad and it was for you only, then no one would use it to poison Mr. Dumfries. That means whoever put the poison in the chicken salad wasn't after him..." He let the horrible words die on his tongue as he helplessly watched Tori's understanding slowly dawn across her face.

"Me?" she squeaked. "Me? You think someone wanted to poison me?" Her voice rose with each word, and Mitch quickly pulled her into his embrace. "Babe, I swear, we'll find out who did this." He locked eyes with Ginny and Burt over Tori's head, and they knew he was making a vow for all of them.

Mitch, back in the police station, stewed as he stared at the large board hanging on the wall in the staff room. Mr. Dumfries' picture had now been moved to the side and a picture of Tori was front and center. As the other officers worked on various angles at their desks, he stared at the picture, his heart not willing to accept what his mind was telling him; and that was the woman he was falling for was in danger. He did not need to look down at the notes in the file on the table in front of him. The interview with Tori was burned into his brain.

. . .

As they had continued her interview, Burt asked who would benefit from her death and as much as I knew we needed to know, I hated the expression on Tori's face.

"I...I don't know," she admitted.

"Let's start with your ex-husband," Ginny suggested.

Shaking her head, Tori replied, "We're divorced completely. I got a settlement from the house when it sold, but I didn't even want alimony. I wanted nothing of his. I had a job while we were married and made decent money. Thomas didn't want his indiscretion to become public, so we had an arbiter come up with an equitable division of our money when we divorced. We basically just walked away. My death would gain him nothing."

I hated to bring her up, but I said, "You need to tell them about your sister and her visit two days ago."

She pinched her lips together tightly, but admitted, "Vanessa is...well, not a very nice person and a pain in my ass, but she'd never try to kill me!"

"Just tell us what you know about her," Burt prodded.

"She hasn't been to Baytown since she graduated from high school, except for grandma's funeral when she popped in and out as quickly as possible. She showed up on my door, two mornings ago, and grumbled about me getting the Inn. Grandma settled money and bonds on her in the Will, but I got full ownership of the Sea Glass Inn."

"Any chance she can contest the Will?"

Shaking her head, Tori added, "I've checked with the attorney, Mr. Benfield, and he says grandma's Will was simple, direct, and no one would win if they tried to argue against it."

I looked at Tori and realized her mind had not even begun to go down the path that the other three of us were thinking. *Damn, this is fucked!* "Tori," I said, pulling her attention back to me. "If you die, without a Will, then your property would be divided amongst your relatives?"

"I've talked to Mr. Benfield," Tori admitted. "Since my mom is still living, it would go to her."

"Do you see your mom wanting to deal with the Inn? If Vanessa wanted it, how difficult would it be for her to get her hands on it?"

Tori's face fell as her shoulders slumped. "Mom would give it to her in a heartbeat, although what she would do with it is a mystery!"

The group was quiet as I watched Tori's face contort before she lifted her gaze, pinning me with her stare. "Mitch, there's no way Vanessa would try to kill me."

"Honey, you don't know tha—"

"Yes, I do," she argued. "First of all, she may be a bitch, but she's not going to kill me. She doesn't hate me...she's just an unhappy person who doesn't like to see anyone else happy. Second, she's not that smart! She'd have no idea how to go about poisoning someone and then actually doing it!"

I glanced at Burt and Ginny, silently warning them not to say anything else, and was grateful when they took their leave. Holding Tori in my embrace, I kissed the top of her head. "Babe, we need to get you moved out of here."

Her head jerked back, bumping my chin. "Out? I'm not leaving!"

"Someone wants you dead," I argued back, wanting her to listen to reason. The argument lasted for several minutes before I finally realized that barring me throwing her over my shoulder and carrying her off, she was not going to leave. With a call to Jillian to come stay with her for the afternoon, earning me a glare from Tori, I left to go back to the station.

"So, what's next Chief?" Sam asked, walking into the staff room, leaning against the table alongside Mitch to stare at the board.

Before he could answer, Burt, Grant, and Ginny came in as well.

"Right now, stick to basics. Motive, Means, and Opportunity."

"Opportunity is the hard one," Grant said. "During the day, when Tori is around, anyone could get into her kitchen. Guests, someone who walks in since she doesn't always keep the front door locked. It's on the website which areas are for guests, and which are off limits. Her food rules are also there, so anyone could easily discern that what is in the kitchen is for her consumption. I also found the sliding glass door leading from the patio to the kitchen is sometimes kept unlocked. Her backyard is fenced, so she probably feels safe."

"Jesus," Mitch growled, deciding a discussion with Tori about security was overdue.

"I've written down a timeline from when she made the chicken salad and placed it in the refrigerator until the time that Mr. Dumfries died," Ginny stated, taping the printed information on the board.

"So, she made it in the evening for the next day's lunch and was not out of the house after that until the next morning. She claims by that time, the house was locked and secure for the night. Her ex, Thomas, shows up the next morning and by curious coincidence, her estranged sister, Vanessa, comes by later in the day. Since the back door may not have been locked, there was opportunity there and the sister certainly had motive." Mitch looked at the group and said, "I'll be heading to Virginia Beach first thing in the morning. Burt, you go with me to interview Vanessa."

"What about her ex?" Ginny asked.

"Don't know," Mitch admitted, "but I'd like you to follow up on him. Stay here and dig up whatever you can on the suspects. Finances. Businesses. Burt and I'll take a trip to Williamsburg and interview him as well. Sam, check out Tori's house and backyard, and talk to the neighbors to find out what they could see. Grant, follow up on the cyanide and see where it may have come from." Glancing up, he noted Grant's raised eyebrows and said, "I know. It could have come from anywhere but see if the lab has any indications. Let's meet back here tomorrow afternoon and see what we've got."

Mitch watched as the others filed out of the room then shifted his gaze back to the board, hoping something would jump out at him.

15

Brogan and Aiden looked up from behind the bar as Tori and Jillian walked in that evening. As Tori took a look at their tight-jawed expressions, she knew Mitch had already told them of his findings. *Great, first the town hears rumors that my food killed a guest, and now someone is trying to kill me.*

Forcing her lips into a semblance of a smile, she proceeded to the bar.

"Nuh uh," Brogan growled, causing her to stop in her tracks. He prowled around the bar and motioned for the two women to follow him. Curious, if somewhat dutiful, they did. Finn's had a small room near the back that was part of the pub or could be used for small parties, and Katelyn was already there putting plates of sliders and wings on the table before turning and pulling Tori into a hug.

Before she could sit, Brogan placed his large hand on her shoulder and bent to focus directly into her eyes.

"We got you, girl. We know Mitch has to be out looking for the killer but, while he's not with you, one of us will be."

"Brogan, I'm sur—"

"Nope, not another word. You might not have grown up all the time in Baytown, but you were part of us then and part of us now. We take care of our own."

He turned and walked back to the bar, glaring at any of the townspeople that got in his way.

"Wow, I think that's more than I've heard him say at one time in…forever," Jillian commented, staring after their friend.

Before Tori could process the changes in her life, Katelyn hustled back with a huge plate of cheese fries. "It's times like this that call for calories and beer," Katelyn pronounced, "and Finn's has an abundance of both!"

Laughing, glad for the ease in the tension, Tori slid into the worn leather, padded booth. She was soon joined by Zac, Grant, and Aiden, while Brogan kept his eye on the bar. The group avoided the topic on everyone's mind, keeping the conversation light and the food coming.

Mitch came in a half-hour later, his eyes immediately finding, and pinning, hers. Sliding down next to her, his arm quickly snaked its way around her shoulders, and she lifted her face to his. As much as he would have liked the kiss to last longer, he pulled back, a smile curving his lips for the first time that day.

"Hey," she whispered, her wide blue eyes twinkling.

"Hey back," he grinned.

The sound of heavy boots came from the front and, as the group looked up, a large man appeared around the corner. His long hair was pulled back in a ponytail with a strip of leather. His face was covered in a shaggy beard, not cropped close, but not long either. Tori thought it looked more like someone who shaved when the spirit moved them. A faded, tight T-shirt strained at his arms, but the worn, leather vest fit like a glove. His jean-encased legs were muscular and as her eyes dropped, she realized the heavy boots were clomping as he walked toward her. Glancing sideways, she watched Mitch eye the stranger warily until Zac called out, "Jason! Thank God you got here when you did!"

As the stranger's eyes landed on Zac, he grinned and Tori saw beneath the rough exterior to a handsome man, whose eyes relaxed as soon as he recognized a friend.

Mitch stood immediately, his hand out to grasp Jason's firmly. "Any friend of Zac's is welcome here. Good to have you."

Jason's gaze dropped to the police logo on Mitch's shirt and his eyes moved back to Mitch's. Anticipating Jason's reaction, he said, "I know you're a top-notch mechanic and hear you want to run a tattoo parlor as well. Got no problem with me, and I'll see what I can do to run interference if the town council wants to quibble about a veteran opening a business."

Jason's smile returned as he shook Mitch's hand. Introductions were made as Brogan made his way over to the table as well. Tori smiled at the newcomer, then noticed the others shifting nervously in their seats. Turning her face toward Mitch, she shot him a questioning gaze.

"Babe, I haven't had time to talk to you about this, but we need your help. Jason is new in town and needs a place to stay. We would like him to stay at your Inn until he can get established."

Smiling, she said, "Sure! I have plenty of room." As soon as the words were out of her mouth, she looked back at Mitch. "Oh, wait a minute. Are you setting me up with a babysitter?"

Jason, already briefed by Zac, softened his gaze at Tori. "Ms. Bradford, please don't think of me as a babysitter. I understand you're having some troubles and, honest to God, I need a place to stay. If you're willing, I'd be glad to barter some of the cost off in odd-jobs until I can get my business started."

Mitch smiled at Jason, already liking the man. Rubbing Tori's shoulder, he said, "I hate to put you on the spot, but what do you say, babe?"

"Of course you can stay," she smiled at Jason. "It's true that my life suddenly went crazy two days ago, and don't worry about the price. I've got a couple of guests now, but have had several cancellations, so I've easily got a room."

Letting out a breath he did not realize he was holding, Mitch leaned back, pulling Tori along with him. She twisted around to look at him and said, "You needn't have worried...I'm not unreasonable!"

A fun-filled hour later, Mitch and Tori escorted Jason to the Sea Glass Inn. Mitch waited as she showed Jason around and got him settled into the Blue Room. Hesitating at the door, she suddenly stopped, placing her hand on Jason's arm. He looked down, his eyes concerned.

"I'm sorry," she blurted, "but you should know that this is the room where Mr. Dumfries died. I promise it's been scrubbed. He died in his sleep, but I'd understand if this is not where you want to stay. It's just the largest room and I thought you'd be more comfortable here."

Jason glanced in, seeing the blue walls, large, four-poster bed, antique chest of drawers, a desk and comfortable chair by the bay window over-looking the Chesapeake, and a flat-screen TV mounted on the wall over a small bookcase. Through the open door, he could make out a white and blue tiled bathroom. Looking back down, he smiled at her concern.

"Miss Tori, this room is a lot nicer than where I've been spending my nights. And where I was stationed when in the service, I've slept where death was at my door. I assure you, this is more than generous of you, and I'd be honored to stay here."

Releasing her worried sigh, she smiled once more. "Then welcome to Baytown and to the Sea Glass," she replied and walked back down the stairs.

Tori, at Mitch's suggestion, took a long bubble bath, complete with scented candles lit and Brian Crain's piano music playing in the background. The desire to step into the bathroom where she lay naked was over-whelming, so he left the room and jogged down the stairs to the second floor, heading straight to the Blue Room. It only took one knock, and the door was thrown open.

Jason nodded at Mitch as though expecting him and stepped back allowing Mitch to enter. "I figured you might want to come by," Jason said. "Zac gave me the lowdown in general terms, but I reckon I need more from you."

"I appreciate it," Mitch admitted. "It kills me that I can't be here all the time, but I've got some suspects that live in Virginia Beach and Williamsburg that I need to interview, and I don't want her unprotected." Rubbing his brow again, he added, "I don't expect you to be her bodyguard, but just being here at night if I can't be, will be a big relief."

"You got it, man." Jason hesitated a second before asking, "With you being the Police Chief...you're not concerned about me wanting to open a mechanics shop or tattoo parlor?"

Mitch considered the man in front of him carefully. "Any reason why I should be concerned?"

"I got no priors, if that's what you mean," Jason replied. "Zac told me there was a garage here in town that's for sale since the former owner died. Heard his daughter was wantin' to get rid of the place so I can probably get a good deal on it. If I get it up and runnin,' I got a couple of my Navy buds that're mechanics too. Like me, they've got no real home and I'd be wantin' to offer them a job."

"Can't see anything wrong with that plan."

"Zac also said there was a small store that's just sittin' empty next to the garage space. I plan on trying to set up a tattoo shop there as well. Some people don't like people who ride motorcycles or have tattoos."

"You're right," Mitch admitted, "and if the Harleys are running up and down the road at night making a lot of noise, then I won't be a big fan either. But I got nothing against a man working to make an honest dollar."

The two men stared at each other, both appearing to like what they saw.

"'Preciate it, Mitch."

"Did Zac talk to you about what we're trying to do with the American Legion?"

Nodding, Jason said, "Yeah. Funny, my granddad was in an American Legion. I never paid any attention when I was a kid, but after coming home and realizing I needed a group around me that understood, I'm ready to help you all get one started. I'd consider it an honor."

Shaking hands, Mitch added, "Zac's been a friend since we were babes. Any friend of his is welcome here in Baytown."

Leaving Jason's room, he took the stairs two at a time, getting back to Tori's room. Seeing the bedroom empty, he walked over to the bathroom door. Knocking lightly, he waited but heard no answer. His hand on the knob, he hesitated.

"Tori?" he called softly but still received no answer. Opening the door slightly, he peered in, his breath catching in his throat.

She was reclined in the tub, her body cloaked underneath the bubbles, eyes closed as the soft music played. Her hair was piled in a messy bun on top of her head, with a few reddish tendrils falling all about, their ends in the water. Before he could close the door, she opened her eyes and turned, gifting him with a smile. Unsure what she wanted, he hesitated until she lifted her hand up toward him, beckoning.

He closed the door behind him to keep the warm air inside. The candlelight cast shadows about the room, and the scent of honeysuckle filled the air.

"You've got to tell me what you want, Tori," he said, resting his hip on the counter, battling the desire to rush to her side. "I don't want to make any assumptions."

She twisted in the water, her upper body against the tub, and rested her head on her arms, crossed on the side. Her sky-blue eyes shone in the minimal light. "I fell in love with you when I was six years old...I'm not six anymore."

His eyes moved over her face, wanting to dip his hands in the water and feel her skin, which he knew would be like silk. Grinning, he shook his head slightly. "No, you're definitely not six anymore."

"I want you, Mitch, if you'll have me. I want you and

I want this. Right now. Tonight. Not when the case is solved. Not when we're both more settled. But now."

He crossed the room in two steps, kneeling at the tub. Taking her face in his hands, he leaned down, his breath warm against her cheek. Kissing the edge of her mouth, he breathed in her scent, before his lips captured hers. He placed his hands under her arms, lifted her easily out of the tub, and set her feet gently down on the cushy bathmat. Grabbing a plush towel, he began to dry her off. He knelt at her feet, drying each as she balanced herself with a hand on his shoulder.

As she looked down, she was overcome with the sexy sight of a man tending to her. *Never...I've never had this.*

Making his way up her legs, he grinned as she moaned and felt her fingers grip into his shoulders as he kissed his way up her body, his lips trailing the towel. Over her belly, he kissed her belly-button as he continued to drag the towel over, drying each inch.

He barely heard her hiss, as his own blood roared through his ears. Moving over her silky skin, the fact that he had stopped drying her was forgotten, until he felt water drip onto his face from her hair.

Lifting his gaze up to hers, he apologized. "I'm sorry...it seems as though I became distracted."

Her breath coming in pants, hands still on his shoulders, she smiled. "No apology needed. I can't remember ever being so happy to be wet. I might have to bathe constantly from now on, just to have you dry me off."

Laughing, he claimed, "That'd be fine with me."

Lifting the towel, he ordered, "Turn around." As she obliged, he kept his eyes on her hair as he rubbed the towel through the tresses. Hanging the wet towel over the bar, he stood and watched her in the vanity mirror over the double sinks.

Not wanting to waste a minute, she grabbed a wide-tooth comb and quickly ran it through her hair. Her gaze lifted to his in the mirror as he came to stand behind her. Wrapping his arms around, he placed one hand on her belly and the other across her chest as he kissed the top of her head.

They stood there for a moment, holding each other's gaze, saying nothing. She finally broke the spell.

"Make love to me, Mitch."

His worshipful expression broke into a huge smile. "Anything you say, Tori. Anything for you."

16

Mitch's hand fisted in Tori's still-wet hair, holding her close as he devoured her lips. Hard. Demanding. As though neither of them could get enough. His tongue delved inside of her warm mouth again and again, capturing her moans.

She squirmed in his arms, her body aching as she pressed closer against his chest. As she moved against him, she felt the rough material of his jeans between them — a delicious friction that threatened to undo her entirely. She tried to slide her hand down toward his zipper but found it captured in his, brought above her head. He held both wrists in one hand as his lips continued their assault down her body.

He wanted to take his time...explore...suckle... nurture. But his action was now playing against him. With her arms trapped above her head, her naked beauty was vulnerable. The realization that he had to get out of his clothes as well — as quickly as possible — shot through him.

Letting her go, Mitch pushed himself off the bed. With a flip of his hands, his polo flew over his head and landed on the floor.

She watched his biceps swell and bunch as he tossed his shirt away. Her gaze drifted down the sculpted lines of his chest, the definition of his stomach — and she had to grip the sheet beneath her to keep from reaching for him. He unzipped his jeans before she had a chance to move, and she found she couldn't look away.

As he stripped off the rest of his clothes and stood over her, a slow grin crossed his face as he watched her. She held his gaze and let her fingers trail slowly down her own body — collarbone, ribs, stomach — until she reached the place that ached most. His breath caught. A groan tore from him.

"Please. Now," she whispered, her need overtaking all other thoughts.

Crawling over her, resting his weight on his arms, all rational thinking left him. He gazed down at her face as her legs wrapped around his waist, her heels pressing into him, pulling him forward. He joined them in one swift movement, and the word arrived before he could stop it. *Home. I've finally found home.* He began moving slowly, watching her eyes go heavy with desire.

She was having none of that. "Harder," she breathed, grabbing him and pulling him closer as her hips rose to meet his.

He answered, and their bodies found a rhythm that made thought impossible. He leaned down to capture her lips, his kiss mirroring everything else happening between them. He had been with other women in years past, but none of it had felt like *this*. Something about the sight of her reddish hair spilling over the pillow as it dried, the way she moved with him, felt right. From the little girl he'd known to the woman in his bed — he knew she was it.

The tension between them built and coiled, and she moved her hips with urgent purpose, chasing what she needed. She let her hands roam — his back, the line of his shoulders — reveling in the feel of him, the solid warmth of his body connecting with hers.

He knew he was close but wanted her there first. He shifted his weight, one arm supporting him, and slid his free hand down her body until his fingers found her — circling, pressing — and she came apart.

She threw her head back against the mattress as the wave crashed through her, her whole body trembling beneath him.

His own release followed, cresting hard and sudden, a low groan tearing from his throat as he drove through it.

Breathless, he dropped onto her before he remembered himself and rolled to the side, pulling her with him so she was draped partially across his chest. They lay without speaking for a long time. Coherent thought was simply not available.

As the air around them began to cool, he reached for

a light blanket and drew it up over them both, tucking it around her with quiet care.

Sated, he pulled her tightly against him — one arm wrapped around her, the other slipping beneath her neck. "Sweet dreams, babe," he murmured.

She hadn't been sure she could sleep with the man of her dreams holding her close. She was wrong. She drifted off quickly, her breathing slowing to match his.

Tori rolled over, once more enjoying the sight of Mitch in her bed with the early morning light on his face. Unable to stop herself, she reached over, barely tracing her finger along his jaw.

He grinned before opening his eyes, then turned toward her. "Mmmm," he greeted, kissing her. "I could get used to this wake-up call."

"I hope you do," she admitted.

At that, his eyes focused squarely on hers and his smile brightened, dimples deepening. Rolling over, he pinned her beneath him, but she welcomed his weight, wrapping her arms around his waist. She fell into his kiss, not paying attention to the passage of time.

Lifting his head slightly, he said, "I've got to get going. I've got to go to Virginia Beach today."

"Then I guess we'd better get busy," she teased.

Growling, he took her mouth…then went about taking his time…taking her body.

A few hours later, Mitch parked his jeep in the driveway of a gated community, each large house seeming to outdo the next in size and landscaping. He had checked and discovered Vanessa and Nelson Hurkamp had only been married for six months. It was his second marriage and her third. *Vanessa always wanted the biggest and brightest...looks like she kept trading up until she found it.* His mind rolled back to a simpler time, but one that left an indelible impression.

The baseball game had finished, and we'd talked to the girls gathered to cheer from the stands. Tori, with her russet hair, large blue eyes, and smattering of freckles was the best part of the summers in Baytown. She had been coming to visit ever since I could remember. This year she had just turned thirteen and had shown up with a body that had matured, and my fifteen-year-old brain short-circuited every time I was near her. Vanessa, now at almost sixteen, had the looks, but was such a stuck-up bitch, no one wanted to hang around her. Thank goodness she usually only stayed a week and Tori stayed all summer.

But I noticed a difference with Vanessa this week—she was definitely interested in getting me, or maybe any of the guys, horizontal.

Agreeing to meet at the diner for hamburgers and cokes, I headed to the small locker rooms connected to the public bathrooms by the ballpark. Entering, I heard noises, and adoles-

cent curiosity got the best of me. Looking at the mirror, I could see the reflection of a pale ass pumping into a girl on the other side of the lockers. Recognizing the shaggy hair as Chuck's, one of the county boys who played on our team, I grinned. Then the girl leaned her head back and I was stunned—Vanessa.

Jumping back, I stepped out of sight, my heart sinking. Chuck was a good guy, but I knew enough about her to know she would chew him up and spit him out. Tiptoeing backward to the door, I heard her words.

"Thanks. Someone like you is the only good thing about coming over here to this dump."

God, what a bitch she is, I thought. Quietly closing the door behind me, I startled when a pair of big blue eyes pinned me to the spot.

"Tori!" I squeaked, hating the sound of my voice at that moment.

"I thought we could walk to the diner together," she said, peeking up at me, a smile playing about her lips.

I would have walked Tori Bradford anywhere, but especially at that moment. I wanted to get her away from the bathrooms, so I grabbed her hand and hustled her away from the building. After a moment, I realized her legs were running to keep up with me.

"Geez, I'm sorry," I apologized. "I guess I'm just hungry."

A noise behind us caused Tori to turn around. I saw the expression on Tori's face at the sight of Vanessa walking out of the boy's locker room where I had just exited. It was fast—a flash of hurt.

"I wasn't in there with her," I blurted. "I mean I was...but not with her."

Her smile, less brilliant now, still glowed in her blushing face. "I know...I also know that what Vanessa wants, she usually gets."

"She doesn't want me," I declared, hearing the hateful words she spewed in my mind.

Gazing up at me, Tori said, "How could she not?"

Smiling down at her, an adorable...and adoring...expression on her face, it touched my adolescent heart. Nothing like her sister—thank God!

Now, almost sixteen years later, Mitch still felt the same way. Vanessa shunned the small town and even the simple way her grandmother lived, and it looked like she had what she wanted. *So, why would she want the Sea Glass Inn as well?*

"Chief?" Burt interrupted his thoughts.

"Sorry," Mitch mumbled. "Just remembering the way Vanessa was many years ago. She hated small town life and spent little time there. She married into this lifestyle, so why the Sea Glass?"

The two men exited the vehicle and walked to the front door. The bell was answered by an older woman, her face pinched tight and unsmiling. Identifying themselves, they were shown through the elaborate entryway and into a femininely decorated study.

Vanessa sat, perfectly posed in a coral silk pantsuit,

beige heels, makeup carefully applied and coiffed hair in a demure chignon at the back of her neck.

"Why, Mitch," she purred. "I was thrilled to hear that you were coming today."

Ignoring her greeting, he turned and introduced Officer Tobber.

"Please, gentlemen, have a seat." Picking up a small bell on the table next to her, she rang it twice. The housekeeper appeared with a tray, three coffees in delicate china cups balanced perfectly. "I took the liberty of having coffee prepared for us."

As Vanessa fiddled with the cups for a moment, Mitch observed her carefully. The years had not been as kind to Vanessa as they had been to Tori...*or maybe the plastic surgery didn't do what she'd hoped.* Mitch had never been in favor of the too tight skin, too blown-up lips, or too highly arched eyebrows of a woman attempting to hold on to their youth. He much preferred the softer look of a naturally maturing woman; the thought of his mother passed through his mind. *Tori will look like my mom, too,* he surmised with a slight smile. *Soft...and beautiful.*

He realized his mistake in smiling when Vanessa caught it and must have assumed it was directed at her. She beamed as she handed him a cup of coffee.

Immediately getting down to business, Mitch said, "Mrs. Hurkamp, we have reason to believe that someone deliberately put poison in the food at the Sea Glass Inn and the result was the death of a guest."

Her hand dramatically fluttered about her chest as

she exclaimed, "I read about that in the newspaper. I was so shocked and, well, I would have tried to call Victoria but wasn't sure she'd take my call. I knew she was terribly busy."

"We understand you visited that day," Burt stated.

"Well, yes I did."

When she offered no more information, he continued, "And the purpose of your visit?"

"Why, goodness me, can't a sister drop in and visit? I happened to have a day free and thought I'd like to see Victoria."

"I would think that after you were the cause of her divorce, she wouldn't exactly greet you with open arms."

A flash of panic flew through her eyes as she replied, "I was not the cause of her divorce. It was an unfortunate circumstance and one I greatly regret. But I should have called first. She was busy, and we weren't able to have a chat like I'd hoped." Nervously glancing around, she lowered her voice and said, "I would rather that information not get out. My…um…husband is unaware of that particular regret of mine."

Mitch viewed her carefully for a moment. *So, just how far would you go to keep that information quiet?* "At this time, I have no reason to reveal any part of our investigation, but…I cannot make any promises down the road."

Nodding curtly, she startled as the front door opened and the sound of footsteps came down the hall. The door to the study opened and a tall, distinguished man entered. His dark hair was slightly sprinkled with gray, and his face was tight with anger. Behind him, another gentleman entered the room, slightly portly and balding.

"Vanessa," the first man spoke. "Don't say another word." Turning to Mitch, he said, "I'm Nelson Hurkamp and upon advice from our attorney," he pointed to the man behind him, "I don't want my wife speaking to you without him present."

Unruffled, Mitch leaned back in his chair, watching the nervous glances between Vanessa and her husband.

"Of course she may have an attorney present." Turning his attention back to Vanessa, ignoring the two men, he continued. "And after you left your sister, where did you go?"

"Don't answer, Vanessa," Nelson argued.

Mitch, standing, towered over the other man. Using his height to his advantage, he said, "We are investigating a murder and an attempted murder. Right now, your wife is a person of interest who was in attendance on the day the food was poisoned. We can do this here, or I will obtain a summons, and she will be called to the police station in Baytown for official questioning. Which will it be?"

The older man stepped forward, "Nelson, there's no reason for her not to cooperate in their investigation. If it appears that Vanessa becomes a suspect, then we'll take a different approach."

"Suspect? Why on earth would I want to kill someone I don't know?" Vanessa's voice shrieked.

Turning to pin his hard stare on her, Mitch said, "Because the intended victim was your sister...Mr. Dumfries was simply the unfortunate victim."

At that, the room grew silent, Vanessa's throat working as she swallowed several times, her eyes darting from Mitch's to her husband's to the attorney.

"My client would have no reason to harm her sister," the attorney said definitively. "Even if Victoria did die, without any heirs, her estate in its entirety would go to their mother."

"Yes, that's true," Mitch agreed, then added, "And we'll be talking to her as well."

Vanessa's face screwed into an ugly grimace before she caught it and replaced it with one of concern. "I assure you I had nothing to do with any of this," she insisted, her hands floundering about.

Mitch watched as the attorney's face registered indecision and Nelson continued to glower.

"We have just confirmed that you visited the day in question. Did you notice anything unusual while you were there?"

Nelson jerked his head around to his wife, and said, "Why would you visit?"

Flustered, she replied, "I just wanted to see my sister."

Looking back at Mitch, she nervously shook her head. "As I said, Victoria was busy and unable to see me then, so I left. I'm not around enough to be able to tell you who should have been there and who shouldn't." Her gaze moved back to her husband's irritated face before she turned back toward Mitch and implored, "My sister and I might not be close, but I'd never want to harm her."

"There, you have your answers, and I'll now ask you to leave my house," Nelson stated emphatically before turning to his wife and glaring. "Going there was foolish!" As he looked back and caught Mitch's questioning look, the man hurried to add, "Of course Victoria would be busy at that time of the morning. Vanessa should not have dropped by without calling first. It was a waste of time."

Not looking at him but holding Vanessa's gaze for a moment until she dropped hers, Mitch nodded. As he and Burt exited the room, Mitch turned back around, pinning her attorney with his stare. "If we have further questions, we'll be summoning her to the station at Baytown and you may certainly accompany her. Good day."

As he and Burt entered the hall, the housekeeper suddenly appeared and showed them to the door. Stepping out into the sunshine, the two men slid on their sunglasses and walked to the jeep. As Mitch drove out of the driveway, he looked back in his rearview mirror at the ostentatious house. This time he wondered if it was Vanessa's dream house...or a gilded cage.

17

Driving in the car, Mitch called Ginny. "Do me a favor and check out the Hurkamp's finances as well as anything else you can think of. Their house is a mansion, but I got the idea perhaps not all is well in paradise."

After he disconnected, he glanced over at Burt. "You got any thoughts?"

"I wonder if Nelson knew about his wife's indiscretion with her brother-in-law, even though it occurred before they got married."

"I have a feeling there's little he doesn't know," Mitch replied. "He's too smart to just get married to any gold digger. He probably had her investigated before they married."

"What's the attraction? She didn't come from money. She can't bring a daddy's trust fund to the marriage."

"Some men like their women to need them...to be

dependent on them. Maybe that was what he was looking for."

Within an hour, they arrived at another gated community, this one full of exclusive condos instead of mansions. Burt glanced over at Mitch and asked, "Are you okay?"

Mitch shook his head and replied, "You know what? I've got Tori and that's possible because Thomas screwed her over with her sister. So, I hate like hell Tori had to go through that pain, but his loss is my gain, so I'm all good."

Thomas Porter answered his own door and Mitch immediately reassessed him, having seen him at Tori's Inn. Tall, blond, hair slightly thinning. He was wearing khakis paired with a light blue polo. *Handsome, but the way his eyes are shifting back and forth...I don't trust the guy.*

Showing their identification, Thomas invited them in and, as Mitch stepped into the elegantly appointed living room, a woman came from the back. Her reddish hair was pulled back with a headband, but the length was left to flow down her back. Her blue eyes landed on the logos on the officers' shirts and her gaze jumped to Thomas'.

"Honey, is everything all right?" she asked, stepping closely to him.

"Yes. This is my fiancé, Hailey Bernard." As the woman nodded toward Mitch and Burt, Thomas turned to her and said, "Please leave us to talk." His voice was firm, but he grimaced a smile toward her. "How about some iced tea?"

Nodding, she pinched her lips together tightly but did not argue. Mitch watched her walk away and wondered if Thomas had specifically gone for a woman who resembled Tori.

Sitting down, Thomas said, "Now, how can I assist the Baytown Police?"

"We're investigating a murder at the Sea Glass Inn—"

"Tori? Is Tori all right?" Thomas blurted, interrupting Mitch.

"The victim was one of her guests," Burt explained. "Why did you seek out Tori the other morning?"

"Me? Why would you be questioning me?" he sputtered. Looking up as the woman came back into the room, he remained quiet while she loitered before leaving with a huff when it was obvious he was not going to ask her to stay.

Mitch watched as Thomas took a long sip of his tea, biding for time. "You were going to tell us about the last time you were at the Sea Glass Inn."

The officers stayed silent with the desired effect of watching Thomas squirm in his seat. "I had not seen Tori in over a year and...and...decided to make a trip over the bridge to see how she was doing."

Burt, taking notes, lifted his head, a quizzical tone to his voice, "Just to take a stroll down memory lane?"

Blushing slightly, Thomas shifted once more. He darted his eyes over to the doorway where Hailey had left, then cast them down at his hands. "Sure. I mean, I had just gotten engaged and thought maybe I should let Tori know in person."

"And how did she take the news?" Mitch asked.

Sucking in a sharp breath, Thomas admitted, "She wouldn't talk to me so..." he lifted his hands up in the air.

"Were you surprised?"

"Well, yes. I thought enough time had passed that perhaps...I don't know...we could talk."

"You slept with her sister and then assumed that she would want to see you again?"

At those words, Thomas' face contorted. "I never meant for that to happen. Jesus, Vanessa is such a bitch."

Once more the officers remained silent and were rewarded as Thomas continued to talk. "Tori had gone to visit her grandmother, who was beginning to slow down. Vanessa and I were at the same function, had too much to drink and...I tell you, she came on to me. She seduced me!"

"So, you just happened to take her to a hotel and leave the receipt in your coat pocket?"

Red faced with anger, Thomas bit out, "What does this have to do with anything? It happened...Tori came back, found out, and walked out! I never got a chance to make it up to her...she just left!"

Unimpressed with the poor-me-pity-party Thomas was exhibiting, Mitch continued, "When she closed the door in your face, what did you do?"

Blinking, Thomas appeared surprised by the question. "Um…well, I came back home."

"Straight away?" Burt asked.

"Um, I stopped at a restaurant in town. It was a new one, and I was early for lunch, so I figured it would be a good place to get served quickly."

"You did not stay in Baytown any longer?"

"No!" Sitting up straighter, Thomas leaned forward, pinning the officers with his glare. "I won't answer any more questions until I know what this is about."

"The victim was not the intended victim," Mitch said deliberately. "The murderer was after Tori."

Sucking in a gasp, Thomas visibly paled, flopping back into his seat. "Oh, fuck, no."

"Since the incident occurred on the day that you appeared at her door, we are questioning everyone who came in contact with the Sea Glass Inn."

His eyes darting back and forth once more, Thomas said, "Um, Tori'll tell you when I was there at her place. And then I was at the restaurant. Surely someone there'll recognize me."

Nodding deliberately, watching the other man sweat, Mitch finally said, "Can you think of why anyone would want Ms. Bradford dead?"

Shaking his head back and forth slowly, Thomas' voice croaked as he replied, "No, no. Not at all. She was…well, I was just a fool. Such a fool."

Standing, Mitch concluded, "Those're all our questions for now, but I'm sure I'll be following up with more as we see where the investigation leads us."

Burt walked out onto the front stoop followed by Mitch, who hesitated for a second to slide on his sunglasses. Behind the closed front door, he clearly heard the screech. "You went to that fucking bum-fuck town to go visit your fucking ex-wife?"

Interesting, he thought as he moved toward his jeep. Anxious to get home to Tori, he hustled in and gladly left the picture-perfect-on-the-outside community.

Jason walked down the stairs and saw Tori standing in the living room staring out the window. "He'll be here soon," he said softly so as not to startle her.

She let the sheers drop from her hand and turned, offering a little smile. "I know…it's just…I don't know… weird." Seeing Jason cock his head to the side, she explained, "The day that someone must have tampered with my food I had two visitors. One was my ex-husband, who I haven't seen in over a year. Then a couple of hours later, my estranged sister showed up. And Mitch went to interview them today."

Nodding his understanding, Jason asked, "Is there anything I can do?"

"No, no. In fact, I feel badly that you're hanging around here when I know you need to be working on getting the shop ready."

Chuckling, he replied, "Don't worry. The realtor has placed the bid for the building, and I've got nothing to do until I find out if I can get it. I've already put in my application for a business permit."

Just then a jeep honked in the driveway and Tori squealed as she saw Mitch drive up. Rushing past Jason, she tore through the door and down the sidewalk to meet Mitch as he alighted from his vehicle. Jumping into his arms, she held on tight. "How was it? Was it awful? What did they say?"

"Hang on, babe, let me greet you first," Mitch said, pulling her head from his neck so that his lips could meet hers. After being in the presence of both Thomas and Vanessa in one day, he reveled in the freshness of Tori.

Out of the corner of his eye, he saw Jason move toward his motorcycle with a grin and a wave. Holding onto Tori's ass with one hand, he tossed up his other in a return greeting, before carrying her up the steps and into the house.

Regretfully, ending the kiss, he peered down at her, visually taking her pulse. "Everything okay here?"

"It's been fine, Mitch. But I want to know what happened today. Please don't keep me in suspense."

Nodding, he said, "Let's go out back so we can talk privately." He linked fingers with her, leading her through the kitchen and out to the patio.

The scent of freshly mown grass filled the air and the sound of children playing next door reminded her of playing with Mitch many years ago. Sighing, she willed her heart to stop pounding as she wondered what Mitch would report.

Sitting next to her on the glider, he said, "Okay, we'll start with Vanessa. She reacted the way we expected... very defensive. She claims she went right back to Virginia Beach and didn't stay in town at all. I met her husband...he came in with their attorney."

Eyes wide, Tori admitted, "I've never met him. They got married about six months ago and I tore up the invitation. I assumed by the way she was dressed and the way she looked at grandma's funeral that she had married a man with money. Something she always wanted."

"Well, he shut her down pretty quick, and I got the feeling he probably did that often, so all may not be as hunky-dory as she had hoped."

"I know she looks suspicious but, honestly Mitch, she's got money now. We don't like each other, but I can't convince myself she would try to poison me." She looked out over the yard for a moment, noting the flower gardens that she and her grandmother meticulously planted over the years. This little oasis was one of her hideouts when she was a child and Vanessa was on one of her rampages about being stuck in Baytown for a week. Sighing deeply, she said, "But maybe I just don't want to believe that she could do something so horrible."

Mitch wrapped his arm around her shoulders, pulling her into his warmth. Kissing the top of her head, he said, "We're not ruling anyone out yet."

Nodding, Tori leaned up and twisted to look at him once more. "And Thomas?"

"He claims he came here to let you know he's getting married again." Mitch did not have to wait long to see her reaction.

Barking out a laugh, she said, "Seriously? He thinks I would give two hoots about him getting married again? God, what a conceited ass!"

Laughing at the expression of disgust on her face, he asked, "I take it you don't care?"

"Nope, not at all. You know, I was more upset over their betrayal than I was when we actually got divorced."

"Well, I overheard him and his fiancé as we left, and I have the feeling she was extremely pissed that he came over here. I believe it was something he planned on keeping from her. And to be honest, I don't think they've got the perfect relationship either."

Giggling, she said, "Would you think less of me if I told you that I'm not exactly torn up over their lives not being perfect?"

Laughing along with her, he shook his head. "Nope, I would think it made you perfectly normal!"

They sat quietly on the glider for a few more minutes, she tucked into his embrace.

"Just to let you know, I've let Jason off the hook tomorrow. Katelyn and I are going sea glass hunting early in the morning and then we're going to her house to do some baking for the Fisherman's Fair." Sighing, she said, "My kitchen is far superior, but we're afraid no one will buy anything if they find out it was made here. I know you all kept a tight hold on the information, but with a few of the other guests staying at different B&Bs in town, I'm sure the rumor mills have been working."

"It should die down soon," Mitch assured. "And we will find who did this." Standing, he held out his hand and gently pulled her up from the seat. Taking her face in both hands, he soothed her cheeks with his thumbs, lost in her gaze. "I've got to go home to check on things there. The guys and I are having a meeting about the American Legion, and then I've got a staff meeting first thing in the morning."

"I'm fine here," she replied. "I've got Jason and another couple staying here so I won't be alone."

Kissing her longingly, he admitted, "It's only been two nights, but I don't want to be apart."

Reveling in the warmth of his lips moving over hers, she muttered, "Then come back here after you're done. I don't care how late you are." Reaching into her pocket, she retrieved a key. "Here...this is for you."

Grinning, he took the key in his hand. Kissing her once more, lingering over her lips until he forced himself to pull away, he whispered, "I'll come back as soon as I can."

18

Mitch walked into the bar and headed straight to the back room, coming up short when he turned the corner and saw who was in attendance for the American Legion planning meeting. The Baytown boys were all there, plus their fathers, a few of their grandfathers, Jason, Ginny, Burt, two younger men he did not recognize, and about six older men, including the ones who had spoken to him earlier.

"Wow, looks like we have the support we need," he joked. Getting down to business, he said, "I've got the American Legion Development and Revitalization Procedures here. I have completed the questionnaire with the help of Dan." Nodding toward one of the older gentlemen sitting at the table, he continued, "From what I can see, the closest American Legion is at the most northern end of the Eastern Shore, and its membership has dwindled. The building it's located in is being sold as part of a redevelopment plan, and so they need a new home. It's still a viable chapter, but the hour and a half it takes from someone down here to drive there has become prohibitive."

He handed a stack of papers to Aiden to pass out and continued. "I have applied for the new location of the chapter to be near us, and the Legion Commander of that chapter has already agreed. He's quite elderly and no longer wants to bear the burden of running it. In your packets you'll see what we'll need to make this happen. I need signatures from all of you and anyone you know who will take part in this organization. You will also find forms for volunteering and what the program needs to look like."

He pinned the group with his stare and said, "You need to understand...this is no old-war-horse-sitting-around-telling–war-stories kind of organization. We're to support each other, other veterans, the community, assist with youth groups...and it cannot be done by just the same people over and over again. So, take the packet home tonight and look it over. We will have a meeting in three days to vote to see if we can support moving the American Legion to Baytown."

The attendees applauded, stunning Mitch, his blush evidence of his surprise. As the group began looking over the forms, one of the unknown younger men walked over. Tall, with shaggy hair, and dark-brown eyes, he stepped up, his hand out for a shake. "Chief Evans," the man's deep voice greeted. "I'm Gareth Harrison. Four-year tour with the Air Force."

"Nice to meet you," Mitch said honestly, gripping his

hand firmly. "Call me Mitch. I haven't seen you around town, but I've been meaning to come by. I heard there was a private investigator in Baytown."

"I've got a little house about three miles south of town," Gareth explained. "I've been wanting to come in and introduce myself to you, but knew you were busy... and now even more with the murder investigation."

Mitch waited, seeing what Gareth wanted to talk about.

"I've got my business here in town, but my office is more understated...the town council won't let me have a huge sign on my window," he said, a smirk on his face. Rubbing his chin, he explained, "Look, I know you probably don't need my services, but...if you ever do... I'm available to assist. I want to get my business off the ground."

He held Mitch's gaze, but Mitch observed a mixture of pride and uncertainty there. Smiling, Mitch nodded. "I've got no problem working with a PI," he assured. "In fact, when I worked with the FBI, I had a private investigation firm I worked with on a regular basis...and am proud to call them my friends."

Grinning, Gareth heaved a sigh. "I'll look forward to helping anytime you need me." Looking around at the others in the room, he added, "And this, helping veterans, this is a good thing, Mitch."

The gathering cheered once more as Aiden called out, "Beers all around!"

Slipping back into the Sea Glass Inn an hour later just as a storm was brewing, Mitch quietly made his way into the bathroom, taking care of business before shucking his clothes. Walking back into the bedroom, he saw the moonlight reflecting off the bay and through the glass door, covering Tori in a mist of light. He stood for a moment staring down at the beauty as her chest rose and fell in sleep.

I heard Tori was back in town and ran over to the Sea Glass Inn to see if she wanted to play. Her grandmother opened the door with a big smile and said Tori was in the hammock in the backyard. Sending me through the house, she instructed me to grab some freshly baked cookies on my way out. Never one to turn down cookies, I grabbed a handful.

Running out onto the patio, I saw Tori on her back in the new hammock strung between two old trees. She wasn't moving and I almost decided to sneak up and scare her. I tiptoed over, but instead of shouting "Boo!" I simply stood and stared. She was asleep.

She was only ten and I was a big, almost-man at twelve, surely too old to be staring at her. But I couldn't help it. She was so pretty. Her red hair had lightened to a gentle reddish blonde and the splash of freckles across her nose called to me.

She looked like a princess in a fairy tale...one where the handsome prince needed to kiss her to wake her up. Without thinking, I bent over and kissed her cheek softly, then watched in fascination as her eyes fluttered open. It took a second for her expression to change from confusion to a huge smile.

Suddenly embarrassed, I shoved my hand out to her, saying, "Um...your grandma wanted you to have a cookie."

We both looked down and saw that the chocolate chips had melted in my hand, leaving the cookies a gooey mess. Before I could pull my hand back, she grabbed it and dragged a finger over my palm, scooping up some of the chocolate. Grinning, she stuck her finger in her mouth, licking the sticky sweetness. "Can't let chocolate go to waste!" Her smile was huge...and I knew it was just for me. If I didn't know it before then, I knew it now...I was in love with Tori Bradford.

In the middle of his memory, he startled when Tori's eyes opened, taking a second to break into a wide grin. The smile pierced his heart and, before he could hold back the words, they slipped out. "I love you."

She lifted her arms, reaching out to him and drew him in. Holding each other close, she whispered in his ear, "I've been in love with you since I was six years old."

He rolled her over, pinning her underneath him, kissing her until they were both breathless and made love far into the night.

The five officers reviewed the interviews from the previous day along with the information that had been gathered.

Using the old-fashioned whiteboard on the wall, Ginny taped up a few more pictures. "So, we've got an ex-husband and sister, both having had an affair…or at least a drunken night of sex…and both, uncharacteristically, visited Baytown the same day as the poisoning. Both had opportunity."

Burt spoke as Ginny taped a picture of Vanessa's husband and Thomas' fiancé up on the wall, "These two didn't have opportunity that we know of and probably no motive, but after yesterday's interviews, I think they have influence over the others."

"Hailey was definitely not happy that Thomas came to visit his former wife. He claims it was to let Tori know in person about his upcoming marriage, but, according to Tori, they had not had contact since the divorce, and she had given him no indication she was interested in what he did."

Mitch added, "I thought it was interesting that Hailey looks so much like Tori . The reddish hair…blue eyes. She had a hard look about her…not Tori's easy smile, but definitely I'd say Thomas either has a type or he's trying to replace his first wife."

"I got the same feeling," Burt agreed.

"What about the sister?"

"She's got anger issues and a dominating personality, until it comes to her husband. I got the feeling he definitely runs the household there," Mitch reported. "He showed up with his attorney and shut us down fairly quickly."

"Nelson Hurkamp is an investment broker in the Virginia Beach area. You saw his house," Ginny said. "He bought it recently, after he married Vanessa. He's been married before but divorced his first wife about four years ago."

"Reason?"

"Infidelity—hers not his, according to the court records. It also appears she walked away with a modest settlement."

"Okay, let's get back to motive," Mitch said. "The only reason I can see as motive is money. Tori's beach-front, large, brick home is valued at almost a million dollars. Her grandfather would never have thought the old home he bought and restored would be worth so much, but it is. As the Hurkamp's attorney pointed out, if Tori dies intestate, then the mother will receive everything, not the sister."

"Did you talk to the mother yet?" Grant asked.

Shaking his head, Mitch replied, "It was too late yesterday, and I wanted to speak to Tori before doing so. When we first re-connected, she commented that her mother was not well, but Vanessa made no such claim when I mentioned the mother to her yesterday."

"So, we might want to ascertain how ill she is," Sam said, leaning back in his chair, patting his stomach, eyeing the box of Jillian's pastries on the counter. Shaking his head, he said, "Damn diet. My Martha's got me on a strict regimen…which of course I broke when I had a donut this morning."

Ginny twisted around and plopped the lid down on the box of pastries before turning back to grin at Sam. "Temptation resolved."

Shaking his head, Sam continued, "If the mom is at

death's door, maybe that would provide Vanessa's motive."

"I can't imagine Mrs. Bradford is extremely ill, or Tori would be more concerned, but you're right," Mitch agreed. "I'll have you check into it, and I'll talk to Tori as well."

"Are we possibly overlooking someone else?" Burt asked.

"We're at the stage where anyone and everyone could be of interest," Mitch pointed out. "What are you thinking?"

"Anyone jealous of Tori? Anybody want her business? After all, she's got prime real estate here in town."

"Who would benefit?" Sam asked. "Other Inns? The small hotel in town? I can't imagine any of those people being so desperate as to drive her out of business."

"Right after Mr. Dumfries died, several of her guests left and moved to different lodging, Burt replied, "and she certainly has had cancellations."

"That would be more of a consideration if her business was being sabotaged and someone stood to gain from owning her estate...but an attempt on her life?" Ginny answered.

The group looked to Mitch who, throwing his head back in frustration, said, "All right, let's go over the rest of what you have, starting with Thomas' and the Hurkamps's finances. And keep our minds open to anything."

As the group headed out of the room, Mitch called Sam back. Nodding toward the chair the older man had just vacated, he watched as Sam settled down, eyes narrowed in curiosity.

"Something wrong, Chief?"

Cutting to the chase, Mitch eyed the veteran police officer and said, "I want to know what Corwin, or Silas, has said to you. Because from what I've heard, your treatment of some of the townspeople might be a little different than that of the vacationers who aren't following some of our rules."

Sam's eyes widened for a second as he opened his mouth to protest, then heaved a sigh instead as he looked down at his hands on the table. The silence between the two men stretched long and heavy.

Sam sucked in a deep breath before lifting his eyes directly back to Mitch's. His face registered a combination of resignation and relief, both noted by his Chief.

"It started when Silas Mills became the city manager. About the time your dad had his heart attack." Sighing again, he added, "Sure as hell wouldn't have happened on your dad's watch."

"What was it you were asked to do?"

"Silas spent time riding around the town and started noticing some things. He didn't like how the kids were playing basketball over at the Methodist church parking lot." Looking up sharply, Sam said, "We patrolled that area...didn't want drugs being involved and, honest to God, they were just good kids playing ball. But Silas didn't like the *look* of it."

Mitch said nothing, but his lips pinched tightly.

"Then, when we would patrol the beaches, we would

always warn anyone who had glass bottles or dogs off a leash about the rules. We never had any problems. Hell, we even carried plastic garbage bags for them to toss bottles in so they wouldn't have to walk to the receptacles. Kids would come up and talk to us. Townspeople and vacationers alike would smile and wave...like they were glad to see us."

"What changed?"

"I got called into the mayor's office one day, and Silas was there, too. Sat me down and began to tell me how the image of the town was important. How we had the only public beach around and that we wanted the town to prosper by making sure the vacationers had a good experience."

"Did you get the feeling it was more the mayor or city planner?"

"Corwin Banks knows he gets elected by the townspeople, so he kept pretty quiet. But Silas Mills...he's a piece of work. Hell, he came to work in Baytown...a quiet, sleepy little bayside town and yet he acts like he's going to turn it into some big vacation destination." Shaking his head, he added under his breath, "Dumb shit."

"What did they want from you?"

"I was told that, in the town's interest, I needed to work on cleaning up the streets...keep the kids off the basketball courts, tell them to stay on the periphery of the beach and not wander through the crowds."

Mitch leaned forward in his seat, pinning Sam with his gaze. "Why you, Sam? Why not the others?"

Sam's face contorted in a grimace as though the answer pained him. "I'd hate like hell to think it's because they think I'm dirty...or maybe not as squeaky clean. Fuck..." Sitting up straight, facing his firing squad, he replied, "I reckon they figured Ginny and Grant were former military and they always exuded a *by the book* attitude. Burt? I don't know, but he also flies straight. It kills me to think of it this way, but they probably figured since I'm the oldest and closest to retirement, and I suppose because I'm more of a local *good ole' boy*, they'd have a better chance of me doing their bidding."

The silence once more hung heavy over the table. Neither spoke for a long minute. Finally, Sam asked, "You want my resignation?"

Mitch shook his head. "Nope. Absolutely not. What I want is your allegiance to me, to this department, and not to the city manager. I want the cop that my father served with back serving with me."

Surprise and relief shot across Sam's face as he sagged slightly in his chair. Nodding, he said, "You've got it, Chief." Standing, he turned to walk out of the room, stopping at the door and looking back. "Your grandfather was a good man as well as a good cop and chief. So was your dad. If anyone wonders if it can happen a third time...well, you've just proven it can. Proud to serve under you, Mitch."

19

As Mitch pulled up to the Inn, Tori bounced on her toes in anticipation. It had been many years since she attended the Fisherman's Fair on the harbor. She had alerted her guests to the events taking place and they had already headed over to the fun. Jason came down the stairs just as Mitch walked through the door.

"We'll see you there," Tori yelled as Jason moved out the door at the same time Mitch came in. Throwing her arms around his neck, she grinned, planting a kiss on his mouth. "Are you ready?"

Mitch allowed her to own the kiss for a moment before taking over. Moving his lips over hers, he wondered how he had so quickly become addicted to her scent...her touch...her taste. Pulling away, he settled her back to her feet and grinned down at the excitement on her upturned face. "Looks like you're ready for the Fisherman's Fair."

"I remember it as a child, but I swear it's been so long, and Jillian told me that it's even bigger and better!"

Grabbing her hand, he twirled her around several times, enjoying her giggles as her long hair streamed out in a curtain about her head. "Oh, save those moves for the dance floor," she laughed.

A couple of minutes later, Mitch parked near the edge of the harbor, the crowds already formed and swirling about. Tents were set up along the boardwalk and the walking path between the harbor and the town. Their nostrils were immediately assaulted with the food tents' tantalizing scents. Fried oysters, fried clams, fish and chips, fresh roasted corn on the cob, popcorn, sautéed zucchini and yellow squash, funnel cakes and cotton candy. Several church groups and women's organizations had tables full of homemade bread, cakes, and pies.

The fire department had one of the large fire trucks parked nearby, and children were able to see it up close and even sit in the driver's seat where their parents could take pictures. One of the local farmers brought his little ponies and, with them in a fenced-in pen, he offered pony rides.

Local artists and vendors had their wares for sale in other tents, now filled with beachwear, jewelry, paintings, carvings, seashells, and hand-painted silk scarves.

"God, I'm hungry," Mitch said as his stomach growled. "This will put me in a fried food coma!"

"Why does food that's cooked out in the open in a fun atmosphere smell better than any fare from a fancy restaurant?" Tori wondered aloud, her eyes darting around.

"I know what you mean," Mitch replied. "I never thought about it as a kid, but after being away from it for several years, it now just feels like..." he faltered, looking for the right word.

"Home," Tori supplied, smiling up at him.

He dropped his gaze back to hers, eyes warm as he saw the same reflected back in hers. "Yeah...home."

"Hey, you two," Aiden called out from behind Finn's tent, selling draft beers. "Come on over. Of course I have to card you, just so the Police Chief won't shut our tent down," he joked.

Laughing, they pulled out their IDs and received yellow alcohol bands around their wrists. Each taking a beer from him, they moseyed down the food aisle and made their selections. Mitch went for the fried oysters and Tori had her eyes on the fried clams. With French fries, onion rings, and slaw, they settled on a picnic blanket on the ground near his parents.

The mayor walked past with Silas at his side. As Corwin nodded to the crowd, he threw up his hand toward the couple, but Mitch observed Silas' assessing gaze on Tori before sliding to Mitch's face and immediately plastering on a smile in greeting. *What's up that man's ass? I may need to have Gareth look into him as well.*

Soon, joined by other friends and family, the group settled back to listen to one of the local bands. Mitch sat with his knees crooked up on either side of Tori as she rested her back against his front. The sun began to drop in the sky, creating a panorama of swirling colors behind the band. He nudged her, whispering in her ear, "Dance with me, baby."

Standing, he reached his hand toward her, and she allowed him to pull her to her feet. He led her toward the area in front of the band, fingers linked. With a twirl, he tucked her into his embrace, arms around each other, swaying to the music.

Tori, lost in the moment, remembered a night at the fair many years before.

The Fisherman's Fair was in full swing, and grandma let me run off with my friends after I helped her carry her famous pies. Well, famous to me, and I was sure they were famous to the whole world as well.

Jillian, Katelyn, and I ran around, looking at all of the food tents, picking out just what we wanted to eat. Staring at the cotton candy vendor, I whirled around to tell Jillian what I wanted when I ran into a wall. Stumbling back, arms reached out and grabbed my shoulders, steadying me. I looked into the blue eyes of Mitch Evans. At fifteen, he was so gorgeous...much more so than I remembered from last holiday.

"Hi!" I grinned, blushing as he smiled back at me.

"Hey," Mitch's whisper broke through her memories. "Where were you just then?"

Blushing, she ducked her head, attempting to bury it in his chest.

"Oh, no," he chided, lifting her chin with his fingers. "No secrets."

Huffing slightly, she said, "Well, if you must know, I was thinking about the fair when I was only thirteen and ran into you at the—"

"Cotton candy vendor," he finished.

Eyes wide, she exclaimed, "You remember?"

Leaning down to place a sweet kiss on her lips, he revealed, "Baby, I remember everything about you. Every time you came to be with your grandmother. Every game you sat and watched. I remember playing tag when you were seven and wanting to play something else when you were sixteen and in that tiny blue bikini." Seeing her incredulous expression, he kissed her lightly once more. "Every. Single. Thing."

The following kiss lasted longer, although he restrained himself, knowing they were in a public place.

As the song ended, and he twirled her one last time, she came back into his chest and said, "I remember everything too. While I was always excited to see the whole gang, it was you that I wanted the most."

Tucking her under his arm, he led her back to the blankets, and said, "Well, now, many years later, you've got me. All of me."

Mitch and Tori barely made it to her suite on the third floor of the Inn. Jason and the other guests were still at the Fisherman's Fair, so the couple decided to take advantage of the privacy to continue what they had started on the dance floor.

Kicking her bedroom door shut with his booted foot, he barely caught her as she whirled around, throwing her body against his.

Slamming their mouths together, with tongues tangling, they vied for dominance as the kiss flamed hot.

Tori grabbed his face in her hands, holding him in place as her lips moved over his, pulling him deeper into the kiss. Pushing her gently back, Mitch set her on the bed, his hands sliding beneath the hem of her dress to find the scrap of lace underneath.

She released him long enough to scoot back on the mattress, laughing as he slipped off her sandals and tossed them aside.

Her rosy lips were kiss-swollen and his beard had slightly abraded her chin. Catching his gaze, she whispered, "I want to feel your beard everywhere."

Halting, he cocked his head to the side. "Everywhere?"

Her only answer was a saucy grin as she lay back.

He shoved her sundress up and made quick work of her panties. With one sharp tug, and the lace gave way.

"My panties!" she complained, although her breathless voice gave little credence that she was upset.

"I'll buy you more," he murmured, and lowered his head.

She had known desire before, but nothing like this... nothing so patient, so deliberate, so wholly focused on her. He took his time learning her, unhurried and thorough, and she understood with startling clarity that she was in serious trouble. He had just found his addiction, and she had just found hers.

She fell apart slowly at first, then all at once in a cascade of warmth and sensation that left her trembling, her hair a riot on the pillow behind her. The cool of the room eventually drifted back in, and she lifted her head to find him watching her with that slow, easy smile.

She smiled back, a twinkle in her blue eyes. "Oh, damn."

"I'll take that as a compliment," he teased.

"Oh, yeah. Absolutely a compliment."

He rose from the side of the bed, and she watched, unabashed, as he stripped away his shirt and stepped out of his pants.

"Better than Christmas," she moaned.

He laughed softly and pulled her to a seated position, making quick work of the rest of her clothing until there was nothing between them but moonlight. He took her hand and stepped back, just looking at her. Her porcelain skin was luminescent in the soft glow streaming through the white lacy sheers on the balcony doors, and the way he looked at her made her feel like something rare and precious.

He drew her close again, his hands moving over her with reverence, his mouth following. She held onto his shoulders as sensation overtook her, sounds escaping her lips that she was barely aware of making. He was thorough and devoted and utterly unhurried, and she was undone by all of it... the warmth of his hands, the scratch of his beard, the focused tenderness that felt entirely different from anything she'd known before.

She reached for him, and his breath caught. *Jesus, I'm gone. Totally. Completely. Gone. No woman could compare.*

He kissed her again, slow and deep, and she tasted the heat of the moment on his tongue. She pulled him close, legs wrapped around his waist, arms around his neck. "I need you now, Mitch. Please..."

He pulled away just long enough to take care of protection, then settled himself over her again.

"I fell for you when I was eight years old," he confessed. "There's no other woman for me."

Her brilliant smile was his reward.

He joined them together slowly, a long exhale leaving him as his body found its home. He refused to give into the urge to rush. They found their rhythm together, unhurried at first, then urgent, her body rising to meet his as the tension between them built and coiled. Her arms moved over the hard lines of his back and shoulders, anchoring herself to him as the world narrowed to just this room, just this man, just the way he made her feel.

The pressure built from somewhere deep inside and she threw her head back, eyes shut, sparks blooming in the darkness behind her eyelids.

"Come on, babe," he urged, his voice low and ragged. "Let go and come with me."

She did. His name left her lips as she came apart, and

the sound of it broke the last of his control. His own release followed and his arms trembled before he collapsed onto her waiting body.

They lay breathing hard, the euphoria washing over them both. When he finally remembered himself, he rolled to the side and pulled her with him, her soft warmth tucked against the solid length of him. Heartbeat to heartbeat.

Several minutes later he slipped out of bed and disappeared briefly into the bathroom before padding back into the room, entirely at ease. Her eyes moved over him with the same undisguised appreciation she knew was written all over his face whenever he looked at her.

Sliding underneath the covers, he pulled her body into his, as had become their habit at night. His mind drifted to the future and how they could make this work. *I don't want to live in a room above the Inn, but my cabin doesn't have enough space.*

Hearing him sigh heavily, she twisted in his arms, her gaze seeking his. He stared into her face and inwardly cursed himself for causing her worry. Before she could ask, he said, "Sorry, babe. I wasn't sighing about us. Promise."

"Then what? The case?"

He lifted his hand to caress her cheek. "Actually," he smiled, "I was just thinking about how much I love having you in my arms. And...how I don't want it to end."

He said no more, wondering if her thoughts would

take her down the same path. He did not have to wait long.

"I don't want us to end either." Holding him closely, she ran her fingers over his beard. "Mitch, I had a bad marriage and honestly thought that I'd never want to be involved with someone again. I thought I could never trust anyone again." Smiling in the dark as the moonlight cast a glow over his face, she continued, "But I never imagined that life would bring us back together. Not even when I moved here. I thought you were gone for good." Sighing, she added, "But if living here made me happy and allowed me to have my childhood memories of times with you, then I was good with that."

He leaned forward the bare inch it took to claim her lips and placed a whisper soft kiss there. "I thought of you every time I thought about my childhood here in Baytown. Sometimes, remembering this place was the only thing that got me through my time in Afghanistan and Iraq." Chuckling, he added, "But I always just thought those were memories to hang on to. I never dreamed I'd come back here to live. And I sure as hell never thought I'd have a chance to make love to my Tori."

"So, what now?" she asked timidly.

Kissing her softly once more, he said, "First on my list is keeping you safe and finding out who the hell is after you. Then...we'll talk about our future. And believe me," he kissed her again, "we're going to have a future."

20

A few days later, just as the sun began to rise, the lonely beach welcomed the walkers, searching for the ocean's treasures.

"Last night's storm helped bring more glass up on shore," Katelyn commented, bending over to pick up a few more pieces of sea glass. "Ooh, look at the deep green of this one," she cooed, holding it up for Tori to admire.

Tori loved the sea glass, but as soon as Katelyn mentioned last night's storm, she blushed at her memories. Mitch had made it to her place just as the lightning crackled across the bay and the thunder echoed overhead.

Woken up by his kisses, they made love as wildly as the wind raged outside, knowing the storm would keep their cries of passion from being heard by anyone else.

"What's on your mind this morning?" Katelyn asked,

as she stopped dead in her tracks, her hands on her shapely hips.

"What?"

"That look on your face tells me the storm wasn't the only action last night!"

"I...I...oh, none of your business," Tori spouted, knowing her propensity for blushing just reached new heights.

Laughing, Katelyn said, "Hey, I'm glad for you. Everyone knows you and Mitch were made for each other." Wistfully looking out onto the bay, she added, "At least you're getting some business. I'm having a serious drought!"

The two women walked beyond the cement factory that was on one side of town where the beaches were not populated, and the vacationers were not also searching for shells and sea glass.

Tori looked toward the dunes, saying, "The golf course is right over there, isn't it?"

Katelyn nodded, her gaze still down on the sand at her feet. "Yeah. Aiden and Brogan go over occasionally to play. Now that Mitch is home, they'll probably all go. I thought about getting a job there as a hostess in the clubhouse, but," shrugging, "I've got enough waitressing with the diner and the bar."

Looking at her friend, Tori asked, "Did you ever think of leaving Baytown?"

Barking out a laugh, Katelyn said, "Of course. I think every kid who grew up in this tiny town wanted to get out. But when Aiden and Brogan joined the military, I knew mom and dad would have been so sad for me to leave, too. So, I stayed. My two years at the North Heron Community College gave me an associate's degree in business, but that's about it."

"Did you ever take any computer tech classes?"

"Sure. I can't do a lot, but I can do business reports, payroll, design a website."

Grabbing Katelyn's arm, Tori said, "Oh, would you work on the webpage for the Sea Glass Inn? I am desperate!"

"Hey, girls!" a shout came from behind and as they turned, Jillian came running up. "I didn't think I'd have a chance to get away from the coffee shop, but all my help came in today, so I decided to find you two. Have you got any good pieces?"

Katelyn showed Jillian the pieces of sea glass she had collected as Tori walked along the beach a little further. Suddenly a shot rang out and Tori jumped at the sound.

"They're not supposed to be shooting geese this time of day," Jillian complained.

"Did The Dunes Resort give the hunters permission to shoot the geese on the golf course again?" Tori called out.

The other two women nodded as they walked toward her.

"Yes, but not this early in the day," Katelyn explained as another shot ricocheted nearby. "Damn, we'd better get out of here. I'd hate to—"

A third shot rang out, this time causing Tori to scream out as she dropped to the sand. Her leg was on fire with pain as she grabbed it, looking down to see blood running between her fingers. "I've been hit!" she screamed.

"Holy shit!" Jillian yelled, crouching down as she low-crawled over to Tori.

Katelyn was already on her phone calling 911 as Jillian reached Tori and ripped off her bandana to wrap around the injured leg. Looking up, she saw two men in a Dunes' Gator used for collecting trash from the beach coming toward them over the sand. Jillian waved, calling out to them, and they immediately drove over, hopping out as soon as they reached the women.

"Who the hell is letting geese hunters out now when there are people on the beach?" Katelyn yelled.

As one man crouched next to Tori, the other replied, "We heard the shots, but there are no hunters allowed on The Dunes Golf Course today."

Kayelyn ran over, her phone to her ear and said, "Can you take us to where an ambulance can get to us?"

"Sure, miss. Tell 'em to come to the front security gate of The Dunes."

The two men carefully lifted Tori, but the burning pain was excruciating. Blood had soaked her sock where it had run down her leg. *Oh, no, I'm going to faint.* Her pale face flopped back as the world darkened.

The driver yelled, "Hold on!" to the other four as he drove straight up the dune and across the golf course, racing toward the gate.

Mitch and the other officers were moving from the staffroom to continue their investigations or move out on patrol when Mildred raced around the corner skidding to a stop in her orthopedic shoes.

"911 call just came in," she panted. "Shooting at the golf course. Zac is in the ambulance. A person was shot." With that parting information, she ran back to her desk, listening to the emergency radio.

"Who the hell is shooting on the golf course?" Mitch growled, already moving out the door.

Grant, right behind him, said, "The Dunes golfing community occasionally gives local hunters rights to shoot geese off the golf course, but not this time of year and certainly not this time of day. Not with golfers around."

As Mitch and Grant were almost out the door, Mildred yelled out, "Chief! It was Katelyn that called in the shooting! Tori was shot!"

"Fuck!" Mitch roared, throwing open the door as he rushed to his jeep.

Grant grabbed his arm, yelling, "No, Mitch!" Grabbing his friend, he shoved him toward the police SUV's passenger side and said, "I'm driving."

It took less than three minutes to arrive at The Dune's guard entrance where they could see the ambulance parked, back doors open, and Zac grabbing his equipment along with the other EMT. By the time Grant parked next to it, several SUVs and trucks had pulled up beside them, filled with volunteer firefighters and rescue workers.

Pushing through the crowd to the arriving Gator, Mitch stared in horror at the image of Tori, pale and listless, lying in the arms of one of the groundskeepers, blood covering her leg and foot.

"Tori," he breathed, moving to take her in his arms.

A strong hand on his arm halted him. "Mitch, let me do my job," Zac said. Mitch turned his stricken gaze to his friend, unwilling and unable to let go until Grant moved in as well.

Jillian hopped out and ran to Mitch, babbling, "They were shooting. We were on the beach, and they were shooting at us."

His mind tried to process what she was saying while keeping an eye on Tori as Zac had her laid on the stretcher so he could assess her injuries.

Grant's gaze darted to Jillian, quickly assessing her from head to toe. His fingers curled into fists as he saw the panic on her face and fought the urge to hurry over to her, as she continued to shake.

Katelyn, the calmer of the women, stepped up and wrapped her arm around Jillian, but kept her eyes on Mitch and the other men who had gathered around. "We heard shots. Two of them hit near Tori. It was the third that hit her in the leg. I think it was just a glance, but it bled like crazy." She nodded to the groundskeepers, "They said there was no geese shooting today, so I don't know who it was."

Mitch, still standing right next to the stretcher, his eyes not leaving Tori, pulled himself together and barked out, "No one leaves the community until checked by us. Grant, you work the gate with The Dune's security guard." He turned to the others gathered around and said, "I'll take any volunteers who'll scour the grounds, especially over by the dunes near the bay, to see what you can find. Any evidence, call for Sam or Ginny to bag it up. Katelyn, go with Burt and show him where you were when Tori was shot. The tide is going out, so we have a chance to recover the bullets."

With that, the group immediately dispersed, the volunteers jumping in their vehicles and heading into the gated community. Mitch looked up as a golf cart came into view, recognizing The Dune's general manager.

Roger Thorpe, informed about the shooting by radio calls from the groundskeepers, hopped out of his cart as soon as it stopped. "Chief Evans, I heard what happened. I've called a halt to all golfers on the courses and had them come back to the clubhouse for their own safety. Thank God there were only a few out this early. If it had been later in the day, it would have been a publicity nightmare!"

Mitch glared at the man, but Grant deftly moved the manager over to the guardhouse to talk with him there. Kneeling by the stretcher, he took Tori's pale hand in his own, breathing easier as she opened her eyes.

"Sorry," she whispered, tears sliding down her cheeks.

"Babe, you've got nothing to be sorry about," he said, leaning down closer to hear her over the noise, his thumb reaching out to brush the tears away.

"I faint when I see blood," she explained, her voice shaky. Glancing down at Zac, she said, "How is it?"

Zac addressed Tori but moved his gaze between her and Mitch. "We're going to take you to the clinic here in town. I want you seen there first. Then Dr. Warren or Dr. Turner can let us know if you need to be taken to the hospital."

Nodding her understanding, Mitch growled, "Why don't we take her to the hospital now and not waste time?"

Zac said patiently, "The bullet grazed her leg. It was a deep graze and needs to be treated but the trip to the hospital is over thirty minutes away. A doctor can treat her at the clinic in about three minutes. We've called ahead and they're expecting us."

Pinching his lips tightly, Mitch knew his friend was right. His gaze searched out Tori's but found her leaning back peacefully.

"I want to go to the clinic, Mitch. I'll go to the hospital only if they think I need to. Honey, why don't you stay and work if you nee—"

"Not leaving your side, babe," he said, his right hand still holding hers closely while his left hand brushed her sweaty brow. Leaning down, he kissed her forehead before looking at Zac. Climbing into the back of the ambulance as they loaded her, he said, "Let's go." Looking out the back to Grant, standing nearby, he ordered, "You're in charge of the crime scene."

Two hours later, Mitch walked out from the back examining area of the clinic, into the waiting room on his way to get his jeep. As he entered the large waiting room, he stopped quickly at the number of people present. Brogan had his arm around his sister, Katelyn, while Aiden stood next to them holding on to Jillian. Zac had come back from the firehouse and waited with several other friends.

His parents rushed over to his side, his mother's face showing her concern and his father's a mask of anger.

"How is she?" Nancy asked, grabbing her son's hand.

"She's going to be fine, mom," Mitch replied. Hugging his mother, he looked to the others and said, "The bullet deeply grazed her leg but didn't penetrate the bone."

The room filled with *Thank God and Hallelujahs* before he continued. "She doesn't have stitches because the wound is like a burn across her thigh and there isn't two edges of skin to pull together. It will be painful and cause scarring, but Dr. Warren says it should heal in several weeks."

He wiped his hand across his forehead and said, "I need to jog over and get my jeep to take her home. She's all worried about the Inn, but I told her that she has to stay off her feet for at least two days, so she's coming home with me."

Jason, who had been leaning against the wall, spoke up. "I'll be at the Inn in the mornings and evenings, so I can take care of everything there if someone can do the breakfast."

"I'll bring breakfast," Jillian volunteered. "She doesn't need to worry about a thing."

Katelyn piped up, "If Jason will be there at night, I'll manage the afternoons. It's slow at the bar anyway, so I can keep an eye on things while Jason is out."

"Honey," Nancy said, "why don't you bring her to our house. I can keep an eye on her while you're working."

Mitch pondered this suggestion for a moment and then said, "Tell you what. I'll bring her there now while I get with the others to find out what they've learned, then I'll come by and take her to my place for the night. I'll bring her back tomorrow."

Ed stepped up to his son, placing his hand on Mitch's shoulder, and said, "We're here for whatever you need, son. And as for me, I want to assist in any way I can. I'm sick and tired of being cooped up in the house, so I'll be more than happy to do some investigating."

A slight gasp was heard and the group turned to see Tori sitting in a wheelchair the nurse had rolled out. Swallowing a sob, she cried, "I don't know how to thank you all."

Stalking over, reaching her side in four steps, Mitch crouched down next to her, taking her hand in his. "Babe, there's not a person in this room who wouldn't do whatever they could to keep you safe." Taking her face in his hands, he brushed his lips over hers. "And I promise," he vowed, "I'll get to the bottom of this."

21

While the sofa was very soft, Tori shifted in discomfort. The pain meds had made her drowsy and now, as she slowly awoke, her gaze tried to focus on her unfamiliar surroundings.

Nancy appeared in her line of vision, a concerned expression on her face. "How are you feeling? Can I get you something to drink?"

Parched, Tori's tongue felt dry and swollen as she nodded. "Yes, please," she croaked.

Without having to leave the room, Nancy produced a tall glass of iced tea with a sprig of mint resting on top. "This should help revive you a little."

Gratefully taking the proffered cold drink, Tori lifted it to her lips, drinking deeply. Nodding, she smiled, handing it back to Nancy before pressing down on the sofa to shift her body up to more of a sitting position.

Looking down at the large, gauze-wrapped bandage

circling her thigh, Tori shook her head. "Wow, I still can't believe what happened. Shot?" Her gaze jumped up to Nancy's. "That's so crazy. None of this makes sense."

Nancy set the glass down on the large coffee table and then plopped down on it as well, her hands reaching out to grasp Tori's. "I'm so sorry, sweetie. I can't even express how shocking this all is." Leaning down slightly to hold Tori's gaze, she continued, "But I'm sure my Mitch will get to the bottom of it all."

At the sound of Mitch's name on his mother's lips, Tori could not hold back the blush rising from her chest to the top of her forehead. *I wonder what his mother thinks about us?*

Before she had time to ponder that question further, Nancy laughed. "Oh, my dear. Don't worry—Ed and I are thrilled that Mitch and you are together. I think we always hoped it would happen one day."

Smiling shyly at his mother, she admitted, "Well, then you hoped for what I assumed would never occur. After he left for the military, I finished high school in Virginia Beach, went to college, worked, even got married...then divorced." Her gaze nervously shot to Nancy's, uncertain as to how much Mitch's mom knew about her life.

Patting her uninjured leg, Nancy said, "Just like sea glass, my dear. We all take some time to let life wear off some of our rough edges and polish us to be admired. You and Mitch needed to experience life outside of Baytown."

Staring at Nancy in curiosity, Tori thought about those words. *Like sea glass. Funny, how those of us who grew up with the surf-polished slivers of beauty understand.*

Nancy continued, "Mitch was a good boy, and we were very proud of him. But he was also a bit of the town's golden boy. All those kids in that group were special. You know, as parents you always hope your children make good friends, and Ed and I certainly got our wish. The group of young men the town affectionately nicknamed the Baytown Boys, were good kids. But Mitch needed to mature. It terrifies a mother when her son goes off to war, but he needed the opportunity to grow. To become one of many...not just the leader of a small-town group of kids. He had to learn fear to become fearless. Learn to serve to know how to lead. He needed to learn loneliness to know who he wanted to be with. He needed to work in a big job in a big city to learn that, for him, the small town was where he wanted to be."

Nancy continued to smile at Tori as she said, "And I have a feeling you needed your life experiences to shape you into the young woman that's ready to have a relationship with Mitch."

"My grandmother used to talk about sea glass the same way," Tori admitted. Sighing, she added, "Sea glass is what Katelyn, Jillian, and I were out looking for this morning. I'm glad neither of them was hit."

Nancy began to say something, but halted, hating to give voice to her fears...and what she knew her son assumed.

Tori watched Nancy's face carefully, reading her easily. "You think I was hit on purpose, don't you? That's what they all think."

Reaching out to grasp Tori's hand again, giving it a gentle squeeze, Nancy replied, "Sweetie, I was the daughter-in-law to a police officer and chief, and then the wife of one, and now the mother of another. Believe me when I say it doesn't help to speculate on something until the evidence is in." She hesitated and then added, "But you need to be very vigilant. I know that is what Mitch wants for you as well."

Standing, Nancy took Tori's empty glass and headed to the kitchen to refill it, returning a moment later. "Now, is there someone we should call? Your mom, perhaps?"

"Oh, goodness, no. I wouldn't want to bother her." Seeing Nancy's surprised face, Tori added, "She hasn't been feeling well lately, so this would only be unnecessarily worrisome." She watched Nancy's understanding nod, and said, "It's no secret mom and I aren't overly close. I love her and know she loves me, but we have always been so different. Vanessa and she were more alike."

Nancy plopped back down in the chair opposite the sofa and nodded. "Yes, I remember that about her. Vanessa was more like Vera, and you always took after your father's side of the family. He loved Baytown, and I always thought he left only because Vera wanted to live a more upscale life." She immediately leaned forward, "Please forgive me if that was impertinent."

Laughing, Tori replied, "Oh, no. Believe me, I have a good grasp on what my family is like. Vanessa and mom were two peas in a pod; that's why my sister rarely spent time here." Sighing, she added, "My summers here with grandma…and my Baytown friends, were the best times of my life." Looking at Nancy, she said, "I'm going to be very candid, Mrs. Evans, and I hope this doesn't offend you, but, well…my divorce was because my husband slept with my sister."

Eyes bugging, Nancy barked, "What? You're kidding!"

Realizing she could speak about it without grimacing, she shrugged. "Both said it was over, but I left him the night I found out and filed for divorce the next day. I told him if I didn't get the divorce, I'd go public, and his business reputation would take a hit. I haven't spoken to my sister in over a year…until she showed up last week, but I closed the door on her."

"May I be so bold as to ask about your mother's reaction to all of this?"

Now the grimace broke free. Sighing heavily, Tori said, "Mom…was hurt and angry with me divorcing Thomas, but I couldn't tell her why." Rushing on as she observed Nancy's wide-eyed, incredulous look, she added, "I told mom that I didn't expect her to choose, but I would no longer be around Vanessa because she had hurt me irrevocably and…I think I knew that mom would always have wanted me to forgive and forget Vanessa's transgression." Looking up at Nancy, she added, "It would have killed me to have listened to mom take Vanessa's side just for the sake of appearances, so I never told her."

Before Nancy could reply, the front door burst open, and Ed stalked into the room. His worried gaze moved quickly to Tori, visually assessing her before landing on his wife. Nancy leaped up to hurry over and rested her hand on her husband's chest.

"Ed, I know you're frustrated, but please...don't make me worry about you."

Tori smiled as his face softened and his hand smoothed Nancy's cheek.

"I'm good, I promise. I did all I could and decided I needed to be here at the house taking care of you two." Dropping his gaze back to Tori, he asked, "You doing okay, darlin'?"

"I'm fine. I took a little nap and then Nancy and I've been talking." Her gaze implored him as she asked, "What can you tell me?"

Sighing, he sat down in a chair, Nancy settling on the arm of it with her hand resting on his shoulder. "They found the bullet near the site where you were shot. Wasn't long range ammunition, so the person must have been just over the dunes."

"So, it wasn't a hunter by mistake," Tori said, her shoulders slumping.

"Still an ongoing investigation, but my gut tells me no. Someone that close, shooting over the top of the dunes...they knew what they were aiming for, and it wasn't a goose."

"But how would someone know where I was? That

makes no sense! It's not as if I go sea glass hunting there every day."

Rubbing his hand over his chin, he said, "Well, Katelyn's got a theory she talked to Mitch about." Seeing both Tori and Nancy's curious gazes on him, he quickly continued. "There was a big meeting at the pub last night about getting the almost defunct American Legion in the area revitalized and moved closer to us. The bar was crowded, and we occupied the back area, but it's all open. Anyone could have been around, listening. Katelyn remembers talking to Mitch about going sea glass hunting by the golf course. Anyone could have overheard your plans."

"But that would imply someone here wanted to harm me," Tori cried. "I don't understand!"

Nancy hopped up and rushed to her side as Ed leaned forward, "Not necessarily. The bar was crowded and, with Aiden and Brogan in the back with us, a couple of girls were handling the front. There were so many people there you wouldn't have noticed a stranger lurking about. So, we've got no idea who it could have been."

Anger coursed through Tori's veins as she fought to keep from yelling. Wishing she was off somewhere alone so she could give in to the urge to scream without fear of Mitch's parents thinking she was losing her mind, she simply pinched her lips as she looked out the front window behind the sofa.

She saw Mitch prowling up the front walk, his face resembling his father's when he walked in...*furious.*

Sucking in a deep breath, she attempted to calm herself, knowing Mitch was angry enough for both of them.

The ride to his house was mostly silent but it only took about ten minutes. She watched in fascination as they made their way down a long gravel drive to a small cabin near the ocean. She was reminded of when his grandfather was still living and kept the fishing cabin.

Katelyn had gotten her driver's license and drove me and Jillian to the beach bonfire party. Nervous, I kept checking my hair in the little mirror in my purse.

"You're gorgeous, silly," Jillian said. "Anyway, your hair will just blow around once we're on the beach."

"Who are you wanting to kiss tonight, Jillian?" Katelyn asked. "I've got my eye on Phillip Bayles."

"Yeah, well you might have to fight Stacey Usher for him."

"Nah, she cast her claws toward Mitch."

At the sound of Mitch's name, my ears perked up. I knew Mitch dated...why wouldn't he? Since I went to school in Virginia Beach and only came to Baytown for holidays and summers...it wasn't like he could be my boyfriend. But...I wish. When he's with me, it's as though we're together.

"Tori, Tori. Earth to Tori," Katelyn laughed. "I would ask where your mind was, but I bet it starts with M!"

Jillian smiled at me and said, "Don't worry. I don't think Mitch likes Stacey. She's just...convenient."

Offering a weak smile in return, all I could think about was what a horrible time I was going to have tonight. Sighing, I wondered if it was too late to have a stomachache and go home. Looking around at the cars parked outside the little cabin, I knew I had no such luck.

It did not take long to head down to the bonfire, but longer to be able to see who all was there. Aiden and Zac were already off to the side, making out with a couple of girls. Brogan was talking on the porch with some other guys, a group of giggling girls hanging desperately on their every word. But no Mitch. Sighing deeply, I hung my head. Great... he's already off with someone.

Just then, arms wrapped around me from behind and a whisper at my ear said, "Hey, beautiful. I heard you were back in town."

Grinning, I twisted around to see Mitch beaming down at me. My stomach fluttered, but not with an ache. Instead, it was filled with a type of longing I've never experienced before. His seventeenth birthday was just around the corner, and I could not imagine a more handsome man.

"Hey," I answered back. "I got here today."

"All summer?"

"Yep, I'll be here until school starts."

"Perfect, beautiful."

Then with a squeeze, he let me go, walking over to talk to Brogan. As we three girls grabbed sodas and headed down to walk on the beach for a few minutes before sitting by the fire, I chanced another glance back at him...earning a wink. Grinning, I carried his wink in my heart.

The sound of a guitar strumming and people laughing

filled the air. A volleyball was smacked back and forth across a net on the beach, and I watched as several girls shrieked when some boys kicked water on them down by the surf.

Fifteen minutes later, we walked back toward the bonfire and my overfilling heart stumbled. There was Mitch, along with many others, sitting near the fire, his back against a log, and Stacy was pressing up close to him. I felt Katelyn and Jillian bristle next to me, but as soon as his eyes landed on mine, he jumped up, a smile spreading across his face. His motion caused Stacey to almost tip over, earning another grin from me.

Mitch jogged to me, taking my hand and leading me toward the fireside. Settling us on the opposite side of the huge bonfire from Stacey, we sat next to each other. I tried not to look at her but could feel her bolts of jealousy through the fire's flames.

"Um...I think maybe someone is unhappy you're here with me," I ventured.

Mitch twisted his body so it was close to mine, while still maintaining a proper distance. "Forget her. She's always trying to get my attention. She's okay, but you're the one I've been waiting for."

Looking up at his face, I saw his twinkling eyes and more...sincerity. "I'm glad. I've been dying to be with you too."

He leaned forward and I was sure he was going to kiss me, but just then Aiden and Zac, and their two girls, all jumped in the group loudly and someone turned up the music. Disappointed, I watched as irritation crossed Mitch's face, only to be replaced by another wink, and then we settled back for the evening.

I not only carried his wink, but the almost-kiss in my heart that night.

"Tori? Babe? Are you all right?"

The sound of Mitch's worried voice broke through her memories. "Yes, yes, sorry. I guess the pain meds are making me loopy," she lied.

She waited as he walked around the front of his jeep and carefully took her in his arms. Carrying her bride-style, she felt self-conscious as he stooped to unlock the front door before carrying her into the small living room.

Setting her gently on the sofa, he bent to kiss her head before crouching on the floor in front of her. Scooting over, careful of her leg, she patted the sofa next to her and said, "Mitch, please stop fussing. Talk to me. Tell me what's going on."

"Don't want to hurt you, babe, so I'll sit here and just be close." With that, he pulled the coffee table over so, as he perched on it, he was right in her space. Sighing, he said, "We scoured the beach and found the bullet. It was not from a rifle but from a gun. The Dunes' manager said that other than a few early-bird golfers, there was no one else on the golf courses. He also said The Dunes' community was not having any hunters for geese until the fall. The security guard has a record of who came to play golf, but there were some other cars with Dune's Resort ID stickers that went through, so there's no way to find out who they were. We did have someone talk to the outgoing guests today to ask if anyone was on the course or beach and saw anything. And of course, we talked to the groundskeepers."

"And?" she asked hopefully.

Blowing out a frustrated breath, he shook his head. "Nothing so far."

Shoulders slumping, she said, "Oh." Lifting her eyes back to his, she asked, "Who would want to do this? I'm nobody. Absolutely nobody."

"Babe, I don't know yet, but you aren't nobody," he replied, tucking a strand of her hair behind her ear as he gazed deeply into her blue eyes.

Taking a big breath, she sat up straighter and said, "Okay, then let's look at this logically. If I die, my mom will get everything, and I talked to her a couple of weeks ago, and we're fine. Maybe not the closest of relationships, but we're fine. So, no one benefits from my death." Her voice rose with each word.

"Shhh," he said, placing a finger over her lips. "We're not doing this now, babe. You need to rest, and I've been processing the intel all day." Leaning forward to replace his finger with his lips, he said, "Let's get you to bed. I want to hold you close all night and pretend that I did not spend part of my day watching you bleeding from a gunshot wound."

22

Mitch indulged in what he wanted by holding Tori all night, but sleep did not come easily. Even the sight of her in his large Army T-shirt was not enough to knock out the image of her lying in the cart, blood running down her leg. The pain pill she took made her fall asleep quickly, but every time she turned and bumped her leg she groaned in her sleep. Finally, he carefully slipped out of bed and pulled on a pair of old FBI sweatpants and headed through the house and out onto the back deck.

Standing at the rail, watching the undulating surf in the moonlight, he breathed deeply. The clean, fresh air of the Bay filled his lungs and helped to clear his mind of the events of the day, filling his thoughts instead with a long-forgotten memory.

"Marco!"

"Polo!"

The screams of us kids in the bay, splashing around, filled the air. For as long as I could remember, we'd spent our summers in the water and on the beach when we weren't at the ball fields. At thirteen, I wondered if this would be our last summer of freedom since I hoped to get a job next summer.

I kept my eye on Aiden, who had his eyes closed while yelling "Marco!", attempting to find the others so he could tag them. He kept moving closer and closer to Tori. Cheating Aiden—he must be peeking!

I moved closer to her, wanting to protect her, when she suddenly disappeared under the surf. Twisting around and around, I searched for her, my heart pounding. Just when I was about to yell for the others to look for her, she popped up fifteen feet further in the bay.

My breath left me in a whoosh as I observed her huge smile. Aiden and the others forgotten, I dove under the water and swam toward her. Surfacing a foot in front of her, she squealed in surprise. Before she dove under again, I grabbed her arms.

"You shouldn't swim out too far, Tori," I warned. "It can be dangerous."

Wiping the water droplets from her eyes, she smiled at me. "But I've seen you swim out here."

"Yeah, but I swim out here all the time. I've learned how."

Her face scrunched as she considered my boast. "Will you teach me? I want to swim as good as you do."

Grinning in pride, I let go of her arms, swimming in a circle around her. "Sure, I can teach you, but you're a girl, so you can't swim as good as me."

*At that, she punched me in the arm, and I was surprised...
it hurt. Startled, I frowned—but only for a second, 'cause the
sweet smile on her face made my heart beat faster. "Well,
maybe I'm wrong," I admitted. "I'll teach you and then we'll
race."*

"You're on!" she laughed.

*"Hey, you two! You gonna make goo-goo eyes at each
other or join the rest of us?" Brogan yelled.*

*Shooting him a warning glare, I watched as Tori swam
back toward the game before I followed.*

*The rest of the summer, Tori and I met almost every day
and swam in the bay. Never going out too far, I taught her
about riptides, staying away from piers and rocks, and
judging how far from shore she was. And she surprised me.
By the end of the summer, I still won the race, but she wasn't
too far behind.*

*"Swimming in the ocean isn't easy, but you're a really
good swimmer, Tori. You're better than most of the boys I
know," I admitted, admiring the way her smile made her face
light up.*

*Swimming up to her, offering what I convinced myself
was nothing more than a congratulatory hug, I could not stop
the thought that this girl felt perfect in my arms.*

Mitch, still standing at the rail, staring out toward the
bay, relishing the calm, remembered another night,
many years before, when he saw Tori as a teenager
standing on this very deck. It was her first night of
summer vacation that year and he had been anxiously

waiting to spend time with her. Seeing her standing at the rail, looking for someone...*hopefully me*...he had come up behind her and had wrapped his arms around her from behind.

It had not escaped his adolescent awareness that when he tucked her close, her breasts were pressed against his arm, and he had forced himself to be a gentleman. Not too much later, another girl had come over trying to claim his attention, but for him it had always been Tori.

Dropping his chin to his chest, he sighed again. *I now finally have her...and someone is trying to kill her. What the hell am I missing?*

No answers came in the night, but with another deep breath of fresh air, he slipped back inside and into bed, drawing her closely once more.

The next morning, Tori insisted that Mitch take her to the Sea Glass Inn, which he agreed to only because Jason and Jillian would be there. Once he had her settled, he bypassed the station and headed to a small business on one of the side streets. Pulling up to the front of Harrison Investigations, he climbed out of his jeep and made his way to the front door. Glad to find it open, he stepped inside and saw a small reception area with a desk where a receptionist could sit. Behind that appeared to be a short hall with four open doors.

Gareth popped out of one, a nod of acknowledgment as soon as he recognized Mitch. "Come on back, Chief Evans."

"Please, call me Mitch, and thank you." Walking toward the door, he quickly ascertained the room directly across from Gareth's office was a small conference room and the other two doors led to a bathroom and small staffroom.

Watching Mitch's gaze move around, Gareth laughed. "I've got what I need for now, except for a receptionist. If you know of anyone looking for a part time job, let me know."

Taking a seat in Gareth's office, Mitch said, "I know your time is important and, God knows, I don't have much time either, so let me get right to the point." Seeing Gareth's nod and interest, he said, "I haven't been here long enough to delve into all the ins and outs of what computer programs I have at my disposal. I've only got four officers, and, as it is the summer, I have to keep one of them patrolling the town. I'd like to hire you to do some computer digging for me."

"Whatcha need?"

"The only motive for someone wanting Tori dead would be someone after her money...or rather the Sea Glass Inn. The beachfront property, the early 1900's brick home, the furnishings, and antiques...all are valued at about a million dollars. I need a little more digging into who might benefit."

"Anyone in town got a motive? Is there something in the old house? Something hidden? Could it be a former disgruntled guest?" Gareth asked.

Shaking his head, Mitch said, "At this point, we're considering anything and everything, but I still feel like it has to do with the inheritance. If you could do more digging into Thomas Porter and Vanessa Hurkamp that'd be helpful. I'll be heading over the bridge to visit Tori's mother today so send me an email with anything you uncover."

Mitch appeared thoughtful for a moment until Gareth prompted, "Anything else?"

Meeting the other man's gaze, he asked, "What are your thoughts about Silas Mills?"

"Man's a prick!" came the growled response. "He's the one who won't let me have a regular sign outside my business...says that a private investigation company has a negative connotation to visitors."

Lifting his eyebrows, Mitch barked out a laugh, shaking his head. "Yeah, sounds about like my impression of him."

"Any particular reason you brought him up?"

"He's made a couple of comments about Tori and the Inn since Dumfries' murder. Made me think that he'd step up to get his hands on the Sea Glass Inn if he could, just to keep any negative press about the town from getting out. Rubs me the wrong way."

"Yep, 'bout my opinion as well. The mayor acts like we're supposedly lucky to get him...but I'll tell you, there's a lot of rumblings. Some of the businesses on the side streets can't have their boardwalk signs on the sidewalks. And he's got some crazy idea about the parking on Main Street."

"Do me a favor, do a little digging on him as well," Mitch requested. "Something about him just doesn't strike me as right."

Shaking hands, Mitch left the PI's office, making his way to the Police Department with a detour by Jillian's coffee shop. Assuring his cousin that Tori was all right and gaining Jillian's promise to spend the afternoon with Tori, he headed on his way.

Once inside the station, Mildred looked up at him, her lips pinched. "The mayor wants to talk to you, but I told him you were out."

"And I am," Mitch replied. "I'm meeting Burt here in about five minutes, and then we're heading over the bridge to Virginia Beach."

A moment later, walking out of his office with his tablet, Mitch ran into Corwin.

"You're a hard man to get hold of," the red faced, puffing mayor said. "I want to know what's going on with the investigation. We can't have people being shot on our beaches!"

"Mayor," Mitch bit out. "Someone is targeting Ms. Bradford, not shooting at vacationers on the public beach."

"Well, we never had these problems until she moved back and took over the Sea Glass—"

Leaning closer, Mitch stepped into Corwin's space. "Don't know what bug is up your ass about Tori, but you're beginning to sound more like the new city manager's crony. Leave the detective work to me and stay the fuck out of my business...or we're going to have problems."

Backpedaling, Corwin immediately clamped his mouth shut. Grimacing, he said, "I'm not an underling of Silas Mills."

"Then grow a pair and act like it," Mitch advised, before turning on his heels and stalking toward the door.

Mitch knocked on the door of a modest home in an older neighborhood in Virginia Beach. As he waited for the door to open, he wondered if she hired out the yard work; it was perfectly manicured.

Tori's mother opened the door, and he stood shocked. Her appearance was much older than he remembered, and he had to remind himself that he had not seen her in almost fifteen years. Compared to his mother, she either had not aged well or was more ill than Tori thought.

"Come in, Mitch…I mean, Chief Evans," she invited, her arm sweeping the air toward the living room.

Vera Bradford settled herself on the sofa, her thin hands in her lap. Her hair, neatly coiffed, framed a face that at one time had been beautiful. Now, she appeared fragile.

"It's been a long time since I've seen you," she began. "Not since you were a child, I'm sure. I…" she hesitated, "haven't traveled over to Baytown in quite a while."

"Mrs. Bradford, I don't want to give you a shock, but

I came today because I'm investigating two attempts on Tori's life."

She blinked, saying nothing. Then blinked again, as though the words were heard but not understood. Mitch grew concerned as she opened her mouth several times without saying anything, her appearance fish-like.

"May I get you some water?"

Clearing her throat, she gasped, "No, no. It's…it's just that…I don't understand."

"When was the last time you spoke with Tori?"

Her hand fluttered about her neck, eyes darting as her mind searched before she replied, "About two weeks ago. I had gone to the doctor, and she called."

"I need to ask you some difficult questions, Mrs. Bradford. Are you sure you don't want a glass of water before we begin?"

"Perhaps I'd better," she agreed. Before Mitch could stand, she called out, "Cora!" A small woman appeared, and she asked for iced tea for the two of them. A moment later, the woman returned with two tall glasses of the refreshment. Tori's mother took a long sip, seeming to revive.

"Chief Evans, I simply cannot believe that anyone would want to harm Victoria. She's a harmless girl, if somewhat fanciful. Her sister was always much more level-headed."

Her description caught Mitch off guard and his eyes darted back to hers. "Fanciful? Tori?"

"Why, yes. As a child Victoria loved Baytown and living with her grandmother. Vanessa preferred golf and tennis lessons at the country club. We didn't belong, you understand, but we could pay for tennis and golf lessons, which afforded us use of their facilities. Including the pool, which she always tried to use to her full advantage. But Victoria...she refused to better herself."

"I take it you didn't approve of how she spent her summers?"

Pinching her lips, Mrs. Bradford gazed out of the window for a moment, and as Mitch's eyes followed hers, he noticed a lawn-care service pull up out front, men piling out of the truck like clowns from a Volkswagen.

"When I met Victoria and Vanessa's father, I was a senior in college and he was a few years older, already working for a bank in Virginia Beach. I thought he was quite the catch. After dating for a while, he was so excited to take me to meet his mother; his father had already passed away. We drove over that God-awful bridge out to the Eastern Shore." Sniffing delicately, she said, "I admit the Inn was beyond beautiful, and I was thrilled to see it...but the town...the rundown, almost non-existent town! How anyone lives there, I'll never understand!"

Deciding to let her talk instead of peppering her with questions, Mitch sat back, his expression blank.

"I hated it. The golf course community had not been built yet and the town was just dismal. I convinced myself that as long as we kept our visits there short, I could accept it." Smoothing her hands down her skirt, she continued, "It was only after we had been married for several years that Reginald first mentioned the idea of moving there! I told him I would never, ever consider a move to the Eastern Shore. Oh, we argued about it, Chief Evans. I won out, of course. After all, I wanted more for my daughters than to settle for such a provincial way of life."

She cast her glance out the window, her tired but exacting gaze noting the men outside working. Turning back to Mitch, she said, "When Victoria was ten years old, Reginald died of a sudden heart attack. Can you imagine if we had moved? My God, I would have had two children stuck in that town!"

Mitch wanted to be offended, but knew his response when he was younger had been much the same... Baytown at that time was unimpressive. Nodding his encouragement, he listened carefully.

"Reginald's life insurance paid off this house, but there was not much left over. I didn't want to work outside the home, so things were a bit tight. We still couldn't afford the country club, but I went as Vanessa took lessons...at one time I hoped I would catch someone's eyes but," her lips pursed, "that didn't happen, so I pinned my hopes on my daughters. Vanessa, like me, wanted the finer things in life. It took her years," she sniffed delicately, "and a couple of unfortunate marriages, but she finally landed Nelson and what a dream it has been, having him as a son-in-law."

She beamed, her whole countenance radiating. Sweeping her hand around, she said, "He's been so generous. Cora and my landscapers come at his request. He does such sweet little things to make my life better."

Her face settled into a pleasant smile, a few years sliding away. Mitch observed as her face began to take on a frown and knew the instant she was thinking of Tori.

"But Victoria never had such aspirations. She preferred spending the summers with her grandmother. I had hoped the beauty of the Inn, and the antiques would impress her, but she preferred to bake goodies in the kitchen or run rampant around the town with her so-called frien—um," her gaze darted to Mitch, her cheeks pinking. "I apologize, Chief Evans, I...well..."

"No need to apologize, Mrs. Bradford. You are entitled to your opinion, and I welcome any observations you have that will assist me in my case."

At that, her face gathered storm clouds. "Why someone would want to harm Victoria is completely beyond me! She is a sweet girl, as I said, if fanciful. Her only chance at bettering herself was when she married that darling Thomas Porter. Now there was another man who was an excellent son-in-law. So conciliatory, so mannerly, so personable. And what did Victoria do? Divorce him! And for what? She only said he had been caught in an indiscretion! Have you ever heard anything so ridiculous in all your life? I mean, what man hasn't had his little flings?"

Mitch, rooted to his chair, was stunned. Actually, dumbstruck. He knew Tori's mother had not been very nurturing, but Mrs. Bradford's callousness surprised him. *But it also tells me Tori never told her mother that Thomas had been unfaithful with Vanessa.*

"Both Thomas and Nelson were going places...well, Nelson was older and already established, but I would have had both daughters married well, and to men who would have helped care for me. Now, with Victoria's selfishness, I don't have Thomas in my life anymore."

The silence created was uncomfortable as Mitch pondered his next line of inquiry. "Mrs. Bradford, if Tori dies and has no heirs, then her estate would come to you. Have you ever considered that?"

Barking out a socially rude noise, she replied, "What on earth would I do with an Inn located in an ungodly part of Virginia? I'm certainly not going to move there and run it!"

"Do you not realize the property and its contents are worth about a million dollars?"

At that pronouncement, Mrs. Bradford's head swung around as she pierced Mitch with her gaze. *Agog.* That was the only term Mitch could think of to describe her expression.

"I...well...I never...I hadn't thought..." she floundered.

"So, now, what I want to know is, in light of that information, do you have a different opinion as to who might want to see Tori dead?"

"No! Certainly not me...I love Victoria as I love Vanessa." Her breathing grew rapidly as she leaned forward, "Chief Evans, I know it seems as though I might not, but I do. It's just, in my opinion, Victoria has not always made wise choices and, well, Vanessa was always so much more compliant, so much more like me. But I have no idea who might want to harm Victoria. I wish she'd have called me."

"She mentioned you had been...unwell..." he prompted.

"Yes, I seem to have had a stomach bug for several months now. I have been to a specialist, but they think I just have a nervous constitution. I am on some medication for heartburn, which seems to help. My internist seems to think I may have some complications from having the flu. Do you think that's why she hasn't told me of what is going on?"

She stared at him, searching for acceptance, and Mitch found himself understanding Tori so much. Her mother was irritating. Self absorbed. Totally clueless. But, ultimately, not malicious. Sighing, he nodded and said, "Yes, ma'am. I'm sure that's it."

Leaning back, her face was now relaxed and once more pleasant. "Good, I'll be sure to call her this weekend."

"One last question, Mrs. Bradford. If you die, who will inherit your estate?"

"Oh, goodness, other than this house, I have very little," she replied.

"Yes, but who is in your Will?"

Her brow crinkled in confusion, then she looked up to where Mitch was standing, "Why, my daughters of course."

Smiling, he thanked her as he headed back out of her

house and began the drive over the bridge back to Baytown, his mind whirling with possibilities. *Tori never told her mom about Vanessa and Thomas' infidelity. Vanessa would inherit everything if Tori and her mother both died. Does Nelson know of his wife's affair with her brother-in-law? How far would Vanessa go to keep it quiet...or to inherit the estate? Is Thomas involved in some way? Is there the possibility he and Vanessa have something ongoing?*

Crossing over to the Eastern Shore usually brought a sense of peace to Mitch...the feeling he had moved from the noisy, crowded land-of-the-incessant-strip-malls to a place where much was left as God intended. But today? His mind could not appreciate the beauty when his thoughts were filled with only one thought—*who wants Tori dead?*

23

Tori limped stiff-legged from the kitchen into the dining room where Jillian and Jason were cleaning up the breakfast dishes and platters. Seeing Jillian open her mouth, Tori threw her hand up, and said, "Nope. Don't say it. I'm resting, but I can't sit around all day. Anyway, I need to exercise my leg. Doctor's orders."

Jason laughed as he passed by her on his way into the kitchen.

"Well, excuse me for being worried," Jillian snapped, then immediately apologized. "Oh, I'm sorry. I'm just on edge for you, Tori."

The two women hugged, both resting their heads on each other's shoulders for a moment.

"I know," Tori confessed. "It still doesn't seem real. I feel as though I've been caught up in some horrible joke. Now, a guest is dead, and I've been shot. My brain isn't catching up to what's happening around me."

A knock on the door had both women jerking apart, hands still clasped. Jason hustled into the hall, peering through the security viewer. Breathing easier, he opened the door, allowing Grant entry.

Grant's eyes landed on Jillian and his smile widened. "Hey," he called out.

She returned his greeting politely, then walked to the kitchen, her arms piled with dishes.

Grant's smile dropped slightly as he watched her move away, before turning back to Tori. "How're you holding up?"

Swinging her curious gaze from Jillian's retreating back to Grant, she smiled. "I'm really doing fine. Have you heard from Mitch yet?"

"I know you're dying to talk to him, since he was visiting your mother this morning, but I haven't heard. He should be back soon." Nodding toward Jason, he said, "I've heard through the grapevine that town residents are excited to have a mechanic interested in coming to town. I think if the town council tries to give you any grief, the residents'll back you up."

Grinning, Jason clapped his hands, rubbing them together as he said, "Good news, man. I've been itching to get my hands back in the business."

"Believe it or not, when word got out about you being a veteran and wanting to help with the American Legion project, I've even heard that a tattoo shop shouldn't be too hard for you to obtain the proper permits."

"Hell, yeah!" Jason's grin broke out into a full-blown, teeth-showing smile.

With a glance down the hall toward the kitchen, Grant nodded toward Tori as he said his goodbyes. Closing the door behind him, Tori turned to smile at Jason.

"Congratulations," she said, placing her hand on his arm as her gaze dropped to his tattooed sleeve. "I haven't even told you that I think your designs are beautiful."

"Thanks," Jason said, holding his arms out. "I did the designs, and a buddy did the actual work. Got it finished when I got out of the service." Dropping his arms, he asked, "You ever get a tat?"

"Oh, no!" she laughed, "I pass out at the sight of blood...and needles. I'd be the last person to ever get a tattoo! But if I were, I'd trust you."

"Fair enough," he grinned. "Well, why don't you rest, and I'll check on the guest rooms upstairs."

Smiling her thanks, she settled on the sofa, waiting for Mitch to come by. As she was drifting off, her phone vibrated, causing her to jolt. Looking down, she did not recognize the number. Answering, she discovered Thomas was on the other end of the line...*great, just great.*

"Thomas, I don't know why you are call—"

"Please, Tori, I really want to see you. I need to see you."

The pleading in his voice gave her pause. A slight pause, but a pause nonetheless. *What could he possibly want? And from what Mitch reported, I hardly think Thomas's new fiancé wants him visiting.*

Her silence gave him another opportunity to press his advantage. "I understand you don't want to see me, but I really want to meet with you. Somewhere… anywhere we have a chance to talk for a few minutes."

"Look, I've had a…slight injury and am somewhat housebound for a few days," she replied, not wanting him to know what was going on. "If you want to come by in a couple of days, I'll give you fifteen minutes. That's all."

"I'll take it and, I promise, it'll be worth your while."

She disconnected without answering, tossing the phone onto the coffee table as Mitch drove into the driveway. Jumping up without thinking, she winced. *Damn!*

By the time she hobbled to the front door, Mitch was already there. Her gaze drifted over him, the view always eye-catching. From his cowboy boots, up his khakis and to the navy BPD polo fitted over his thick chest. His attractive face split into a grin as he swept her into his muscular arms.

"Hey babe," he greeted. "You been resting?"

"Yes, and I'm tired of sitting. Anyway, my leg was getting stiff so I'm trying to stretch it some." Searching his face, she asked, "How was it? I can't tell by your expression. How was mom?"

Brushing strands of hair behind her ear, he was about to answer when Jillian came from the back.

Greeting his cousin, he excused himself for a moment as his phone vibrated.

As Mitch walked back to the front porch, Tori grabbed Jillian, "Hey, what's going on between you and Grant?"

Eyes wide, Jillian tossed her long blonde hair over her shoulder and, avoiding Tori's gaze, shrugged.

"Come on, girlfriend," Tori cajoled. Seeing Jillian's reticence, she added, "It's okay if you don't want to talk about it, but just know I'm here for you."

That brought Jillian's eyes back to Tori's and she sighed heavily. "I've been crazy about Grant for as long as I can remember...even back in high school."

Shocked, Tori admitted, "I knew that back then, but you've never said anything or even indicated that your feelings still went that way."

Jillian dropped her head down, staring at her feet for a moment before lifting her gaze back to Tori's. "You know the feeling of wanting something so bad you think you can't breathe without it? And yet you know it'll never be yours?" Seeing Tori's understanding expression, Jillian continued. "Of course you do. That's how it was for you and Mitch. That's how I've felt about Grant ever since he came back from the military and finished his degree in police science. Once he came back to Baytown, I thought for a fleeting second, we might have a chance."

"And you don't think that anymore?" Tori asked, her heart breaking.

Jillian's eyes filled with sadness as she shook her

head. "Nope. For the past few years, since he moved back...I've been relegated to the friend-only zone. The barren, wasteland, friend-only zone. And what's worse, I've had to watch him as he's dated several women, not to mention the one-night-fucks of summer visitors."

Before Tori had a chance to throw out her opinion, Mitch walked back into the Inn. Jillian pasted a huge, albeit fake, grin on her face and tossed her goodbyes out before leaving quickly.

Tori, torn, wanting to help her friend, knew Mitch needed her attention now. He walked right back into her arms again.

"We've got lots to choose from for lunch today," she said. "Seems like half the town brought over food."

"Whatever's fine with me. We'll talk and then I've got Katelyn coming to spend the afternoon with you."

"God, I hate having babysitters," Tori complained, limping into the kitchen.

Several minutes later, the two were ensconced at the family table in the kitchen eating chicken casserole, as Mitch ran down the interview with Tori's mother.

Nothing he told her gave her a surprise...or a shock. "Honey, you have to understand...mom never loved Vanessa more than me, but my sister was easier for her to understand. I was like my father and Vanessa was like mom. She was perfectly happy to leave me here for the summers because I loved it and would have made her life miserable if she'd forced me to take tennis lessons at the country club. Vanessa was a social climber...and I also know that came from mom as well."

Mitch observed her, hating to ask the next question. "Babe, why didn't you tell your mom about Vanessa and Thomas?"

A grimace shot across her face before being replaced with a deep sigh. Spearing a helpless piece of chicken as she toyed with her food, she admitted, "Even though mom loved me...I knew Vanessa was her golden girl. If mom had even hinted to me that I should ignore what happened just to hang on to Thomas...I don't think I could have taken it. It would have pierced my heart. So, it was easier not to say anything."

"Doesn't she wonder about the distant relationship you have with Vanessa?"

"My sister and I never exactly got together for Thanksgiving dinners...at least not since becoming adults. She and her revolving door of husbands are usually off on a cruise or some holiday trip. Thomas and I would take mom out to eat." Shrugging, she added, "Mom was never the domestic type. Last year, I came here and spent it with grandma. She had one childless couple staying in the Inn and we had a lovely celebration."

The silence stretched between them until she felt she would snap with the tension. "Mitch, you've been asking me a lot of questions, but what did you find out about any suspicions you have?"

"I agree with you that it is highly unlikely your mother had anything to do with any of this...but she did confirm you and Vanessa would inherit everything when she dies."

"So? That can't be unusual. And mom has little other than the house she lives in."

"No...but if something happens to you, your mom would get your estate and then, if something happened to her, it would go to Vanessa."

Eyes wide open, Tori shook her head. "It just can't be my sister."

Katelyn's voice could be heard from the front as Mitch's phone vibrated again, and he cast a regretful glance toward her. Bending over, he gave her a quick kiss and promised, "I'll be in your bed tonight," earning him a wicked smile.

Good, she mouthed as he answered his phone. Nodding toward Katelyn, he headed back to work. As he drove to the center of town he thought, *time to find out what skeletons Gareth has dug up.*

After Mitch left, Tori turned to Katelyn and said, "Grab some lemonade, let's talk!" After settling in on the shaded back patio, Katelyn turned her curious gaze toward Tori.

"Look, I don't want you to reveal any private info, but Jillian was here earlier, and Grant dropped by—"

Katelyn responded with an eye roll before Tori could finish. "And Jillian wasn't too happy, right?"

Nodding, Tori agreed. "She told me a little but, well, I was curious."

Taking a deep sip of the tart lemonade, Katelyn

leaned back in her chair and elevated her feet onto the footstool as though settling in for a long talk. "When we were growing up, the Baytown Boys spanned more than one year in school, but the group that seemed to be the tightest was Mitch, Grant, Callan, Zac, Aiden, and Brogan. You were the different one...not being related to any of them. I think at one time, they probably all had the hots for you, but you only had eyes for Mitch and the others respected that. Hell, it's not like they were hard up!"

Following suit, Tori lifted her leg to the footstool, moving around slightly to find a comfortable position before turning her full attention back to her friend.

"For me, I was always just Aiden and Brogan's little sister, so none of them would ever look at me, knowing those two would probably kick their asses. Phillip was the teenage crush I hoped would come back and declare his everlasting love for me...but, well, that wasn't meant to be. Zac and I have gotten close, but just friendship close, which is all either of us want. For Jillian, she fell for Grant a long time ago, but she was Mitch's little cousin to the guys. But they did date in high school before he graduated and left for the Army." Casting her eyes out toward the yard, she added, "I thought at one time when he came back, they might get together. But all the boys came back with some heavy memories, and I heard him and Jillian arguing one night at the bar a couple of years ago. Since then...just friends."

"I hate that for her," Tori sighed, thinking of her burgeoning relationship with Mitch.

"Me too, but she puts on a great game face when we're all together. She says she'd rather be his friend than nothing at all, but I know it stings."

For a few minutes, the two sat, sipping lemonade and listening to the birds chirping. Finally, turning back to Katelyn, Tori asked, "And you? I know at one time you wanted to escape this town, but here you are. Anyone keeping you here?"

Tucking her long black hair behind her ears, Katelyn smiled. "Nah – just family. I told you that when my brothers left for the military, I didn't leave even when I graduated. Just couldn't leave my parents. And then, by the time Aiden and Brogan came back and took over the bar, I wanted to stay close. Keep an eye on them. And now? I'm twenty-nine and too old in my mind to start over anywhere else. Plus," she winked, "I love Baytown. I can't imagine living anywhere else. Who knows? Someone may come along that catches my eye!"

"Gareth?" Mitch called out.

"Come on in," Gareth replied, sticking his head out of his office. "Sorry, I'm scarfing down a burger from the diner, but I've got some info for you."

Mitch walked into the office, taking a seat across from Gareth, who was wadding up the hamburger wrapper and tossing it into the trashcan. "You found something for me?" he asked.

"I've been looking at the mom, the sister, and the ex-husband. I've only begun to scratch the surface, but I'm looking into their finances. What I've found so far on the mom is that she owns the home she lives in—looks like she paid it off when her husband passed away. She has a small investment account from the remainder of his insurance policy and so she lives well, although modestly. Can't find an employment record for her, but I'll still look."

Interrupting, Mitch added, "You won't find one. She told me this morning she didn't work outside of the home when the girls were younger nor after she became a widow."

Gareth made a note on his pad of paper that he used for scribbling, and then continued. "I'll keep looking deeper into the mother because sometimes things are hidden under layers, but perhaps she is just what she seems to be...a woman of a modest, fixed income."

"And one who would like to be more, according to what she told me." Seeing Gareth look up at him, he explained, "She wanted more of a country club exis-tence and pinned her hopes on both Vanessa and Tori to help her achieve that goal. Tori disappointed but it seems Vanessa did not."

Nodding, Gareth looked back down at his pad as he continued to scribble. Glancing back up, he asked, "Do you want to hear about Vanessa first or the ex-husband?"

"Let's go with the sister first. I'll save Thomas for the end," Mitch replied, his lips pinched in irritation.

"Okay. Vanessa Hurkamp. She and Nelson Hurkamp

married about six months ago after meeting at the most exclusive country club in Virginia Beach. She was not a member but was there with a friend. He is ten years her senior and a financial planner that, from all accounts, appears to do very well for himself. You've seen their home, so you know they live in an expensive, upscale, gated community neighborhood. Vanessa fills her time with charity events and social activities. Their finances, on the surface, do not raise any red flags but, usually, the richer a person is the more they can bury their assets under layers of bullshit accounts. This can be to hide some from taxes or for more nefarious reasons. On the other hand, they can be living in a make-believe world, where they give off every image of being wealthy, but underneath, they are actually living in a house of cards that could come tumbling down at any time."

"Pre-nup?"

"Oh, yeah. She screws around, she gets nothing."

Nodding, Mitch wondered how solvent the Hurkamps were, but trusted Gareth to dig deeper to find what he could. As he pondered, he felt the man's stare on him, realizing it was time to talk about Thomas.

"Now for the ex-husband. Thomas and Tori were married for two years, having met through a mutual friend. They lived in a modest house in Richmond. I haven't had a chance to check with any former neighbors but, again, on the surface there didn't appear to be any major problems. They shared a joint checking account but, like many couples, they maintained separate savings accounts. I found there was some transference of funds from one savings account to the other occasionally, but not enough to raise any concerns, such as he was siphoning money off of her. When they divorced, they paid off the legal fees from his savings account, sold the house and split the profits." Gareth chuckled and added, "It also appears she didn't pay him the real estate agent's fee for having sold their own home."

Mitch grinned knowing that Tori, with the grounds of adultery, had Thomas by the balls. Gazing back up, he asked, "What else?"

"He's dated some and, as you already know, he's now engaged to a woman who appears to be somewhat of a social climber. She comes from a fairly poor background but, with looks and a few good connections, I think she has now landed someone she thinks will take her to the social heights she would like to achieve."

Shaking his head, Mitch replied, "Sounds like he's marrying someone that was very much like his former sister-in-law--the same one he had an affair with and lost his marriage over. I need to dig more into her as we focus on Thomas."

"I had the same thought. Now, here is where it gets a little more interesting. Thomas has remained somewhat solvent during the housing crisis, but his investment accounts have taken a hit. I'm not sure, but I see withdrawals and some deposits that don't jive with his income. My guess is perhaps he's trying to play catch up with his money."

"Gambling?" Mitch asked, leaning forward, pinning Gareth with a stare.

"Don't know, but that's what I'll be looking into next."

Standing, Mitch shook his hand. "Can't thank you enough. Keep track of your hours, of course, and I'll make sure you're paid."

Placing his hands on his hips, Gareth said, "I'll give you a discounted rate." Throwing up his hand before Mitch could retort, he explained, "Got a new business started here and not a lot of people walking through the door. So far, Mrs. Parson wanted to know if I could figure out who her husband was cattin' around with and the Johnson kids wanted to know if I could find their actual cat that was lost."

Mitch threw his head back and laughed. "Watch out for Mrs. Parson. If she gets really mad at her Henry, she'll go after him with a frying pan, and the neighbors will have to call us."

"Thanks for the warning. I'll stay on her good side," Gareth laughed. "So anyway, I want to help you out, so I'll give you a good price on my services."

"I appreciate it. I'm still figuring out the police department's budget."

As Gareth escorted him to the front door, Mitch turned and looked at the empty receptionist desk. "You know, if you're still looking for someone competent to help you out part-time, you might want to consider

Katelyn MacFarlane. She works early mornings at the diner and then late afternoons or evenings at her brothers' bar. She might like having something a little different to do and she'd be good. At least you can consider it."

Watching the Chief walk to his jeep, Gareth remembered the dark-haired beauty from the last time he was at Finn's. Rubbing his chin, he pondered the idea.

24

The next morning, Mitch pulled up to the station and noted a North Heron Sheriff cruiser in the lot. Walking in, he noted Mildred smiling at a tall, dark-haired man, lean muscles stretching the short sleeves of his uniform. As the man turned his way, his eyes crinkled at the corners when his gaze met Mitch's.

"Chief Evans? Colt Hudson. Sheriff of North Heron County."

Mitch knew of the neighboring law enforcement agencies but counted it as a failing that he had not had time to meet them. A firm handshake later, he invited the man into his office.

Colt settled into a chair as Mitch sat behind his desk.

"I'm real sorry I haven't been down to meet you before now," Colt began.

Mitch shook his head in protest, and said, "Been meaning to come up myself but, I swear, the first part of my job was dealing with the mayor and every committee and organization in town and then..."

Colt's face grew serious. "Yeah, I heard about your troubles. I wanted to come down and offer my assistance whenever possible. Your dad and I worked together on a couple of cases that moved between the town of Baytown and the surrounding North Heron County."

"Good to know," Mitch admitted.

"In fact, there's not many of us on the Eastern Shore and we get together about once a month. Good officers, all of them, and we work well together. Your dad was a good man to deal with...we're all looking forward to having you in the fold."

"When's the next meeting?" Mitch asked, his eyes bright with interest.

"Next Tuesday morning. The Easton Café," Colt said. "It'll be me, you, the Easton Police Chief, Hannah Freeman, the Accawmacke County Sheriff, Liam Sullivan, the Manteague Police Chief, Wyatt Newman, and the Seaside Police Chief, Dylan Hunt."

"Sounds good," Mitch said, standing once more. "I look forward to it."

As he walked the other officer out to the lobby, they shook hands once more. Colt nodded as he turned to leave. "You need help, ...or backup, ...give a shout. We work that way out here."

Mitch watched Colt leave and smiled at the laid-back offer of assistance. Thinking of the Saints he used to work along side, he welcomed the camaraderie.

"What have you got?"

Mitch wanted to know what the other officers had discovered about the alibis for their suspects.

Grant reported, "Vanessa was at home getting ready for an event...a flower garden show, and the show checks out. She was there by ten a.m. But before that, she was at home alone. And before you ask, the house-keeper wasn't there yet. Mr. Hurkamp was not there either. He'd already left for work, and it was the house-keeper's half day off."

"According to Thomas' fiancé, he was at home getting ready for work as usual and left the house about seven a.m.," Ginny added.

"Her word can't be trusted," Burt commented, shaking his head, gaining agreement from the others. "She'd lie for him in a heartbeat."

Sam glanced over to Mitch. "I know keeping an eye on our intrepid city manager is on the down-low, but I know his lawn-care man. Got to talking to him the other day, just about how nice Silas' yard looks and what grass fertilizer he uses...you know, just shootin' the shit. Asked him how early he got to work, and he said he's there on Mondays and Thursdays by about seven-thirty a.m. Just so happens that Silas was gone early last Thursday."

"How the hell did you manage to get that info?" Ginny asked.

Chuckling, Sam admitted, "He was running a loud

blower when I saw him, and I asked if the owners minded him using such a noisy gasoline engine right next to the house. He said that he usually does it in the afternoon, but last Thursday, he noticed Mr. Mills' car was out of the driveway, so he took advantage and did it early that morning."

Shaking his head, Mitch grinned. "Good thinking."

"Chief," Sam began. "What exactly are you thinking with Silas?"

Rubbing his chin, he said, "There's something off about him. On the surface, he seems like a good catch for the town, but his comments about Tori and the Sea Glass Inn make me cautious. I don't know what his angle is, but I'm not willing to ignore it."

"How could he profit by the Inn failing?"

Still shaking his head, Mitch replied, "Don't know. I'll tell you, though, I've also got Gareth working on it."

At this, he gained cautious looks from all his staff, so he threw up his hands and said, "Hear me out. This is nothing against any of you...this is about a town that only has a police staff of five. Granted, we are a small town, but we are stretched with normal duties and petty crimes. Add a murder and attempted murder on top of that, and...we are really extending our resources. Even in the FBI I used a high-powered security and investigation firm at times. We worked well together. I've talked with Gareth, and he seems capable."

"Hate to point out the obvious, Chief, but if we're struggling as a department, how're we going to pay for a private eye?"

"Right now, I'm working on our budget and, for the time being, I'll pay for his services. For next year, I'm going to work in a line-item for his fees up to a certain point. He needs the work, and we need his research abilities. At least, until we can beef up our own."

The others nodded, accepting his explanation. Mitch glanced around the table, appreciating the unwavering support. As the others began to rise, he added, "Just wanted to add, ...I'm proud to be serving with you. I know this is a stressful beginning to my career here, but...well, thank you."

Smiles came his way as Grant said, "Mitch, we'll find out who's doing this to Tori. We will give it our all, no matter what, 'cause she's one of us...we've got her back...and yours."

As the others left the room to complete their duties or patrols, Mitch turned his gaze back to the board on the wall, Tori's picture still front and center. Staring at her beauty, he felt a familiar pang in his chest and reached his hand up to gently rub over his heart. Then he allowed his eyes to continue to roam. Thomas. Vanessa. Silas. Motive. Opportunity. Means. *What am I missing?*

Several days later, Tori made her way into the breakfast room to tidy up from the guests' morning meals. Jason had beaten her to it, his arms full of dishes.

Grinning at him, she said, "You seem comfortable

with the china. Most men are afraid they're going to break the pieces just by looking at them."

Chuckling, he passed her on his way into the kitchen where he set the delicate plates down gently. "I've been a jack-of-many-trades," he joked. "My parents ran a little diner, and I grew up washing dishes, waiting tables, and generally being an all-around clean-up guy."

"Where was home?"

A dark expression flashed across his face before he carefully schooled his features. "North Carolina. A little town...not a whole lot bigger than this place."

Tori hesitated, wanting to know more about Baytown's new resident and rapidly becoming new friend, but did not want to pry.

Jason caught her reticence and running a hand through his long hair, heaved a sigh. "Not really a pretty story."

Placing her hand on his arm as it rested on the counter, she smiled softly. "You don't have to explain. I'm glad you're here now. Baytown always called to me when I was growing up...maybe you can find healing here as well."

His eyes drifted from hers to a glass bowl on the oak sideboard behind her. "I've been meaning to ask about all the colorful glass your grandmother had in bowls sitting around."

Smiling, she stepped over and picked up a few pieces, letting them sift through her fingers. "It's sea glass. Pieces of glass that were tossed into the sea by shipmen and then, with the pounding surf and sea, became polished and beautiful as they washed up on shore."

"Sea glass," he repeated. "Hence the name of her Inn."

"Well, my grandparents both named their Inn. They bought the place, refurbished it, and then grandpa left for Vietnam. He was twenty-eight years old...kind of old for who the Army was sending, but he felt it was his duty. He never came back. He left grandma a widow, a single mom of a little boy, and a big Inn to run. But she always said it was the rough and tumble seas of life that turned her world into a beautiful piece of glass."

The two stood silent for a few minutes as she watched Jason's inner battle show across his face.

Finally, he said, "Got out of high school, knowing I didn't want to work in the diner. Had a neighbor who taught me about cars and engines. I worked in his garage for about two years. Had a good friend who owned a tattoo shop and discovered I had an artistic side as well. Worked in the garage during the day and the tattoo shop at night. Made decent money...thought it was a good life."

He grew silent and she leaned her hip against the counter, knowing he would continue when he was ready to reveal whatever was next.

His fingers turned the piece of sea glass over as his thumb ran over the smooth surface. "Had a couple of cousins who joined the Navy, and their letters home made it sound great. By then I was feeling choked being in the small town. Wanted to see more of the world. Joined the Navy as a mechanic. I was such an idiot...

thought I'd never be in danger out in the ocean. I had no idea the real nightmare was going to be back home. Stupid asshole came into the diner late one night to rob my parents and shot them both in the process. I got notified that they were killed, and I was on a fuckin' ship."

Tori's grip on his arm tightened reflexively. "Oh, Jason, I'm so sorry."

"Left the Navy at the end of my enlistment and never looked back. But didn't want to stay in North Carolina. Felt lost…till Zac gave me a call and said to come here. I figured I had nothing else to lose."

"For what it's worth…I'm glad you're here," her soft voice wrapped around him.

Nodding, he looked up at her, a wistful smile on his face. "Yeah, me too." Looking back down at the sliver of glass in his hand, he said, "Guess I've got a lot in common with this piece of sea glass…like your grandmother."

"We all do," she smiled. "We all do."

The older man rapped the gavel on the podium. Wearing his navy blazer with the American flag pin in one lapel and the American Legion pin on the other, he eyed the group as they sat down, and the Sergeant-at-Arms closed the doors of the meeting room in the basement of the Baytown Community Center. With another three raps of the gavel, the few older members stood as the newer recruits glanced around quickly before standing as well.

"The Color Bearer will advance the Colors." As the assembly stood, Mitch watched as an elderly man from the back marched forward, the American flag and pole in his hands, and set it in the floor stand.

"The Chaplain will offer prayer." The Baptist minister, a member of the American Legion, stood and prayed as the group bowed their heads in unison.

The POW/MIA Empty Chair Ceremony followed as the few older members recited the procedures and the newer recruits watched, interested and eager. A chair was designated as a symbol of the thousands of American POW/MIAs still unaccounted for from all wars and conflicts involving the United States of America. The POW/MIA flag was placed on the Empty Chair.

The assembly appeared eclectic to the untrained eye. Men...a few women...ages running from about twenty-five to almost ninety. But all with their faces turned toward the Empty Chair. Mitch found his breath caught in his throat at the remembrance of his friends who did not make it back. His eyes glanced at the others, seeing the same haunted expression in most of them.

After the Pledge of Allegiance and the Preamble to the American Legion Constitution, printed on small cards for the newer members to learn, the gavel was rapped once more to indicate that everyone could take a seat. It took several more minutes for the previous business to be worked on before the attendees discussed the upcoming election for chapter officers.

Mitch, stunned, watched as the group unanimously nominated him to be the next Commander of the Post. The group then nominated First Vice Commander, Second Vice Commander, Post Adjutant, Finance Officer, Post Chaplain, Post Historian, Post Service Officer, and Sergeant-At-Arms. The Commander agreed to be nominated as the Second Vice Commander, to assist the new men in their positions, but smiled as he shook Mitch's hand.

"Been part of this organization a long time," he said to the group, "but I'm looking forward to newer, younger blood taking us forward."

The chaplain led them in a prayer once more and then, with three raps of the gavel, the saying of the Commander's Charge, and the retiring of the colors, the meeting came to a close. The group hung around for a few minutes talking, and Mitch observed the easy camaraderie between the older members and the newer ones.

As the members trickled out, Mitch stood at the front with Grant, Zac, Ginny, Aiden, Brogan—all who had been nominated. Jason walked up, a grin on his face as he addressed them. "Glad to be in this town. Glad to be with you all."

"We need to meet after the elections and see what we want to propose to the group as our first projects," Ginny said.

"Hell, looks like life just got more complicated," Zac commented good-naturedly.

Brogan, rubbing his chin, nodded. "This just might

bring in a few more old buddies that need a positive to land."

Closing the door behind him, Mitch followed the group outside. The evening air was warm and unusually still for the seaside. *Peaceful.* Calling out *goodbyes and goodnights,* he headed toward his jeep, thoughts of the beautiful Tori filling his mind.

25

———————

Making his way to Tori's attic bedroom, he did not see her but heard the shower running. Not wanting to scare her, he called out as soon as he got to the door.

"Babe? It's just me."

Her head popped out from behind the shower curtain, her face brightened with her grin.

Glancing down, he furrowed his brow as he asked, "Are you supposed to get your leg wet?"

"The doc said I could now, but I still have a bandage on it to keep the water from hitting it directly. I figured that would sting, but to get all clean feels amazing."

Pulling the blue curtain back slightly he let his eyes drift from her bandaged leg upwards. The water streamed from her hair, now dark as it flowed down across her shoulders. The droplets dripped down her body, and he battled the desire to catched the lucky drops. The curve of her waist as it arched out to her hips made his hands itch to grasp her, pulling her closer.

His nostrils flared as he leisurely lifted his gaze back to her face, her exuberant grin now replaced with an expression of unbridled lust.

"Wanna join me, cowboy?" she teased, flicking her tongue over her moist lips, stepping backward in the tub to give him room.

She watched in amazement as he stripped quicker than she could have imagined and moved directly into her space. Leaning back to keep her hungry gaze on him as he reached for her, she shuffled slightly so the water was not in her face.

With his hands on her waist, he turned so that the spray was on his back, protecting her. Sliding one hand to her face, he cupped her cheek, his thumb caressing the soft skin. Leaning down, he nibbled the water droplets on her lips before taking her mouth. Aligning his lips with hers, the kiss rocketed from gentle to scorching.

Her arms wound around his neck as her fingers weaved through his hair. Sighing in pleasure, she allowed him to take over, owning the kiss as she wanted him to own her body.

Lips following the same trail as the water drops, he made his way down her neck, sucking gently at her pulse point before hoisting her into his arms. She instinctively wrapped her legs around his waist, immediately feeling his body pressing against her.

Pulling his head back, his gaze raked over her, assessing her comfort. "Your leg okay, babe? We can take this to the bed where you'll be more comfortable."

Grabbing his jaw, she pulled him back in, barely getting the words, "Don't you dare stop," out of her mouth before latching onto his lips once more.

Not one to need to be told twice, he obliged. Pressing her back against the blue and white tiled wall, he held her firmly with one hand under her as the other hand roamed freely.

She leaned her head back against the hard tile, her moans resounding in the confined space. Her fingernails scraped against his back and shoulders as sensations poured over her.

He lifted her slightly, bringing her close as he slowly joined them together, fighting every instinct that urged him to rush, easing into her warmth instead. *Hang on, man. Hang on.*

Her hands found his shoulders for leverage as they moved together, the sensation building between them in slow, coiling waves. "Close...close..." she gasped.

Feeling her tremble against him, he shifted to give her what she needed, watching in quiet satisfaction as her head fell back and his name left her lips. He buried his face in her exposed neck as his own release crested and broke, holding her through every last tremor until there was nothing left in either of them.

His hand, braced against the tile, barely held them upright as his legs went unsteady. The force of it had emptied him completely of energy and thought... of everything.

He set her down carefully, his hands at her waist until she found her footing. Reaching behind him, he flipped off the water and stepped out, then helped her out as well, lifting a thick, plush towel from the rack and wrapping it around her. He draped one across his own waist and turned back to her.

She reached for the towel, but he gently moved her hands aside. "Here, babe. Let me." He drew the towel over her slowly, following each pass with a soft kiss against her skin. When he reached her stomach, she squealed and jerked away.

"No, not there!"

He cocked an eyebrow, grinning. "I seem to remember you being ticklish."

She backed toward the door, hands up defensively. "Oh, no. No way, Mitch. I swear I'll pee on the floor if you tickle me!"

Laughing, he scooped her up and carried her into the bedroom, setting her gently on the bed with careful attention to her healing leg. He leaned over her, pressing a kiss to her stomach, then lower. "Well," he murmured against her warm skin, "let's see if we can find another place that'll make you wet in a different way."

What followed left her completely undone. She dropped her head back against the mattress, lost in sensation, unable to hold a single coherent thought. He was thorough and patient and entirely focused on her, and by the time he finally crawled over her body and settled his weight on his forearms, she was already floating somewhere above herself.

"Mmmmmm," she managed, torn between keeping

her eyes closed and opening them to see his face. The desire to see him won, and she found his deep blue eyes already on hers.

He joined them together again, and she pulled him close with her hands moving over his shoulders, down his back, urging him on. He needed no further encouragement. Their bodies moved in unison, perfectly matched, his weight warm and solid above her, her softness yielding to the hard lines of him. He dipped his head to kiss her, their breath mingling as they moved together toward the edge.

The tension coiled tight. "Babe, you close?" he breathed against her mouth.

"Oh yeah," she managed.

And then she was there... her whole body shuddered as the wave broke over her. He followed seconds later then barely managed to roll to his side, pulling her with him and tucking her close against his pounding heart. He couldn't speak. He could only hold her and hope that everything his body had just said was enough.

She rested her head on his chest, his heartbeat sounding steadily in her ear. *Strong. Sure. Safe.* Several long minutes passed as their warmth slowly settled. Then she leaned back to meet his gaze and whispered, "I love you."

Sweeter words were never heard. Mitch kissed her softly. "I love you, too." He pulled the covers up and helped her ease into a position that wouldn't strain her healing leg, and just that small act sent a shadow across his peace. *Somewhere out there is the asshole who tried to kill Tori...twice. No more. No—*

Her soft hand on his cheek brought him back.

"I can hear your thoughts, Mitch. I'll be careful and I know you'll catch whoever did this."

Humbled by her confidence in him, he squeezed her gently and pressed a kiss to her forehead. "Sleep, babe."

With that, they both drifted into slumber as the moon moved across the night sky over the bay.

———

Mitch looked at the map of Baytown spread out in front of him on the workroom table. He had studied the map before but now, in the quiet of the morning, he opened his mind as the possibilities flowed through him.

The dunes at the edge of the golf course where someone hid, waiting for Tori to walk by. The tall, scruffy grass would have provided the perfect cover. The Dunes Resort has several different residential sections containing close to fifty homes, forty townhomes, and close to eighty condos.

Peering down at the map, he remembered when the land had been a large farm. A developer from Virginia Beach had seen the potential for a beautiful resort and bought the land. It took years to build and landscape the rural surroundings into a golfing and seaside community. Baytown looked at The Dunes as a double-edged sword—it provided much needed revenue to a town that had been slowly dying, but many of the seasonal residents did little to integrate into the town's life.

Still...Baytown was thriving and had maintained its small-town appeal with the resort lying to the south of the town.

Grant and Ginny walked into the room, interrupting his perusal. Both glanced down at the map, Ginny immediately moved to Mitch's side to peruse it more carefully while Grant stepped to the counter to pour coffee.

"Anything new?" Ginny asked.

"Most of the transitional, vacationing residents have left The Dunes by now," he commented. "So, we're left with the full-time residents and some fall vacationers staying in the condos. I keep going back to thinking that it was someone who was already there that morning, not just coming in."

"Is there a resident who lives there who'd want to hurt Tori?" Grant asked, walking over with two cups of coffee in his hand. Placing one in front of Ginny, he sipped his before leaning over the map as well.

"Can't come up with anyone," Mitch added, pulling out a piece of paper with a list of names on it. "Here are the Baytown residents who live in The Dunes. Even got a few of our American Legion members there. Most came from other areas and retired here. I've poured over the list but can't come up with one single person who'd have any connection to Tori at all."

Ginny tapped her short, manicured fingernail on the condo section of the map and said, "A lot of these are rentals. Is there a list of who was staying?"

Pursing his lips, Mitch shook his head slightly.

"Almost impossible. The Dunes realty office has a list of the condos that are listed as rentals and if someone rents through them, then yeah, we know who was there. But many are owned by people who rent them out to friends or family, and quite a few are owned by companies who use them for their employees to rent."

"So, in other words, there could have been any number of people there when Tori was shot?" Grant growled.

Mitch nodded, his frustration showing as he lifted his eyes to his staff. Burt and Sam had walked in, hearing the last of the conversation. "I'm thinking of asking Gareth to do a search on the owners of the condos...even if for no other reason than future reference."

"But if it were someone from inside the resort, it would have to be a resident or someone staying there," Burt said. "What does your gut tell you?"

Mitch eyed his officer, knowing his FBI reputation for following his instincts preceded him. "I've spent a lot of time focusing on the ex, the sister, even the city manager. I still think they have the most to gain from Tori's death. But I'm now thinking that they didn't have to do the act themselves. They could have had someone else do it for them."

"Murder for hire?" Sam queried, his eyebrows lifted in shock.

"Don't know," Mitch answered, but piercing his staff with his gaze, he added, "But at this point, we can't discount anything."

Ginny nodded slowly, her eyes showing her intelligence at work. "Just because Vanessa doesn't own a gun and probably doesn't know anything about firing one, doesn't mean she couldn't find someone to do the task for her."

Mildred's voice came over their radios. "Domestic disturbance call." She rattled off the address—one that the group was familiar with.

"Jesus, can't she just leave him?" Grant groaned as he and Sam headed out the door.

"It's not that simple," Ginny replied, her face a mask of professionalism belying any personal thoughts.

Mitch knew the caller. Her husband must have come home again from an all-night bender, and he had become a mean drunk before passing out. Heaving a sigh, he nodded toward the others as he called out to Mildred, "Going to Gareth's. Then I've got another meeting with the mayor."

Mildred tossed him a wave along with a look of sympathy.

Mitch pulled up to the security house at The Dunes Resort and nodded to the guard as he was waved in. Earlier, he and Gareth sat in the small room across from his office, since it was unoccupied, and spread The Dunes map in front of them. When Gareth admitted he had never been to the resort, Mitch decided that the town's private investigator needed to see the area firsthand.

Now, Gareth glanced at the guard and commented, "Not a lot of security, is it?"

"No," Mitch admitted. "I've heard the resort management is in the process of stepping up their security. The owners and golf members get yearly passes on their vehicles and a number code for the gate. All other vehicles are supposed to check in with the guard and be placed on a list. But since people can come in only to go to the clubhouse restaurant or to play a round of golf, there can have a lot of visitors."

"I assume you've gone through the list from the day of the shooting?"

"Yeah, but it only had a couple of names on it, so I looked at the previous day as well."

"Thinking someone was lying in wait?"

"Maybe. But that doesn't take into account the people who are there as temporary visitors and are staying the week."

Mitch drove down the main road, lined with tall pine and stately magnolia trees. Rose bushes, mixed with a variety of other plants, scattered throughout the pine mulch brought a blast of color to the area.

"Beautiful," Gareth commented.

"Yeah, the developer of this community spared no expense to make it a real showplace. He went belly-up when the market crashed, but by then the resort was already established." Mitch drove down several streets containing manicured lawns surrounding townhomes. "Most of these are actually lived in by the owners."

He then moved to the next neighborhood, driving through modest single-family homes. "Same here. These people are permanent residents."

The next two neighborhoods were filled with massive, expensive homes bordering the golf course.

"Million-dollar homes?" Gareth asked, his gaze darting around.

"Oh, yeah," Mitch added. "Some of these are lived in... some are just tax write-offs for the owners who have probably never set foot in them." Chuckling, he pointed to one and said, "Got a Washington Redskin player owning that one. Far as anyone can tell, he's never even been here."

"Can't imagine having that kind of money," Gareth admitted. "But then, I've got my own little piece of the Eastern Shore, so I don't need a mansion to be happy."

Circling back around, Mitch turned into the last neighborhood, a quaint space filled with condos. "There are about twenty condo buildings with six condos each. Some are lived in full time...some are used just as rentals by the owners. And some are owned by companies to use for their employees or for retreats."

Nodding as he looked around, Gareth thanked Mitch. "This is good for me to see, since I will have to come here sometimes for investigations. Now I have a better idea of what I'm looking at."

Lastly, Mitch drove to the end of the lane where cars and golf carts parked in order for residents to cross the dune and go to the private beach. The two men got out and walked a short distance to where Mitch determined someone laid in wait for Tori. Pointing out to the beach, he said, "There's where Tori was walking. So, from the angle of the trajectory, I calculated that our shooter was approximately here."

Gareth looked down at the ground, saying nothing, then turned his gaze to the beach before moving back to where Mitch had parked. "Seeing the set up...you're right. It could be someone who was staying here, who did not have to sign in because they had a rental or owner's decal, knew there would be virtually no golfers out, and waited to take their shots. Then a quick dash back to their vehicle and back to where they came from. Later, when they left, they just had to be questioned by the guard and your officers on their way out. Or they could have left immediately before anyone headed over there."

The two men walked quietly back to the Jeep, each lost in their own thoughts, before Mitch turned and said, "This is what I need from you. I need a list of the owners of The Dune's properties and, if it's a company, any information you can get about them as well."

Smiling, Gareth agreed. "No problem, Mitch. I should have that for you soon."

Driving back to the station to talk to the mayor, Mitch heaved a slight sigh of relief. His officers were doing all they could, but the small force made solving a murder and attempted murder more difficult. *Maybe, just maybe, with Gareth's assistance, we'll get somewhere.*

26

The group at the Seafood Shack smiled and greeted one another enthusiastically. The Friday night music was pumping as Mitch and Tori stepped outside to settle at one of the tables on the deck overlooking the Baytown harbor.

Gareth, already there, waved to the couple then kept his gaze on Katelyn as she plopped down near Tori. Mitch wondered if Gareth had given any thought to talking to Katelyn about working as a receptionist for his business. From the way Gareth was eying the tall, dark-haired woman, he had to believe that the PI was at least considering it.

Tori glanced around to see who else was already there. Belle was present, her shy smile peeking out as she sat near the end of the table, next to the wall. Zac winked toward the waitress he had been chatting with, before moving to the deck. Callan came out talking to Ginny as they took seats at the adjoining table. Jason followed, appearing right at home as he greeted the others.

"Look who the cat dragged in!" called the bartender as Aiden and Brogan made their way through the restaurant toward the deck as well.

Tossing up their hands in salute, the two made their way toward the back deck.

"Hell, the way Josh acts, it's like he's never seen us outside of Finn's," Brogan groused.

Aiden laughed, "That's 'cause we're almost never outside of Finn's. It's a treat to go somewhere else."

The two found seats with the others in their group, which was growing by the minute. Soon, most of the deck was filled with the Baytown boys, girls, and their friends. Two young women walked in, both smiling shyly toward Katelyn.

"Rose! Jade! I'm glad you could make it!" Katelyn shouted as she jumped up from her seat. Grabbing the newcomers' hands, she pulled them toward the group and made the introductions.

"Everyone, this is Rose. She's opening an ice cream parlor and has recently moved into town. And this is Jade, a new teacher at the elementary school."

"Fresh blood," Aiden called out, earning a glare from his sister.

Rose stared at the group, her deer-in-the-headlights look giving an indication of her feelings. Katelyn turned toward her and said, "Don't worry about everyone's names now, ...you'll eventually figure them all out. And ignore my dumb-ass brother. I assure you that our parents did teach us manners! Come on, sit with me."

The group welcomed the young women, and their conversations picked back up as their glasses were quickly filled. Belle smiled at Jade and Rose, leaned over, and whispered, "I'm Belle. I'm not new here, but well...this group can seem overwhelming at times, but they really are the best."

Jade settled in next to Katelyn as Rose smiled at Belle sitting next to her. Rose gazed back at the crowd, her eyes stopping on the long-haired, tattooed handsome man sitting near her...his twinkling gaze staring back.

The music continued to play as the sun began its descent in the sky over the bay. Tori, leaning back against Mitch, watched the shimmering water change from blue to orange and pink, with hints of turquoise and jade mixed in. She sighed happily, the realization hitting her that Baytown had never just been her grandmother's hometown—it had always been where she felt at home.

Tori observed in interest as Grant and Jillian, sitting at opposite ends of the table, watched each other when the other was not looking. Grant would stare at Jillian, but as soon as she turned toward him, he jerked his head away. Then the same action would be repeated as Jillian stared at Grant. Shaking her head, Tori wondered when the two of them would ever get past whatever hurt and longings they had buried.

"Whatcha thinking?"

Mitch's voice, his warm breath tickling her ear, had her smiling. Twisting around, she shrugged. "Just wondering about some people and what keeps them apart."

His arms around her middle squeezed as he dropped a kiss on her lips. "Glad that's not us."

"Me too," she grinned against his mouth.

They jumped apart as the food and drinks were delivered to their tables. Everyone began helping themselves to the shared platters. Baskets of fried clams, chicken wings, nachos, and sliders began disappearing as the pitchers of beer were passed.

"Their sliders aren't as good as our burgers," Brogan commented, shoving one in his mouth.

"Yeah, but their menu is pretty different from ours at the pub," Aiden replied. Slapping his brother on the shoulder, he added, "Don't worry, bro. There's room in Baytown for both of us." Looking at the pretty waitress who was refilling beer pitchers, he continued, "And the Seafood Shack closes up during the winter months, giving Finn's all the business."

"Ohhh, fish tacos," Jillian cooed as the waitress plopped down more food. "This is better than each of us ordering our own plates. Sharing is much more fun." As she reached for another mini-taco, Grant's hand snatched it out from under her, a grin on his face. Caught off guard, she rolled her eyes and then reached for another one.

Tori leaned back into Mitch's chest, turning to place

her lips near his ears. "Do you think Jillian and Grant will ever get together?" she whispered.

Cutting his eyes down to hers, he whispered back, "Babe, I don't get into the romantic lives of my friends."

Jerking around, she glared. "Oh, too macho, are we?" she huffed, still whispering. "You can't tell me that you men don't talk about us women."

Chuckling, he tightened his arms around her once more. "Okay, then let me amend that. I know they had a thing years ago and he's changed since coming back from the war. But he's a good friend and a good police officer. Not going to get in his business." Another huff met his ears, and he leaned around to kiss her cheek. "Especially when I've got my hands full with my own love life."

Feeling his soft lips combined with the scruff of his beard against her cheek, she melted. Impossible to keep the smile off her face, she rested her head against him, sighing in pleasure. Looking around at the boisterous group, she grinned wider. The memories of so many times as a child, and then a teen, with the Baytown boys and girls hanging together filled her mind. The ones who left came back a bit more hardened. The ones who stayed were a bit more jaded. Feeling the warm cocoon of Mitch's embrace, she closed her eyes for a moment, realizing *we're the lucky ones in love.* Her eyes suddenly popped open as another thought slammed into her peaceful reverie. *At least, as long as I can stay alive!*

Mitch had been called out and Tori hated the feeling of lying in bed alone. *Has it only been a few days that I've grown used to Mitch's presence in my bed?* Her mind drifted to their growing relationship. Glancing around her shadowed bedroom, she realized he had been spending most nights with her. The pastel décor was suited to her...*at least when I was younger,* but she knew it was not right for Mitch. *So, if we stay together, where will we live? His place is too small...this place comes with all the responsibility of the Inn and only this bedroom suite in the attic.*

No answers came to her, so she rolled over, punching her pillow in frustration as she forced her mind to wander to what was needed for the next day.

Besides Jason, she only had two other couples this week for lodgers so it would not take her long to fix breakfast and clean. *Maybe today would be a good day to work in the yard.* Many of the no longer flowering summer plants needed to be cut back, and she noticed a few limbs hanging low. The temperature was supposed to be milder, so a day spent outside working appealed to her. Smiling, now that her decision had been made, she rolled over once more, hoping sleep would come.

Suddenly the peaceful night was blasted by the screeching of the smoke detector alarm. *Oh shit!* Heart pounding, she threw off the covers and bolted through her door and down to the second floor, slamming into Jason as he plowed into the hall as well. The other two couples had opened their doors, their faces filled with concern and sleepy confusion.

"Please follow me," she called out, willing her voice

to be steady when her heart was pounding. "It's probably nothing, but I'd rather be safe."

Her eyes sought Jason's, who placed his hands on her shoulders. Leaning down, he spoke calmly. "Take them outside and make sure they're comfortable. I'll check it out."

Nodding, she led the others down the stairs and out the front door. Seeing no smoke, she hoped the alarm was tripped by mistake. It would be embarrassing to have woken the guests in the night, but at least there would be no threat.

Opening the front door, the group made their way to the front lawn where a bench sat under one of the large magnolia trees. "Please have a seat and I'll be right back," she promised, turning to go back into the house.

"Miss, you should stay here too," one of the gentlemen said, his arm protectively around his wife's shoulders.

Smiling, she replied, "I'll be careful. I want to check to see what's going on."

Jogging back into the house, she came up behind Jason as he entered the kitchen. "What have you found?"

"Jesus, Tori, get back outside!" he ordered.

"This is my house...My life! I want to know what is going on!"

Their argument was interrupted by a popping sound coming from the laundry room behind the kitchen.

Before she could process what it meant, Jason cursed, "Fuck! Call 911!" Seeing Tori rooted to the spot, he grabbed her shoulders, giving her a little shake. "Tori! Call 911!"

She had left her cell phone upstairs in her bedroom, but ran to the desk in the front hall and made the call with shaky hands. Unable to leave, she ran back to the kitchen and watched as Jason grabbed wet towels and placed them at the bottom of the door leading into the laundry room.

Already hearing the siren of the fire truck, she placed her fingers against her mouth, suppressing the desire to scream her rage at once more being attacked in her home. Jolted when Jason grabbed her shoulders again, she was spun around and pushed out of the kitchen in front of him.

Meeting the firefighters in the foyer, Jason reported succinctly, "Zac, the fire is in the laundry room. I think it's contained."

Zac nodded and ordered them outside as he pushed his way by them. Stumbling down the stairs, Tori held on as Jason assisted. She looked up and observed as more firefighters ran around to the back of the house. Another siren sounded as two of the police cruisers stopped at the sidewalk, just behind the rescue squad.

Mitch and Grant bounded out, running over to Tori and Jason. She threw herself into Mitch's arms, willing the shaking to stop.

Jason, grim faced, looked at Mitch and said, "There's a strong smell of gasoline outside the laundry room."

Mitch's anger grew as he looked up at the Inn, stately and proud, with smoke now coming from the back. Looking back into her frightened eyes, he said, "Stay here with your guests. Do not, and Tori, I mean this…Do not come back into the house."

Accepting her nod of agreement, he sprinted around the back to see what was happening. Furious, he glanced up toward the roof, a tight smile crossing his face. *Hopefully, my little surprise will get us somewhere!*

27

Several hours later, the fire department declared the Sea Glass Inn safe to enter. The fire had been contained in the laundry room, which had been an addition between the garage and kitchen. She overheard the murmurings of the firefighters, agreeing with Jason's assessment that gasoline had been poured on the outside of her Inn.

The house had been thoroughly checked and with the location of the fire, the rest of the house was unharmed. The kitchen had a slight smoky odor, but the fire had been quickly doused before any damage had occurred.

Katelyn drove the two couples to the Baytown Hotel, where they were safely ensconced until they were able to return later in the morning.

Tori walked through the kitchen, seeing the laundry room through the now open door. She realized how much she owed Jason for his fast thinking in placing wet towels at the bottom. She leaned in, seeing the blackened walls, now dripping with water, and the ruined industrial washing machine and dryer. Since the only other items the room held were a large sink and shelves for cleaning supplies, she knew this would not close the Inn...only cause an inconvenience with the laundry.

I'm lucky, she thought and then bit back a growl. *Well, lucky for someone who has a target on her back!*

She looked for Mitch, but did not see him. As she glanced out the kitchen window, she saw Grant talking with Zac and a few of the firefighters, but no Mitch. Startled at the sound of footsteps behind her, she whirled around, throwing her hand on her chest.

"Jason! Oh, you scared me. Sorry, I'm jumpy."

He walked over and leaned down to peer into her eyes. "How you holdin' up?"

She sucked in a deep breath and let it out slowly as her thoughts became untangled. "I'm really okay," she admitted. "The fire was contained. No one was hurt. The damage is only to the laundry room, thanks in part to you." She smiled as he ducked his head in embarrassment.

"Don't thank me," he said. "I just acted instinctively."

Barking out a laugh, she said, "Well, thank God your instincts are better than mine. Running around screaming was my instinct!"

"Hey, don't underestimate the power of a good scream," he teased.

Feeling the mood lighten, she continued, "I just can't believe that someone wants to hurt me. It makes no sense. I am absolutely no one!"

Zac and Grant stepped into the kitchen, hearing her words, as Jason offered her a hug. Zac wrapped his arms around her and kissed the top of her head. "Don't worry, Tori. Mitch is on it. And this time, he had a secret weapon."

Her gaze jumped up to his in question, but he just smiled. "I'll let him explain, but for now, why don't you try to get some rest." Throwing up his hands before she could protest, he added, "I know, I know. But at least lay on the downstairs couch for a while. Katelyn's bringing the guests back later and I know you'll have to deal with them. So, take it easy for now."

Jillian came flying in through the front door just as Grant was walking out. Slamming into him, she grabbed his arms, asking, "How is she?"

Putting his teasing aside, he said, "She's fine. But she could use a friend until Mitch gets back. He's at the station."

Nodding, she offered him a little smile before running through the house toward the kitchen. Grant watched her leave and could not keep the smile off his face as he got into the cruiser and drove to the station to see what Mitch had discovered.

Grant stood in the police station workroom, leaning over Mitch sitting at one of the computers. Ginny, Burt, and Sam peeked over Mitch's back as well and when Gareth joined them, Mitch felt the hot breaths of everyone pressing down on him.

"Does she know you had this done?" Sam asked.

"Nope," Mitch responded. "Two of my friends and their wives came for a day visit and while Tori played tour guide with the wives, I had my friends put up the security cameras."

"Damn, they must be good. The equipment looks expensive."

Sighing, Mitch nodded, fiddling with the playback of the digital security video. "Gotta tell you that's the one thing that I do miss. I had a lot at my fingertips with the FBI, but my friends in the Saints Protection & Investigations Company were invaluable. They have private contracts with industry and government agencies and make a mint."

"Hey, you still have friends in high places," Grant commented.

Shaking his head, Mitch replied, "Yeah, but I don't want to overuse them. I can't pay them and, while they'd help out in any way, I've got to figure out how to get more money from the state, 'cause cases like this really strain the tax base of the town."

"Hey, go back," Ginny called out, her hand jerking over Mitch's shoulder with her finger pointing to a dark patch near the bottom of the screen. "What's that?"

As Mitch's head moved forward to enlarge the picture, everyone leaned closer to his back. In the corner of the screen, a dark figure made its way toward the back of the house. The arsonist was clothed all in black, including a stocking cap on their head. They watched as the person moved from the front corner of the house, around to the back on the side where the guests could enjoy sitting under one of the large trees. The camera mounted on the garage now picked up the movements as the person made their way to the laundry room window.

The lone figure poured liquid from a can along the bottom of the Inn's extension before reaching into their pocket and withdrawing matches. Striking one of them, they flicked it toward the building, jumping back as the flames immediately sparked to life.

The arsonist then ran toward the front of the house and continued running down the street out of view of the camera.

"Damn, we can't even get a make on their vehicle because they parked down the street," Burt cursed.

"This is no professional," Mitch stated, his voice hard but sure. The others looked at him, each silently awaiting his explanation with their own expressions of interest. "A professional would know that starting a fire in an outer part of the house would take a long time to reach the living quarters and, by then, enough smoke would set off the alarms. A professional arsonist would also slip inside the house and start the fire at the staircase in the middle of the house for maximum damage, and to keep the residents from being able to escape that way."

"What do you think?" Ginny asked.

"I can't tell from here if it is a man or a woman, but my instincts tell me it's a man. Look at the way they're running. Men and women run differently."

The group watched as he played the video back for them to observe the details more carefully.

"That leaves out Vanessa," Sam pronounced.

Shaking his head slowly, Mitch disagreed. "Vanessa has the means to pay someone to do her dirty work for her. She might have taken care of the poisoning herself but, if it's her, I'd bet she was the distraction while someone she paid tampered with the food. And she'd likely have no idea how to shoot a gun. No," he said, rubbing his chin, "she's still very much in the running as a possibility."

"And Thomas?" Grant asked.

"Could be him...from what we can see of the lower part of the face, where it's not hidden, they are Caucasian."

Gareth spoke up, saying, "I came over to tell you what I found in doing more digging on Thomas, but wanted to see if you found out anything from the video first. Since Thomas is still a possibility, then this is pertinent."

All eyes turned to him and Gareth explained, "It seems that while they were married, they had life insurance policies taken out on each of them. Tori was listed as the beneficiary on his policy...and he's still listed as the beneficiary on hers." Holding everyone's gaze, he continued, "One million dollars. All his if she dies."

Thomas answered the doorbell, his congenial face quickly turning into a scowl, seeing Mitch and Grant on his front stoop.

"I've told you all I know and if you continue to harass me then I'll contact my lawyer," he declared, keeping one hand on the door barring their entrance.

"That is certainly your right," Mitch agreed, "but we can easily summon you to the station to answer questions. Your choice."

Appearing to fight an inner battle, Thomas wavered for a moment then threw open the door. "Fine, I'll talk to you now. But I'm warning you—"

"I wouldn't do that," Grant said, stepping into the living room and taking a seat on the sofa.

Thomas sat down heavily, his face still sporting a scowl. "What do you want?"

Mitch, casually and deliberately, pulled out a sheaf of papers. "You want to explain the million-dollar insurance policy on Tori that lists you as the beneficiary?"

Visibly paling, Thomas flopped heavily back in his seat, his breath leaving him in a whoosh. His eyes darted between Mitch and Grant. He opened and closed his mouth several times, his fish-like appearance now filled with apprehension.

"I…I tried to talk to her…I had forgotten…I…I knew she had…"

Mitch and Grant sat in stony silence, both waiting for the man to get his words out and to create a sense of nervousness, hoping he would keep talking.

His Adam's apple bobbing, Thomas swallowed heavily a few times before taking a deep breath. "That's why I went to her…why I showed up at the Inn to talk to her." Seeing Mitch's cocked eyebrow, he continued, "Honestly."

Rubbing his face, Thomas started again. "When I proposed to Hailey, she wanted to know about my finances." He hesitated, catching their expressions and hastened to add, "My lawyer suggested a pre-nup, but I didn't want to go that route. Hailey and I did discuss finances and that's when I realized that Tori and I still had life insurance policies set up through my work-place. Tori was listed on mine, and I was listed on hers." His voice became petulant as he added, "We were married, after all."

"Continue," Mitch demanded.

Huffing, Thomas said, "When Hailey saw those, she flipped her shit. Got mad that I still had Tori listed as my beneficiary. Cried, screamed, and generally had a shit-fit. So, I went to the insurance company and had Tori's name taken off and Hailey's added." He lifted his gaze to the officers and added, "But, I knew Tori had forgotten about hers. She didn't return my calls, so I decided to drive over to Baytown to see her. I wanted to let her know that she needed to change her beneficiary to someone else or cancel the policy or…I don't know…whatever. I was trying to do the right thing, but she wouldn't see me." Pouting, he continued, "You even told me to leave."

"So, you left…made no further attempt to contact her nor had a lawyer take care of it since she wouldn't see you? You just left the insurance policy the way it was. And now, there have been three attempts on her life. Kind of coincidental, wouldn't you say?"

Eyes wide, Thomas sputtered, "No, no! I swear I've done nothing to Tori. You don't understand…I still… care for her. I know what I did with Vanessa was stupid…so stupid. But Tori's a good person and I'd never try to hurt her."

"Where were you last night?" Mitch asked, unimpressed with Thomas' declaration of innocence. *Heard too many of those from guilty suspects when in the FBI.*

Licking his lips, Thomas said, "Here. I got home about seven p.m. We ate and then I was in bed by about ten."

"We?"

"Hailey lives here with me. She was here too. All night. I swear."

The two officers stood and walked to the front door, with Thomas trailing. Grant headed to the cruiser as Mitch turned back after Thomas' hand snaked out and grabbed his arm.

"You believe me, don't you?" Thomas whined.

Looking down at his arm until Thomas jerked his

hand back, Mitch then lifted his gaze up. "We'll be in touch."

As the door closed behind Mitch, Thomas turned and looked down the hall. Hailey moved from the shadow of the kitchen and stared at her fiancé.

"Still watching out for your ex?" she bit out.

He wilted under her angry glare.

28

The night sky over the bay sparkled with stars and the breeze tossed Tori's hair behind her as she stood at the rail of Mitch's deck. Sucking in a deep breath of sea air, she closed her eyes for a moment, remembering easier times as a child when her only concern at Baytown was hoping Mitch would come play with her.

Before her thoughts could turn down the darker path of someone wanting to harm her, she felt his arms wrap around her from behind. Leaning her head back against his chest, she relished the warmth in his embrace.

Nuzzling her ear, he whispered, "You good out here?"

"Mmmmm," she replied. "Better now that you're here."

Giving her a little tug, he said, "Come back in, babe. I hate you standing out here where anyone can see you."

Her body jerked involuntarily, and she bit back the

desire to argue that this unknown assailant would not dictate her life. *But who am I kidding? My whole life has been disrupted. ...One person dead...two more attempts on me.*

Sighing, she allowed him to lead her back inside his house and watched as he closed the curtains, keeping out any observers.

Lifting her gaze to his, she said, "What do I need to do about Thomas?" Mitch had shared the news about the life insurance policy when he came back to Baytown earlier in the day.

Linking fingers, he led her to his worn sofa and pulled her down next to him. "For one, contact your lawyer tomorrow to see what headway he's made. I don't want you dealing with Thomas directly, so let the lawyer contact him and get the insurance company and policy information. Once you have that, you just have to list a new beneficiary if you want to keep the policy. It looks like Thomas has continued to have it paid for... the fees just came out of his pay, and he never noticed it along with everything else. Or you can cancel it, and it'll stop."

"I don't really know why I would need it," she said. "The Inn is paid for, and I have no children..."

His eyes quickly searched hers. "Not yet. If the cost isn't prohibitive, you could keep it...for the future."

Her lips pinched together for a moment, causing him concern. The idea of being with her and possibly having children one day was a plan he wanted to pursue, but the expression on her face gave him the realization that she might not share his view.

"But who for now, Mitch? My sister? My mom? I've got no one in my family that I'd leave it to right now!"

Releasing a sigh, he smiled slightly, catching her curiosity. "Sorry, babe. I...well, I was thinking about children down the road and saw your face and thought...well, that maybe you didn't wa—"

Grabbing his jaw with her hands, she pulled him in for a kiss. Soft, then searing. Pulling back, a moment later, she panted. "Oh, that's not what I meant at all! It's just that everything's so...so..." Suddenly a sob tore from her lips, her face crumpling in sorrow.

Tucking her head under his chin, he let her cry it out, her tears wetting his shirt. Rubbing his hand on her back, he murmured soft words, soothing the tension from her body. After a few minutes, she took one last shuddering breath and lifted her face from his neck.

Wiping her cheeks, she leaned over and grabbed a tissue from the end table. She attempted to climb off his lap, but he held firm.

"Mitch, I'm sorry. God, I'm such a mess," she proclaimed.

Cupping her cheeks, he caressed the last of the moisture from them. Leaning down to stare deeply into her eyes, he said, "Babe, you're not a mess. Hell, I'm a mess 'cause I can't seem to catch this asshole and keep you safe."

Concern filled her face. "It's not your fault," she cried.

"Well, it sure as hell isn't yours, either."

The silence filled the couple, circling them in a

warm blanket of care. Smiling slightly, Tori said, "Did you mean what you were saying earlier? About us... kids? Um... you know?"

"Hell, yeah," he vowed. "I want it all with you, Tori. Finding you again after all those years...perfect."

"But we haven't been dating that long," she added, hesitancy back in her voice.

His blue gaze captured hers. "Do you love me?" he asked.

Her smile widened as she answered, "Yes. You know I do."

"When you look into the future, who do you see yourself with?"

"Mitch...you know it's you. It's been you since I was six years old!"

"Then don't you think we're now old enough to know what we want? I know I want you in my life...for as long as you'll have me, and babe, I'm hoping that's going to be forever." Seeing her smile, he brought her in for a kiss...a sweet kiss, full of promise.

Pulling back, he said, "So, if you want, dump the insurance policy. When we have kids down the road, we'll get our own policies."

"When?"

"Oh, yeah...no doubt about it. You and me, staying together? Count on it!"

Mitch stared at the board on the wall in the station workroom, knowing something was staring him in the face and frustrated the culprit's identity did not appear before him. His eyes roamed from the pictures on the board to the map of The Dunes Resort. *Condos. Lots of condos. Many owned by companies for their employees. Who the hell are these companies?*

Picking up the phone, he called Gareth. The phone rang several times with no answer. *Jesus, Gareth...you need a receptionist!* Just as he was about to hang up, Gareth answered.

Before giving the PI a chance to greet him, Mitch immediately asked, "Did you find out what companies own any condos at The Dunes?"

"Working on it today. They would be public records at the courthouse. Whatcha thinking?"

"Thomas works for a big real estate company. I want to know if they're owners. That'd give him the opportunity to be here in town and not have to go through the checkpoints at the security station at the resort. If he had the code, he could come and go at will. He could have stopped by her place, done the shooting, and been around for the fire, all within easy distance from her without having to travel back over the bridge."

"You don't believe his fiancé's alibi statement?"

"Hell, no! I don't trust her to tell the truth where he's concerned at all."

"Okay, give me a little bit of time, and I'll let you know what I find out."

As Mitch hung up, Grant and Ginny walked in from

beach patrol, arguing about who had the best crabcakes in the area as she headed straight to the refrigerator to grab her lunch.

"I'm telling you, the diner's got amazing crab cakes. And don't roll your eyes at me. They may just be a diner, but they fry them up so crisp on the outside and—"

"Yeah, the focus is on *fried*," she argued. "Too much grease. The Sunset View Restaurant broils them and they're healthier."

"It's a crab cake. A little piece of heaven on Earth. Who gives a fuck if they're healthy?"

Before the argument could go any further, Mitch interrupted, gaining the officers' immediate attention. "Got Gareth checking on the companies that own any of condos at The Dunes. I realized that could be how Thomas moved so easily around without detection if he was able to slip back into one."

"You think it's him for sure?" Grant asked.

"Don't know, but he's the only one with motive, means, and opportunity...especially if he's managed to be local during some of this."

Ginny added, "No one would notice him...not with all the tourists in town."

"And Vanessa?" Grant prodded.

"I'm not discounting her either, but that million-dollar insurance policy in Thomas' hands is motive enough for me to want to pursue him." Mitch viewed Grant carefully, seeing his intelligent eyes viewing the board. "What are you thinking?"

"Don't know, but there's something about the sister that I don't trust either. Even if she's not the one who's doing it, ...but hired someone." Dropping his head down to stare at his feet for a moment, Grant sighed. "God, high school seems a million years ago. But I still remember how, even back then, I noticed how condescending she was to those of us who lived here. Maybe I'm holding on to some regressed dislike."

"That's honest," Mitch agreed. "It is hard when you have a personal dislike for a suspect. It can cloud judgment. Doesn't make them innocent...just means you have to look at the facts carefully." He looked back at the board before adding, "I've got the same problem with Tori's ex. Part of me really wants him to be the guilty party."

Cabin fever was stealing her sanity as Tori dusted the same piece of furniture for the third time. Jason had gone for the morning to meet with the town's city manager concerning the architectural plans for his garage and shop. Jillian and Katelyn had gone to the North Heron Gardening Club meeting in Easton and would be gone for the morning. Mitch had mentioned that his dad had a doctor's appointment in Virginia Beach and his mom had driven him.

At her wits ends, she tossed the dusting rag down and flopped on the sofa. *I hate this! It's like being held hostage in my own house!* Just then her phone rang, and she answered, glad for the distraction.

"Ms. Bradford?"

"Yes, this is Tori Bradford."

"This is Dr. Camden from Virginia Beach Memorial Hospital. Your mother was brought in early this morning with stomach pains, and we have admitted her for observation. You were listed as the point of contact."

"Oh, my God! Will she be all right?" Tori forced her grip to loosen on her cell phone as her heart pounded.

"At this point, we can't tell anymore until some tests come back, but she is asking for you."

Interrupting him, she exclaimed, "I'll be there. I'll leave right now. It should take me about forty minutes to get to the hospital." Already jumping up, she barely remembered disconnecting as she ran up the flights of stairs to her bedroom. Throwing on capris and a T-shirt and pulling her hair up in a ponytail, she flew back down the stairs and out the door, pausing only to lock it behind her.

Once in the car, she dialed Mitch as she backed out of her driveway, but she could only leave a message. "Mitch? I just got a call from Memorial Hospital in Virginia Beach. Mom's there so I'm heading over the bay bridge to see her. I'll call as soon as I have any news." With that, she was ready to head out of town and stepped on her accelerator.

Gareth hustled into the Police Station, looking for Mitch. Gaining a nod from Mildred, he jogged toward the back workroom. "Mitch!" he shouted, gaining the attention of the group. "I found something. Not sure what it means but wanted you to have it immediately."

Mitch's heart leaped, sure that the noose was about to tighten on whomever was threatening Tori. "What? What've you got?"

Shoving a couple of pieces of paper toward Mitch, while the others quickly circled around, Gareth said, "Here's a list of companies that own condos in The Dunes Resort. Take a look at the ninth one on the list."

Scanning, Mitch read the name. Looking up, he nodded, then announced to the group, "This may be exactly what we need to get them." Jolted into action, he said, "Sam, you and Ginny have town and beach patrol today. Burt, I need you to stay here and work with Gareth to see what else you can dig up on this. Keep it all legit. Go to the Commonwealth Attorney's office, or at least call her, to let them know what we're doing. Grant, you come with me. We're going to pay them a little visit."

With nods of agreement from everyone, Mitch and Grant hurried out to the cruiser. Looking down at his phone, Mitch said, "You drive. I've got a message from Tori." Before he could listen, he and Grant were on the road heading toward the long bridge. *Time to finally break this case wide open!*

29

Ten minutes after Tori left her house, she heard a loud *whump* and felt her car jerk over to the right. Quickly pulling off to the shoulder, she put her car in park. Getting out, she walked around to the passenger side, staring in dismay at the blown front tire. *No! I've got to get to the hospital!* Glad that the blowout occurred before she got on the long bridge, she opened the passenger door to grab her phone from her purse. *I may be Jason's first customer before he even opens his shop.*

"Miss? Miss? Can I help you?"

Tori leaned back up, noticing a car had pulled directly behind her. A nicely dressed, handsome man alighted from the vehicle and her instinctive nervousness dissipated as she saw an attractive, smiling woman in the passenger seat.

"I've had a blowout," she explained, pointing to the flat tire.

"We were heading into Baytown when we saw you

swerve and turned around to check on you. Can we take you somewhere?"

His voice was pleasant, and she noted he made sure to stand away from her in a conciliatory manner. His grayish blond hair and mustache were neatly trimmed, and she had the feeling she had met him before. Her mind too full of what she needed to do, she dismissed trying to place him. "I was going to call a friend in Baytown to see if he could come tow my car."

"We can give you a lift so you don't have to sit on the side of the road. Just lock up your car, and we can get you there quickly."

Seeming uncertain, she added, "I was on the way to Virginia Beach. My mother is in the hospital."

The woman leaned her head out of the passenger window, concern on her face. "Oh, I'm sorry. If we take you back to Baytown, can you get someone to drive you there? Then you won't have to be sitting on the side of the road waiting with your car before trying to get to the hospital."

Nodding, Tori realized she was right. "Thanks," she replied. "That makes sense. Let me call my friend to tell him about the car."

The man and woman shared a look but neither said anything while she made the call. He did not answer, so she left a message. "Jason, when you have a chance, my car is on the side of the road, about half a mile from the Exxon on Rte. 13. I'm getting a lift back into town with a nice couple and will get Jillian to take me to Virginia

Beach. If you can arrange to check on my car later, I'd appreciate it. Thanks!"

Disconnecting, she grabbed her purse and locked her car. Following the man back to his BMW, she nodded as he held the back door for her. Sliding in, she forced a smile at the woman who turned back to look at her. *Jesus, I just want to get to the hospital! Can this day get any weirder?* Leaning back in the seat, she closed her eyes momentarily, before reaching for her phone. Wanting to call the hospital to let them know she would be late, she startled when the woman in the front seat spoke sharply.

"Put the phone down."

Looking up at the harsh order from the woman, who had just been smiling, Tori's eyes widened in shock at the tip of the gun pointing at her.

Mitch listened to Tori's message then relayed it to Grant before calling her back. The call went straight to voicemail. "Damn, I wish I had listened to this earlier. Her mom's in the hospital and Tori's headed there to be with her. She said it didn't sound serious, but the doctor said Tori was listed as the contact person."

"We can detour and go to the hospital first," Grant offered. "You can talk to Tori, check on her mom, and then we'll finish our interview."

Looking at his watch, Mitch shook his head. "No, I'll let her get there and find out what's going on with her mom. We can do the interview and then head over to the hospital. Maybe by that time, she'll know more."

Thirty minutes later, Mitch's anger simmered as he and Grant climbed back into their cruiser. Glancing at his Chief, Grant asked, "Since he's not at work, you want to go by his home?"

"Hell, yeah," Mitch growled. "Don't know if she'll be there, but we can see. I'd rather not upset Tori at the hospital now if I don't have to."

Soon, Mitch and Grant were standing on the front stoop of the large house. The housekeeper let them in and then moved back as Vanessa walked into the entrance foyer. Her eyes narrowed to slits as she saw them.

"I don't have anything else to say to you," she bit out.

"We're not here to talk to you, but to your husband. Seems you left out the little fact that his company owns one of The Dunes Resort condos."

Vanessa's eyes widened before darting between the two men, her nose flaring in irritation. "Well, even if he does, that hardly means I'm using it to try to murder my sister."

"True, but I'd like to talk to him nonetheless. He's not in his office today so I thought I'd try here."

Mitch observed Vanessa's breathing change as her grimace tightened. And for the first time, he noted she appeared nervous.

"I have no idea where my husband is at the moment. He could be in a meeting or having lunch with a client. He has many important clients."

"I'm curious why you aren't with your mother in the hospital," he commented, watching her reaction. Instead of anger, she met his statement with confusion.

"Huh? Why would I be at the hospital?"

A sliver of fear began to coil around Mitch's heart as he stared at Vanessa. "Tori got a call this morning from a doctor saying Vera Bradford was in the hospital."

Cocking her head to the side, Vanessa argued, "Well, she's misinformed. I was just on the phone to mom when you two showed up. She's fine and planning on attending her Garden Club meeting today."

Forcing his knees to hold his body up, Mitch grabbed his phone as Grant immediately took Vanessa by the arm and moved her to the side.

Calling Tori first and receiving no answer, he then called the hospital. Receiving the news that no Vera Bradford had been admitted, he turned back to Vanessa.

"I would advise you to tell us where your husband is, Mrs. Hurkamp. We need to talk to him...before there's another attempt on your sister's life."

Still standing in her entrance foyer, Vanessa's haughty expression was replaced with uncertainty that slowly morphed into anger. "I honestly don't know where my *husband* is right now. He...keeps...well, let's just say that I've had a feeling that he isn't exactly *alone* on his lunch hour...and he's certainly not with me."

Mitch, his mind struggling to focus on her words, was a step behind. Grant, glancing at his Chief, took over.

"Do you have any idea who your husband's…uh… lunch partner might be?"

Lips tight, Vanessa lifted her chin as she held their gazes. "I have no idea." Barking out a rude laugh, she added, "At first, I thought it was payback."

"Payback?"

"Yes. I wondered if my sister was having an affair with my new husband as payback for my affai—well, indiscretion with Thomas."

"What made you think it was Tori?" Mitch asked, anger simmering.

"I saw him out one day, leaving a restaurant," she admitted. "And before you suggest it might have just been with a client believe me, the hand on her ass and the kiss he gave her made me sure." Her voice had taken on a hard edge, incredulity seeping into her words. "A fucking redhead. He was with a fucking redhead."

Turning, Mitch walked briskly out of the house with Grant on his heels. Pulling out his phone, he called the Station. "Mildred, I need the make, model, and license number for Nelson Hurkamp. Once you have it, put out a BOLO on it and call Sheriff Colt Hudson. I want his deputies on this as well. Grant and I are heading back now. And find someone who knows where the hell Tori is! ETA is thirty minutes."

Grant gunned the SUV, heading to the entrance of the bay bridge. Glancing sideways, he watched as Mitch tried to call Tori's cell again only to curse when it went to voicemail. "What are you thinking, Mitch?"

Before he could answer, Mitch's phone rang.

Answering, he listened as Jason told him about Tori's car. "I found her car on the side of the road, but her tire had been tampered with. The blowout was intentional, man. And she never made it back to town. No one's seen her."

"Get everyone you know to the station," Mitch barked. Hanging up, he called Mildred back. "Call the others. Have them meet back at the station, and that includes Colt and any spare deputies he's got."

Rubbing his hand over his face, willing the shaking to still, he looked at Grant and replied, "Could be anyone with Nelson, but I've got a bad feeling I know who the redhead is. I was looking at the wrong fucking people all along."

Tori sat staring at the gun pointing toward her before managing to lift her gaze to the pretty red-headed woman whose eyes were now hard. Seeing the man make a movement, she watched as he pulled his mustache off.

"Still don't recognize me? My dear sister-in-law, you should have come to my wedding to Vanessa, then you would have recognized me."

"Ne...Nelson? Nelson Hurkamp?" Tori asked, her voice shaking. "But...I...what..."

"It's very simple, my dear. I need you out of the way, but you're proving to be quite the hard young woman to get rid of."

Not understanding, she quickly looked out the window noticing they had passed the turnoff toward Baytown. Jerking her head back, the realization of being kidnapped finally hit. "You can't do this," she cried. "I'm nobody. This is madness." Glancing back to the young woman sitting in front of her, she said, "Who are you? I don't even know you."

"No, but I know you. I know you are the woman my fiancé sees every time he makes love to me. Actually, he just fucks me, but I know in his mind he's making love to you."

Her eyes searched the woman's face, but she still did not recognize her. *She looks familiar...actually she looks kind of like me. Like me...Oh, my God!* "Thomas? You're my ex-husband's fiancé?"

Laughing, the woman said, "Give the woman a gold star! She finally figured it out!"

"But I'm no threat to you. I don't want him back. I—"

"It doesn't matter if you want him or not, bitch. I know in his heart he wants you. And that's enough reason for me to want you out of the way. That, plus the million dollars he'll get off the insurance policy."

"Shut up, Hailey!" Nelson growled.

"But...but, I got rid of the policy," Tori stammered.

"What?" both Nelson and Hailey shouted at the same time.

"I wasn't going to leave it to Vanessa and certainly not to Thomas. So...so...I cancelled the policy."

"Great, just fuckin' great! You cost me half a million dollars!" Hailey screamed.

By now, Nelson had turned the car down a narrow, gravel road, with tall trees on either side. Glancing to the side, Tori acknowledged she had no idea where they were. Not having been a Baytown native, she realized how little of the area she actually knew. Feeling her phone still in her hands, she hoped Mitch would be able to locate her. *How does that work? Does the phone have to be on? Shit! Why don't I know these things?* Unsure, she silently pressed the call button while holding down the sound. She had no idea if Mitch would be able to tell if she called him or where it was coming from, but she hoped it helped.

Stopping next to a farmer's field, Nelson put the car in park. Turning to Hailey, he said, "Let's get out of here. Give me the gun."

Nodding, she turned the gun over to him before getting out of the car. Tori sat, rooted to the seat, her legs not willing to move her. Expecting Nelson to shout for her to get out as well, she jolted violently when the gunshot rang out.

Eyes wide, mouth open, she panted as her mind attempted to accept what she had just witnessed. Hailey's body crumpled to the ground, blood pouring from her chest. As Tori's horrified gaze looked down, all she saw was the expression of shock on Hailey's face as she lay dead in the dirt.

"Get up front," Nelson ordered, the gun now pointed back to her. "Climb over the seat."

Forcing down the bile that threatened to rise, she pulled herself over the seat and console, her muscles quivering, to move into the front. Nelson climbed back into the driver's seat, starting the car with one hand while holding the gun on her with the other.

Answering her unspoken questions, he said, "Hailey was only good for one thing and that was to get her hands on the money from the insurance policy. No policy, no need to keep her around with her big mouth to fuck things up for me."

Tori's mouth opened and closed several times, but no words came forth. Her mind was still filled with the image of Thomas' fiancé, who looked so much like herself, lying in the dirt.

Finally finding her shaky voice, she said, "But you're rich...I don't understand."

Sneering, he replied, "Got too much money tied up in a deal that rests on you dying, dearie. I needed that insurance money to keep my creditors at bay."

Nelson drove for ten more minutes along several winding dirt roads, heading toward the bay. Coming to a stop at an old hut with a small pier sticking out into the water, Nelson got out of the car and walked around to her door. Opening it, he held out his hand. "Let's go, Victoria."

Unable to fight with the gun still pointed at her face, she slid her phone in her purse and stepped out of the vehicle, keeping an eye on him as he walked around behind her. "What are you going to do?" she asked, unsure her voice could be heard over the pounding of her heart. No answer came other than the feel of the gun pressing between her shoulder blades.

30

Mitch and Grant were minutes away from Baytown when the call came in. Mildred's voice cracked, as she relayed the information.

"10-39, 10-50." Mitch's heart rate increased at hearing of a body being reported. Rattling off the address, Grant flipped on the siren and the SUV turned quickly. As close as they were, it only took a few minutes to make their way down the farm road. Seeing a man standing to the side of the path over a body, they pulled to a halt. Recognizing Thadeous Maelstrom as the farmer, the two officers immediately jumped from the vehicle, weapons drawn.

As they neared, Mitch saw a woman lying in a pool of blood, her long reddish hair spread out on the dirt. His knees buckled as all thoughts of procedures flew from his mind and he ran to her, throwing himself to his knees by her body. With shaking hands, he turned her slightly, bracing himself.

Hailey Bernard...not Tori! His breath left his chest in an audible *whoosh*.

"Mitch?" Grant spoke behind him, gaining his attention. Mitch looked up, realizing Grant and Thadeous were staring at him.

"It's Hailey Bernard," he replied, his voice barely a croak. Allowing Grant to question the farmer who had found the body, Mitch took a moment to pull himself together, but then quickly began to work the situation. *Nelson's turned on his accomplice. He'll have nothing to lose by going ahead and killing Tori. Especially if he thought no one would find Hailey's body for a while.*

Forcing his legs to stand, he moved over to Grant and Thadeous as the ambulance came careening to a halt. Seeing the look of horror in Zac's eyes, he hastened to identify the body. Colt and one of his deputies came next, bringing their equipment with them, and started to process the murder scene.

"Colt," Mitch greeted. He filled him in quickly and gained the North Heron Sheriff's cooperation.

"I'll call in more of my men to come here and I'll go to Baytown with you," Colt promised.

Thirty minutes later, Mitch was standing in the middle of the workroom, already filled with people as soon as he arrived. Sam, Burt, Grant, and Ginny were all in attendance as well as most of their friends. Aiden, Brogan, and Katelyn all came together after picking up Jillian. Zac, Callan, Jason, and Gareth crowded in as well. Colt was also in attendance, as well as the small town of Easton's Chief, Hannah Freeman. Mitch heard someone else come in and he looked up to see his father standing in the doorway with his mother right behind. His father said nothing, but held his son's gaze for a moment and, with a nod, indicated he was going to assist in any way possible.

Sucking in a deep breath, Mitch turned to Gareth and said, "Bring everyone up to speed."

"Mitch had me check to see which companies own condos in The Dunes Resort and it didn't take long to find out that Hurkamp Financial Group was an owner."

"Honest to God, when I had Gareth check, I thought it was going to be Thomas' realty company. I felt as though it would have given him the perfect opportunity to be in the area without being seen around town and he would have dune access to be able to watch and shoot Tori. But I was looking at the wrong fucking person."

"Son."

Mitch looked over at his dad and knew he needed to pull his shit together. *All those times I worked cases...but was never involved...now I understand. My friends who worked for the Saints...when their women were in danger... now I get it. Oh, hell.* Sucking in a cleansing breath, he nodded. "Right. As it turns out, it appears we're looking for Nelson Hurkamp. His accomplice, Thomas' fiancé, Hailey Bernard, is dead."

"What the hell?" Jillian bit out. "How did those two hook up?"

Shaking his head, Mitch said, "Not sure, but Gareth has been able to dig into Nelson more and more."

Jerking his head toward the PI, he indicated for Gareth to explain.

Gareth continued, "Here's what we're supposing. He met Vanessa, and on a trip to visit her grandmother, he saw huge potential in the Inn. If he could get his hands on it, then he'd turn it into a money-maker. I've been able to find at least three emails between him and Silas Mills. Can't find that Silas did anything wrong, but Nelson was already planning on the feasibility of how to make the most for the property."

Looking at the stunned expressions from the crowd, he continued, "Nelson Hurkamp has already sold condo sites here in Baytown...condos that haven't been built yet. He expected his wife to inherit the property here... or at least half. He probably always expected to get rid of Tori. He's now strapped for money and living in a house of cards, ready to fall at any time. He can't make good. He's facing financial ruin and prison."

"I knew I didn't like that new town manager," Mitch's mom groused, gaining a shushing sound from her husband, then quickly soothed when he tucked her into his side.

"How can we find them?" Jillian wailed. "They could be anywhere. Even back over the bridge."

Shaking his head, Mitch said, "No, I had the State Police and the Bridge Police checking for Nelson's BMW. It hasn't gone back over the bridge, so we're going to assume he's got her here. What we have going for us is that he doesn't know he's being sought. We have the element of surprise."

Jillian cried out, "Yes, but then he could just kill her and—"

Mildred rushed in, interrupting the group. "Got it!"

Mitch explained, "We've had a GPS trace put on Tori's phone, but we had to go through the Commonwealth Attorney's office."

Gareth immediately sat at his laptop filled with his specialized programs. Turning it so no one could look over his shoulder, he began. Glancing up at a few questioning gazes, he shrugged. "A few of my programs aren't exactly...um...legit..."

"Just search," Mitch ordered. "We'll worry about legalities later." As Gareth worked, Mitch turned back to the group and clarified. "While I'm authorizing Gareth to find a trace on her phone in any way he can, we do this by the book. When we go in, we do everything completely legal. I do not want this slick-shit to get away. And you can bet he'll lawyer up, so no fucking up!"

"Best I can tell, her phone is near the coast, north of Baytown, but not quite to Easton."

"That's my jurisdiction," Colt announced, with a firm expression. "I'll call it in, and you can get our full support."

"Mine as well," Hannah added.

"The more, the better," Mitch agreed.

Ginny, sitting at her computer, shouted out, "Chief! I ran a check on a front company name that Gareth linked to Hurkamp. There's a yacht in the Baytown

Marina that's owned by that company. I just checked and the yacht is out now."

"Get me the info," Callan shouted. "I'll call my superior. The Coast Guard can go out to search for the vessel."

"There's a lot of beach there with no one around," Colt added. "We can spread out and cover more ground."

"Then let's go," Mitch ordered, hoping his voice carried authority and not the fear wrapped around his heart.

Mitch led the group outside of the Police Station, only to be stopped short in his tracks by the small crowd that had gathered outside. At first glance, it appeared to be an impromptu meeting of the American Legion.

"I'm sorry, but I don't have time to talk—"

"Not here to talk," one of the men said. "We're here to help."

Stunned, Mitch was speechless. "I…"

"I've got this, son," Ed said, stepping up. "You head out. Your mom and I'll stay here to organize these good people. I'll send them out to scan the area, give them instructions on what to do or not do," he assured.

Shooting his father a grateful look, Mitch and the others ran to their vehicles.

With the gun at her back, Tori followed Nelson out onto the pier and to the end. The tide was coming in and the water swirled underneath them. A small motorboat was tied to the pier and Tori viewed a larger yacht anchored out in deeper water.

"Get in," he ordered.

Whirling around to face him, Tori felt her momentary bravado flee at the sight of the gun pointed at her chest. Forcing her quivering chin to lift, she said, "Why? What possible reason could you have for this?"

"You have what I want," he said simply.

"What?" she shouted, her hands involuntarily lifting into the air only to slam back into her sides as his eyes narrowed.

"You have a large piece of beach-front property … that should have been split between you and Vanessa. I had planned on getting rid of you anyway, but when you became the sole owner, I had no choice but to get rid of you."

"It's a beautiful Inn, but old. I barely make a profit for the year! How can you want that?"

"You really are stupid, aren't you? I thought you had the brains in the family, but I'm beginning to think you're just as ignorant as Vanessa." He spared a glance to his surroundings. "Look at this place—completely undeveloped beachfront. The potential is worth millions." Turning back, he snarled, "I'm already working with the town's city manager to change the zoning. Once I get my hands on your Inn, that *quaint* dump will be torn down, and a huge condo complex will rise."

Mouth open, she stuttered, "But...but...the town... won't go for that."

Grinning, he said, "Oh, the manager and I'll have it all worked out." As the grin fell from his face, he snarled, "Now get in!"

Forcing more bravado into her quaking body, she said, "And if I don't? You kill me and everything goes to my mom...not Vanessa. You still won't have it."

Throwing his head back in a sharp laugh, Nelson then said, "And you think I'm not already taking care of that? How's your mom's stomach, by the way?"

Her brow crinkled in confusion at his words until it slowly dawned on her and she felt her knees almost buckle. "You're...oh, my God. You're poisoning her."

"So easy for slow cyanide," he admitted. "She'll gladly turn everything over to her capable son-in-law and precious Vanessa." Stepping so close that the barrel of the gun was mere inches from her chest, he stated clearly, "Now. Get. The fuck. In. The. Boat."

Unable to think of an alternative, she turned and moved to step down into the motorboat. She instinctively knew his plan was to dump her into the bay, somewhere close enough to wash ashore several hours after drowning. She would be dead, and he would be long gone by that time. No witnesses. And it's easy for a man like him to pay for an alibi. Or simply get Vanessa to lie for him.

Vanessa. My sister. Whirling around so quickly she

almost ran into the gun, she asked, "Vanessa? Does she know about any of this?"

"I was attracted to your sister for her looks…and the way she put me on a pedestal." Throwing his head back, he laughed, "She's easy to control. Easy to manipulate. And dumb as a brick. So, no, she has no clue. But she'll continue to play the dutiful wife. Hell, as long as she thinks we're the lord and lady of the country club, she's happy. I did some digging into her social climbing background and discovered she would be in line to inherit beachfront property." He pierced her with his stare as he confessed, "If your grandmother hadn't died, I'd have taken care of her, too."

At that, Tori gasped, unable to believe what he was saying. Chest heaving, she hesitated at the end of the pier.

With a jerk of the gun in her direction, she climbed down into the boat, her mind swirling trying to think of a way out. *I can't let him kill me. I've got to get to mom. And who's to say he won't kill Vanessa once he's through with her? And Mitch…I want a life with him!*

As Nelson worked to start the motor and then began to drive, she looked out to the yacht anchored offshore. *If we get all the way out there, it might be too far for me to swim back.* Unable to judge the distance, she looked between the yacht and the shore, wondering how far she would be able to swim. *But he could run over me with the motorboat!* Anger filled her as her hands gripped the sides. *Think, Tori, think!* An image of Mitch's face filled her mind…then fueled her determination.

As she focused her attention on Nelson, sitting in the back of the boat, one hand on the motor handle and the other still holding the gun on her, she heard a noise coming from a distance from above. Chancing a glance behind her, she saw a helicopter moving toward them. *I wonder if I can wave. Or make a sign? Damn, he'd blow me out of the water before I had a chance!*

Turning back toward Nelson, her hands still gripping the sides of the rocking boat in fear, she watched as his eyes moved upward toward the incoming helicopter. His eyes narrowed as he looked into the sunshine, giving her the exact opportunity she had been awaiting.

With a strong kick upward, she made contact with his arm, knocking him backward toward the motor. Losing his balance, he slipped off the seat, landing unceremoniously in the bottom of the boat, but with the gun still in his grip.

Not willing to take a chance on a fight, she stood, rocking the boat as he was attempting to right himself. With a quick decision, she dove into the water, thrusting her arms to move as deeply as she could. Mitch's words to her, almost twenty years ago, flooded back to her as she stroked her way down.

"Swimming in the ocean isn't easy, but you're a really good swimmer, Tori. You're better than most of the boys I know."

31

On the road, Mitch watched the scenery fly by as Grant drove them toward the beach north of Baytown. Listening as various members of the rescue team reported in, his heart leaped as Callan informed him that the Virginia Beach Coast Guard was sending a helicopter over the bay to look for Nelson's yacht.

"We're en route," Zac called, and Mitch knew he and some of the CG stationed at Baytown were on the water.

"Going as fast as I can," Grant said unnecessarily, as the SUV skidded on the gravel road heading between tall pine trees toward the water.

"Helicopter may have visual," Callan's voice crackled over the radio. Rattling off the coordinates, Mitch felt his back press against the seat even more as Grant stepped on the accelerator.

Coming to a stop at the end of the road with a small

wooden hut nearby, they leaped from the vehicle. The other officers behind them surrounded the structure, quickly ascertaining it was empty. Mitch ran toward the water and out to the edge of the pier.

A small motorboat was out a hundred yards but was not speeding toward the anchored yacht. Instead, a man was standing in the small watercraft, firing a gun down into the water. While his heart threatened to beat out of his chest, his eyes searched the surface of the water for any signs of Tori.

Tori's lungs felt near to bursting, but the initial ping of gunfire into the water near her kept her swimming. When she dove into the water, she was pointed in the direction of the shore, but knew she needed to surface soon to gain her bearings. Slowly rising, she tried not to shoot upward, but her need for air overrode her desire to not be seen. Popping up, she gulped air, filling her lungs as her arms moved back and forth to keep her in place.

Still gasping, she twisted around to see the motorboat a distance behind her, but with the water and sun in her eyes she could not tell if Nelson was still looking for her. The large helicopter was near the yacht and two other large boats were gaining on the motorboat. Uncertain of their occupants, she glanced in the other direction, seeing the pier in the distance off to her right.

Deciding against trying to swim to it, she was afraid that would be where Nelson would look first.

With another gulp of air, she dove back down under the surface, pumping her arms and legs in an attempt to carry her to safety.

Mitch watched in horror as Nelson continued to fire into the water before Grant ran up behind him, pointing to the CG boat, saying, "Callan!"

The two police officers watched as their friend, gun drawn, ordered Nelson to drop his weapon. Instead of obeying, Nelson turned his gun toward the Coast Guard vessel and fired. Returning fire, Nelson was struck in the leg and dropped to the bottom of the motorboat, where the CG quickly moved to bring him on board.

"Tori! Where the hell is Tori?" Mitch yelled, his gaze still scanning the surface of the water.

"Both of you used to swim in the ocean together. What would she do?"

Thinking quickly, Mitch yelled, "Get the Jeep! She'll swim parallel to the shore, avoiding the pier."

Within a couple of minutes, the two were driving on the beach, churning up the sand behind them. Getting on the radio, Grant called for backup, as Mitch held the binoculars to his eyes. *Come on, babe. Surface so I can tell where the hell you are!*

Bouncing along, Mitch yelled for Grant to stop. Skidding in the sand, Mitch leaned out the window, carefully searching. Just then a dark spot was seen on the surface of the gently undulating water. An arm moved about, pushing hair away from the swimmer's face. Bringing the person more in focus, he shouted as her face came into view.

"Tori! Tori!"

Hopping out of the vehicle, ripping his polo shirt off his chest, he ran to the surf as Grant called in the sighting. Kicking off his shoes and socks, Mitch jumped out of his pants, tossing them to the ground as he ran into the water, continuing to shout.

Her arms aching with the strain of a much longer swim than she was used to, Tori treaded water as she panted. Trying to slow her breathing, she checked her location once more. The pier was no longer in sight, and she felt no riptide currents. Glancing toward the beach, she wondered if it would be safe to swim toward it and try to hide from Nelson there.

As she wiped water dripping from her hair down into her eyes, she blinked at the object on the shore. A vehicle was parked, and it appeared someone was running toward her. Uncertain what to do, she gave her head a shake to try to dislodge the water from her ears.

Hearing her name, or what seemed like her name,

being called, she wiped her eyes once more, her tired legs still kicking. *Mitch?* Her eyes may have been deceiving her, but it appeared Mitch was stripping as he ran toward her. *Mitch! Thank God!*

Finding renewed strength, she began swimming with long strokes toward the shore and toward the man she loved. By the time the sandy bottom of the bay was under her enough for her toes to barely touch, he had reached her.

Throwing herself into his strong embrace, she allowed him to carry her to shore. Panting, she tried to tell him about Nelson, but he shushed her.

"It's over, babe. I've got you and no one else can hurt you now."

Letting his words wash over her, she tucked her face into his neck as her exhausted body settled into his. Hearing shouting, she managed to lift her head just long enough to see a crowd gathering on the beach, an assortment of vehicles next to the police SUV.

Smiling, she fell back into his arms as her body began to feel the weight of coming out of the water. *Home. I'm coming home.*

Mitch also watched the crowd of friends and family gather in front of him as he staggered out of the ocean with Tori in his arms. Seeing his parents, the American Legion members, friends, and the original Baytown Boys gathering, his chest swelled with emotion as tears stung his eyes.

I came home to Baytown. No regrets. No fuckin' regrets.

With a smile, he made his way to the center of the gathering, glancing down at Tori resting in his arms.

The crowd at Finn's was thick, with barely a place to stand.

Brogan looked over the heads of all the ones gathered and saw Zac eyeing the crowd. Handing him a beer, he said, "Sure hope the Fire Chief doesn't shut us down for cramming too many people in here."

Zac chuckled and said, "Well, just this once, I'll overlook the infraction. Hell, I'd be driven out of town if I tried to shut you down right now!"

Aiden and Katelyn, both pulling beers as fast as they could, insisted Mitch and Tori sit at the bar so they could hear everything that was being said. Mitch eschewed sitting on a stool, preferring instead to stand behind Tori, tucking her closely into his front as his arms wrapped around her body. With her on a tall stool, she came to just under his chin, close to his heartbeat. A position he hoped she would always be in.

As the crowd clamored for answers, Mitch held out his hand, responding, "Right now, Nelson is in the North Heron Hospital, under guard and under arrest. As soon as his leg is patched up, he'll be escorted to the jail. The investigation is still ongoing, but I know he's been arrested for murder, attempted murder, kidnapping, discharging a weapon, firing at an officer, and that doesn't even touch what he'll be charged with in relation to his financial schemes."

"What the hell was he trying to do?" Nancy asked. "I still don't understand!"

Taking over, Tori explained, "He said he married my sister because he found out that her grandmother owned one of the best beach-front properties in Baytown and he saw potential for a huge moneymaker. She also fit his idea of a country-club wife—not a socialite that might be hard to manage, but someone who put him on a pedestal. His plan was to turn it into condos, buy up other properties and do the same. He even had investors who had already paid him for some non-existent condos."

"But the town's building codes would have never allowed that!" someone shouted.

Just then Corwin pushed through the crowd, huffing as he tried to maneuver to the center. "Now, now, you're right," he said, his voice rising over the angry residents'. Mitch watched, narrow eyed, knowing the mayor was desperate to calm the crowd and separate himself from the actions of Silas.

"This town was never in danger of allowing someone to come in and turn our quaint city into beachfront condos," Corwin assured, puffing his chest out in an effort to take control. "I assure you the town council will be reviewing the policies and will have strong words with the town manager, if indeed there was any impropriety."

Most of the residents dismissed the mayor as they turned back toward Mitch and Tori.

"What I want to know is what the hell was he doing with that other chick?" Aiden asked.

"Nelson had no money…not really," Tori continued. "Everyone thought he was rich, but if he didn't get his hands on some money quickly, he wouldn't last to see his scheme through. I have no idea how he and Hailey got together with the plan to kill me and then split the insurance money." Twisting around to look into Mitch's eyes, she added, "I think he planned on killing her no matter what. He would have never wanted to split the money with her."

Cupping her face, he pulled her into his chest, offering comfort as well as to remind himself she was alive and in his arms.

Lifting his head, he added, "It appears that Hailey Bernard worked for the Hurkamp Company at one time, so she and Nelson were acquainted. Thomas let his fiancé know about the insurance policy, but we don't know exactly what happened then. Maybe when she realized Tori looked like her, she took that info to Nelson…or Nelson found out and recruited her to go in with him."

"Hailey got pissed thinking that Thomas was trying to replace me with her. I doubt that's true, but," Tori said, giving a little shrug, "who knows?"

"We'll know more as the investigation continues," Mitch reminded the crowd. "For now, all that matters is that Tori's safe and sound, and he didn't get his hands on a piece of Baytown."

"Hear, hear!" Aiden called out, leading the gathering in more cheers.

The drinks and food were flowing as the laughter filled the pub. As Tori and Jillian headed to the ladies' room, Mitch stood at the bar observing the crowd, especially the Baytown Boys. Aiden with his easy laugh, held secrets hidden inside. Brogan, surly and brooding, who served drinks but never took a drop of alcohol himself, always seemed to need control over every situation. Grant, in the corner holding court over three women at one time, all vying for his attention, but Mitch knew that his friend kept one eye out for Jillian while deep inside feeling unworthy of her.

Zac and Callan sat at the other end of the bar, surrounded with some of the older men from the American Legion as well as a few of the CG, sharing war stories. Jason, beaming since the town approved his garage, was standing at the bar with a few of the locals eager to see his shop open. Mitch had carefully noted some of the tattoos on Jason's arms and saw war memories engraved into the young man's skin, wearing his pain. Mitch watched Gareth approach Katelyn and selfishly hoped she would accept the receptionist job, freeing up the PI's time to do more investigating. And if the young man could erase the sadness in Katelyn's eyes, all the better.

Before Tori returned, Mitch heard the bar door open, and a smile spread across his face as he saw who walked in. He headed toward the large man, who was looking around at the crowd nervously.

"Lance!" Mitch called out, gaining the man's attention.

With a slight smile, Lance stuck his hand out. "Good to see you again, Mitch." His eyes shifted around, and he said, "Didn't expect this kind of crowd."

Recognizing Lance's uneasiness, Mitch nodded back toward the door, and said, "Let's step outside."

The two men stood on the sidewalk, the noise of the bar lessening as the door shut behind them. Mitch clapped Lance on the shoulder. "Glad as hell you decided to come here."

"Well, got back from the war and home just wasn't home. Parents moved to Florida. Sis got married. Got no friends there and my former job was filled. Seemed like I was more alone there than ever."

"This is a good place, Lance," Mitch assured. "Good friends, good people."

"I don't need people so much as just a place to be by myself."

Mitch watched the large man glance toward the bar again.

"Always like this?"

Chuckling, Mitch said, "No, not always. We just solved a big case, and everyone here is kind of celebrating. Something else the town does really well." Sobering, he said, "You'll like it here, Lance. And we've got the American Legion started here."

Nodding, Lance admitted, "I got a place south of

town…not too far, but it's a small house. I'll be able to be by myself most of the time. I can work on my art, and I've already got a contract with a couple of the shops around here…even some dealers across the state."

Mitch smiled, knowing the dourly, large man, with long hair was not what most people would assume was an artist. But he also knew the town would embrace his former Army buddy. "You want to come in? Meet a few people?"

Lance's eyes glanced toward Finn's, where the noise could still be heard, and he shook his head. "No, thanks. Crowds aren't my thing." He turned to walk away, then stopped and grabbed Mitch in a man hug. "Thanks, man. I know I gotta get settled in, but…well…thanks."

He let Mitch go as quickly as he had embraced him and headed off down the sidewalk, soon disappearing into the night.

Mitch turned and looked in the other direction toward the night sky over the Chesapeake Bay. Sucking in a deep breath, he let it out slowly. The door opened, allowing a sliver of light and the noise to escape, and he saw Tori's face illuminated.

"Hey, sweetie? Um, are you okay?"

Lifting his hand toward her, he motioned for her to join him on the sidewalk. She slipped easily into his embrace, once more tucked perfectly next to his heart.

"What were you thinking?" she asked, her soft voice floating into the night.

With his arms wrapped tightly around her, he stared once more at the moonlight glistening over the ripples in the bay. Admiring her upturned face, he kissed her. Gently...full of promises of more to come.

"Home," he said, simply. "I was thinking about coming home."

Smiling up at him, her eyes twinkling, "Coming home? Or going home?"

Laughing, he said, "Let's call it a night...and go home." With her tucked into his side, they walked toward the Sea Glass Inn knowing wherever home was, they were going together.

32

EPILOGUE

The orange ball slowly sunk into the horizon, casting the evening sky into brilliant colors of pink and blue, while the water reflected its brilliance. The large gathering sat in white chairs on the green expanse of grass outside Sunset View Restaurant where the staff awaited the beginning of the reception.

Mitch scanned the gathering as he waited on his bride. It seemed the whole American Legion, all their friends, and many townspeople came out to celebrate the first of the Baytown Boys getting married. Looking down, he smiled at his parents and friends, Jason, Gareth, and Lance sitting in the front. Across the aisle, Vera Bradford sat. Tori's mother, horrified with the actions of her son-in-law, had renewed her devotion to and acceptance of the simpler life Tori had chosen. Vanessa was not present and, while devastated by her husband's crimes, Mitch was not certain of her true feelings. He could not deny that her attitude toward

Tori had been conciliatory, but Vanessa moved shortly after Nelson's trial and imprisonment, deciding she needed a fresh start.

His gaze landed on his group of friends from the Saints, and their wives, all smiling at him in return. Happily remembering his times working with them, he had no regrets. *None at all.* Coming home to Baytown was the right move.

Sparing a glance to the side, he grinned nervously at Grant, Zac, Aiden, Brogan, and Callan.

Now, with the change in the music, Mitch saw Jillian and Katelyn on either side of Tori as the three made their way down the aisle. His breath caught in his throat and if Grant had not whispered for him to breathe, he feared he would have passed out.

The bride walked down the aisle, flanked by her two best friends, breaking tradition. Tori, dressed in a long, fitted, ivory gown, layers of lace hugging her hips and flowing to the long train, walked slowly. Unable to keep the smile from her face, she walked toward the tall man waiting for her at the front. Mitch, his ivory shirt showing off his tanned face, never looked more handsome.

As the sun made its final descent below the gently undulating watery horizon, the two spoke their vows, first led by the minister and then their promises to each other.

"I, Tori Bradford, fell in love with you, Mitch Evans, when I was six years old. You were my hero then…and my hero now. You showed me that I could be like sea glass, becoming beautiful by the twists and turns of life. I vow to love you, with all my heart, for as long as I live."

Smiling, Mitch lifted his hand to wipe a falling tear from her cheek, as he promised, "I, Mitch Evans, first saw you standing on Baytown's beach when I was eight years old. Your hair caught my attention…and then your smile caught my heart. Seeing you each summer became the best part of my year. And when I see you now, I know that our years apart only served to polish the beautiful sea glass that we have become. I vow to love you, with all my heart, with every sunrise and sunset."

The gathering broke into cheers as Mitch leaned over, placing a sweet kiss that soon turned scorching on Tori's lips.

***

Ten years later

Tori stepped out of the Sea Glass Inn after checking on the guests. The managers, a young couple, now lived in her former attic suite. They were more than competent, but as the owner of the Inn, she liked to make sure to take time to greet guests and occasionally still participated in serving breakfast.

"Slow down and hold your sister's hand," Tori called out, keeping an eagle eye on her eight-year-old son,

Eddie, as he ran toward the beach across the road, ignoring her request. Waving to neighbors as she followed her children, she smiled at Mitch as he stepped from the police SUV and scooped their giggling, four-year-old, red-haired daughter up into his arms.

Mitch watched as Tori made her way to them, her hair now swinging just at her shoulders, her curves a little more pronounced, and her smile still lighting his world. As she approached, she placed her hand on his chest and lifted up on her toes, lightly kissing him.

Licking his lips, he said, "Hmmm, cinnamon rolls?"

Before Tori could answer, little Vivian gave her father a huge, smacking kiss then leaned back and shouted, "Yes! Cimmimmon buns!"

Laughing, he settled Vivian on one hip while swinging his arm around Tori. The trio walked across the street and Tori's gaze traveled quickly up and down the beach, looking for Eddie. "Now, where did he get to?"

Mitch spotted his son immediately, nudging Tori who turned her head to watch the scene playing out before her.

Eddie had approached a little girl on the beach and the two of them stared at sea glass in his hand. He appeared to be telling her about the sliver of colored glass before she lifted her beaming face up to his.

Tori's heart stuttered as she watched her son reach down, grab the little girl's hand, and then the two of them began to run toward other children on the beach. Already coming to be known as the second generation of Baytown Boys, their son never let go of the little girl's hand. Turning her gaze back to Mitch's, she felt tears stinging her eyes. "It looks like the sea glass cast its spell over Baytown once again."

Setting Vivian down on the sand, Mitch held Tori's face, gently kissing away her joyful tears.

Don't miss the next Baytown Boy
Just One More Chance

ALSO BY MARYANN JORDAN

Don't miss other Maryann Jordan books!

Baytown Boys (small town, military romantic suspense)

Coming Home

Just One More Chance

Clues of the Heart

Finding Peace

Picking Up the Pieces

Sunset Flames

Waiting for Sunrise

Hear My Heart

Guarding Your Heart

Sweet Rose

Our Time

Count On Me

Shielding You

To Love Someone

Sea Glass Hearts

Protecting Her Heart

Sunset Kiss

Baytown Heroes - A Baytown Boys subseries

A Hero's Chance

Finding a Hero

A Hero for Her

Needing A Hero

Hopeful Hero

Always a Hero

In the Arms of Hero

Holding Out for a Hero

Heart of a a Hero

Hidden Hero

More Than a Hero

Falling For a Hero

Baytown Legacies - A Baytown Next Generation Series

Jack's Legacy

Trevor's Legacy

Jeremy's Legacy

For all of Miss Ethel's boys:

Heroes at Heart (Military Romance)

Zander

Rafe

Cael

Jaxon

Jayden

Asher

Zeke

Cas

Holiday for a Hero (Miss Ethel's love story)

Lighthouse Security Investigations

Mace

Rank

Walker

Drew

Blake

Tate

Levi

Clay

Cobb

Bray

Josh

Knox

Lighthouse Security Investigations West Coast

Carson

Leo

Rick

Hop

Dolby

Bennett

Poole

Adam

Jeb

Chris's story: Home Port (an LSI West Coast crossover novel)

Ian's story: Thinking of Home (LSIWC crossover novel)

Oliver's story: Time for Home (LSIWC crossover novel)

Lighthouse Security Investigations Montana

Logan

Sisco

Landon

Devlin

Home for Justice (LSIMT crossover novel) Tyler's story

Todd

Casper

Bert

Hope City (romantic suspense series co-developed with Kris Michaels

Brock book 1

Sean book 2

Carter book 3

Brody book 4

Kyle book 5

Ryker book 6

Rory book 7

Killian book 8

Torin book 9

Blayze book 10

Griffin book 11

Saints Protection & Investigations

(an elite group, assigned to the cases no one else wants…or can solve)

Serial Love

Healing Love

Revealing Love

Seeing Love

Honor Love

Sacrifice Love

Protecting Love

Remember Love

Discover Love

Surviving Love

Celebrating Love

Searching Love

Follow the exciting spin-off series:

Alvarez Security (military romantic suspense)

Gabe

Tony

Vinny

Jobe

SEALs

SEAL Together (Silver SEAL)

Undercover Groom (Hot SEAL)

Also for a Hope City Crossover Novel / Hot SEAL…

A Forever Dad

Long Road Home

Military Romantic Suspense

Home to Stay (a Lighthouse Security Investigation crossover novel)

Home Port (an LSI West Coast crossover novel)

Thinking of Home (LSIWC crossover novel)

Time for Home (LSIWC crossover novel)

Home for Justice (LSIMT crossover novel)

Meadowlark Creek Mystery

June's First Murder

A Pumpkin Patch Murder

Letters From Home (military romance)

Class of Love

Freedom of Love

Bond of Love

The Love's Series (detectives)

Love's Taming

Love's Tempting

Love's Trusting

The Fairfield Series (small town detectives)

Emma's Home

Laurie's Time

Carol's Image

Fireworks Over Fairfield

Please take the time to leave a review of this book. Feel free to contact me, especially if you enjoyed my book. I love to hear from readers!

Facebook

Email

Website